MY FIRST MURDER

MY FIRST MURDER

LEENA LEHTOLAINEN

Translated by Owen F. Witesman

amazon crossing

Published by AmazonCrossing
P.O. Box 400818
Las Vegas, NV 89140

ISBN-13: 9781612184371
ISBN-10: 1612184375
Library of Congress Control Number: 2012941209

Drifting on the tide, along this endless road we glide
Surges battering bow and keel
But what is man?
A restless will-o'-the-wisp, a restless will-o'-the-wisp
Rocks scraping underfoot we walk
One born to pleasure and another born to pain
But within each heart the tick of a clock
Which when it stops, 'tis time for death to reign
Drifting on the tide, along this endless road we glide
No man, not one, its length may know
Sea and sky and land—all, all shall fade away
How shall the soul be saved from woe?
But in dreams how dear it is to say
That spring will come again and a new dawn yet will break
That from atop the fells, come winds of days soon to wake—
Or have they lied?
Drifting on the tide.

—Eino Leino, music by Toivo Kuula

PRELUDE

Riku woke up to a vicious call of nature. His mouth tasted like it usually did after whiskey, beer, garlic, and too many cigarettes, and he hoped he'd be able to find some blood orange Jaffa soda in the house. That was his drink of choice whenever he was hungover—assuming, that is, that he wasn't in such bad shape that he had to resort to beer.

The morning was beautiful. Tuulia and Mira sat on the porch, consuming a leisurely breakfast. Riku was amused by their friendly sounding chatter about different varieties of cheese—the fact was the two women couldn't stand each other. However, since one of them was the best soprano and the other the best alto in EFSAS—the Eastern Finland Student Association of Singers—they had to make the best of it. Heavyset and somber looking with dark hair, Mira was the classic archetype of an alto. She would have been perfect as the gypsy woman in Verdi's *Il Trovatore*—what was her name...?

When the bright sunlight hit his eyes, Riku's head exploded. He popped two extra-strength Burana tablets for good measure, even though he was basically immune to ibuprofen at this point and even the whole bottle might not have helped.

There was no soda of any kind to be found, so he settled for fresh juice. The world felt oppressively vibrant: the sea was shining, seagulls were screeching down at the dock, and there was already a hint of the warmth the afternoon would bring. Singing in this heat wouldn't be easy.

"Feeling a little fuzzy, Riku?" Tuulia asked. She looked as pale as Riku. None of them had slept much. But it wasn't like it really mattered since it was Sunday and they didn't have to be back at work until the following day.

"Are the others still asleep?" Riku asked, looking around.

"Pia was going for a swim, and I haven't seen the others. Hopefully they'll show some signs of life soon so we can get something done." Mira's tone was bitter—she didn't care for slackers. In her opinion, EFSAS had sent their best double quartet lineup to Tommi's parents' villa to practice for their upcoming concert, not to carouse into the wee hours. As far as she was concerned, it was high time they get up, chug some coffee, and start warming up their voices.

Riku stood up. A swim might not be a bad idea, especially since the seawater was a perfect seventy degrees. So he set off for the boat dock. Pia was on the shore over by the sauna, modestly covered with a bikini. Riku lacked the energy to drag himself that far. He couldn't be bothered with swim trunks, so he just pulled off his clothes and plunged into the water naked.

Tommi was in the water too, lounging against some rocks in the shallow area by the dock. He must have had a devil of a headache, judging from the bloody mess on the back of his head. He didn't look very lively otherwise either. Suddenly, Riku's stomach lurched. He fell to his knees and vomited into the reeds.

It was a full two minutes before he could stand up. When he did, he staggered back up to the veranda, where several more people had gathered. Riku's clear first tenor, the envy of so many, was unable to form a single word.

"Well, aren't we the cock of the walk in our birthday suit?" Tuulia said.

"Tommi…down at the dock. Oh, fuck…he's dead! Drowned!" Riku screamed.

"What the hell are you talking about?"

Antti charged down to the shore, with Mira trailing after him. Moments later she raced back up to the house and ran inside to the telephone. The emergency numbers were written neatly beside it. Everyone on the porch listened as Mira's low, breathless alto summoned first the police and then, only afterward, an ambulance.

1

Drifting on the tide, along this endless road we glide

When the telephone rang, I was in the shower rinsing the salt off my skin. I heard my own voice on the answering machine and then a colleague's urgent message to call him back. I had been able to enjoy a surprisingly long part of my Sunday off without being called into work, but even on the beach I had been unable to relax. Though I generally hated lying around and loathed the scene at the beach, I had, for some reason, felt compelled to spend my first warm summer day off worshipping the sun. I had gone to the gym regularly over the winter, so my body was in more tolerable swimsuit shape than it had been in years—though at the rate I'd been drinking beer, I was never going to get rid of my love handles. I turned off the answering machine and dialed the number for the station. The switchboard connected me to Rane.

"Hey, Kallio! I'm going to be at your door in fifteen. Everything is already packed. There's a body over in Vuosaari. The boys from Patrol called it in half an hour ago. You don't need anything from your office, do you? See you soon!"

Here we go again, I thought, as I looked in the closet for something decent to put on. My uniform skirt was down at the station in Pasila, so my best jeans would have to do. My hair was wet, but the blow dryer would just whip it into a tangled red mess. I dabbed some makeup on my flushed face and frowned at my reflection in the mirror. The face that stared back was quite simply not that of a respectable female police detective: my greenish-yellow eyes looked like they belonged to a cat, and my coarse hemp-rope curls had been intensified with a bottle of red dye ("Everyone will notice, but no one will know..."). The feature most likely to provoke contempt was my snub nose, which was mottled with freckles by the sun. Someone had once called my lips sensual, referring, I think, to my full lower lip.

A hastily thrown-together girl of a woman, I fleetingly wondered whether I was really up to the task of defending law and order in the boondocks of East Helsinki.

Rane's sirens were audible in the distance. Like half of the police officers in Finland, he loved running them at every opportunity. The dead don't exactly run away, but the public didn't need to know that.

"Forensics went on ahead," Rane said matter-of-factly as I clambered into the passenger seat of the Saab. "So, body in Vuosaari, drowned, but it sounds like there's something off about it. Dude about thirty; I think his name was Peltonen. There were about ten people spending the weekend out there at a summerhouse, a choir of some kind, and this morning they found this Peltonen guy in the water."

"Did someone push him in?"

"Don't know. We haven't gotten a whole lot of detail yet."

"What's this choir thing about?"

"Some kind of singers, I guess," he said. Rane swerved so hard onto the East Highway that I lurched and hit my elbow painfully against the door of the patrol car. With a sigh of resignation, I buckled the seatbelt, an obnoxious contraption that

chafed at my neck because it was designed with taller male officers in mind.

"Where's Kinnunen? And all the others? Weren't you supposed to have the day off today?"

"The rest of the guys are still tied up with that stabbing from
yesterday. And I've been trying to get hold of Kinnunen for the
last half hour, but you know how Sundays are. He's probably
nursing a hangover on some pub deck."

Rane sighed. Neither of us wanted to talk about our boss. It
was common knowledge that our section head, Sergeant Kalevi
Kinnunen, was an alcoholic. Period. Since I was next in the chain
of command, I would take over the case until Kinnunen recovered
from his latest drinking jag.

"Listen, Rane. I might know this dead guy. Or used to
know him…"

"My vacation starts tomorrow, and I intend to take it. This
case is yours whether you like it or not. You don't get to pick and
choose in this job."

It was obvious from Rane's tone that he thought I should
have continued studying to be a lawyer, since then I could have
chosen my cases. He had always regarded me with a certain
degree of suspicion, as did many others in the department. Not
only was I young, and a woman, but I also wasn't a permanent career police officer like they were; to them, I was nothing
more than a fly-by-night substitute with a couple more months
to endure on the force.

After my matriculation exams, and to the astonishment of
everyone around me, I had applied to and been accepted by the
police academy. I had always been a quasi-rebel in school, a punk
in a leather jacket who still graduated *summa cum laude*. The other
punk—and the worst truant in our class—went on to become

an elementary school teacher. But my head was full of idealistic notions of social justice. I imagined that as a police officer, I would be able to help both victims *and* criminals. I thought I could change the world and decided to specialize in vice work so I could help all the women and children caught up in prostitution and pornography.

The police academy had proved a disappointment, however, though I had held my own surprisingly well among the men. I had long since gotten used to being one of the guys; in school I had strummed bass in a testosterone-rich garage band and always played soccer with "the guys."

At school I had become accustomed to being at the head of the class, and I felt compelled to do nothing less at the academy. But the actual work of a police officer had been too much for me in the end. After two years of writing reports, doing body searches on female reprobates, and sifting through the social histories of shoplifters, I had had enough. I was using only one part of who I was—the most boring and officious part. No one wanted my compassion, and there was little use for my mind— which I had always made a habit of keeping fit.

Those two years of police work reawakened my desire to pursue higher education, and I quickly worked my way through two officer candidate courses. There was a shortage of women, and it's possible that I rose through the ranks more quickly than usual as a result. This caused no end of jealous grumbling among the boys. But the thing that seemed to rankle my colleagues the most was that I didn't actually think much of the job. When I was accepted to law school, I thought that I had finally found the right fit. I was still interested in the application of the law, and at twenty-three years old, I believed that I knew what I wanted out of life.

While I was in school, I continued to do summer temp work and other ad hoc jobs for the city police department, and now, five years later, I was a police officer again. I had gotten bored with studying, and a six-month substitute posting in the Helsinki Police Department's Violent Crime Unit had seemed like a good idea, especially since I was specializing in criminal law. I had thought that a few months off would give me some distance from my coursework and a new perspective on my life. So far, I seemed to be wrong about this too. As a criminal investigator, I did not have the energy to think about anything but work. Every now and then I'd go out for a beer, but I hardly ever made it to the gym anymore.

Further complicating things, my immediate supervisor did only a small fraction of his work. He spent the rest of his time drinking—or nursing a hangover. I couldn't understand why he hadn't been put out to pasture years before. Kinnunen's work almost always fell to other people, and now, especially during the summer, the situation had become intolerable. The budget appropriations for bringing in extra staff, such as myself, had run out in April, and the vacations everyone had scheduled to recover from being overworked were looming on the horizon.

In addition, I wasn't nearly as hard-boiled as I had been when I was young, but admitting that would have been a big mistake. My male colleagues kept a close eye on my nerves and eagerly monitored my reactions when inspecting evidence—like the rotting, vomit-sodden, eviscerated corpse of a wino who had been drinking water mixed with sulfuric acid. It wasn't as though that didn't turn everyone's stomach, but I was the one who wasn't allowed to show it—because I was a woman. But I was tough and made far and away the most callous wisecracks in the police cafeteria afterward, even though spooning the chicken fricassee into my mouth almost made me gag.

When it came down to it, there was nothing I could do about my appearance: I looked hopelessly female. I kept my hair long because my curls would have frizzed up all over my head if I had cut it any shorter. And I was short. My height had actually almost prevented my acceptance into the police academy, but a doctor I knew had added the two missing inches to my medical certificate. My body was an unlikely combination of feminine curves and masculine muscles. I'm strong for someone so small, and I know my own strength well enough that dangerous situations don't generally frighten me. However, right at this moment, I could have done with the self-confidence that came with a tight hair bun and a police uniform.

Until now, all of my cases, both homicides and otherwise, had been strictly business. But the words "choir" and "Peltonen" sent a stab of fear through me. If my sinking feeling was right, I was about to see several people who knew me in an entirely different capacity than that of a police officer.

During my first year of law school, I had lived in a cramped student apartment in Itäkeskus, near the mall on the east side of the city. My roommates had quarreled constantly because one of them spent half of her time at home singing. At times a whole quartet could be found harmonizing in Jaana's room, with Jaana's boyfriend singing bass. Tommi Peltonen was a dreamboat—eyes like Paul Newman and a face deeply tanned from many yachting excursions. Jaana had spent many a long night agonizing over whether to move in with him, sometimes inviting me into her room to talk it through over a bottle of red wine.

After the years I had spent surrounded by nothing but dull police bodybuilder types, Tommi had been a feast for the eyes.

Jaana's vocalizing never bothered me much, both because she sang pretty well and because I could always put on my headphones and crank up some Dead Kennedys or homegrown Popeda if I got tired of listening to classical.

Then my great-aunt died and the family didn't want to sell her studio in Töölö until real estate prices went up. So I moved in and kept up the apartment, paying only the maintenance fees. When the value of the unit eventually went up, I was afraid I would lose it, but my greedy relatives decided to wait for square footage rates to balloon even further and were left out in the cold when the recession hit and real estate crashed. So there I was, still living in a nicer neighborhood than I deserved, surrounded by restaurants I couldn't afford. I bumped into Jaana now and then at the university and heard that she and Tommi had broken up. Jaana had fallen in love with the son of a host family she stayed with while the choir was on a trip to Germany and ended up becoming a hausfrau. These days, I maintained the typical Christmas card relationship with most of my old roommates.

As I tried to recall that period of my life, the names and faces of Jaana's other friends came rushing back to me. There had been some other eye candy in addition to Tommi; I had even finished off a bottle or two with the EFSAS crowd a few times. Since I knew that many of the choir members had difficulty moving on with their lives, I figured it was quite likely I was about to come face-to-face with several of them. Choir singers were their own breed: a gang of masochists who got off on singing forgettable ditties while standing beside people with worse voices than their own, all being led by a tormentor waving his arms around incomprehensibly.

The road leading to the villa wound through green summer meadows. Although Rane was no longer running the sirens, he was still speeding, which was perfectly legal. I read him the driving directions, and we managed to turn off at the correct spot. It was so damn embarrassing when the police got lost—it had happened to me a couple of times, and I had taken the blame. The sea glinted silver beyond the fields. A hare loped lazily across the road. A wasp tried to fly in through the open car window.

"There are a few old summerhouses out here that rich folks have fixed up for themselves," Rane explained.

We finally crossed a narrow stretch of land about thirty feet wide onto what felt like an island and drove under a high arched gate. A brass nameplate announced that we had arrived at Villa Maisetta. A narrow, overgrown road led to the yard of an idyllic summerhouse, exactly the sort of place I would have loved to live in. The two-story villa had white window frames and was adorned with intricate woodwork on the eaves. A patrol car was parked on the lawn next to the old, beat-up Volvo used by Forensics.

"The guys were quick today. What exactly are we supposed to do here?" I asked, forcing myself to take on a cynical, almost aggressive posture. No tears for the corpses of old roommates' cute ex-boyfriends.

A patrol officer approached with a morose-looking dark-haired girl. They both eyed me suspiciously as Rane and I introduced ourselves. Though I had braced myself for this kind of reaction, it still rankled me. The girl looked vaguely familiar, and her name, Mira, called to mind Jaana's less-than-complimentary comments about the choir's worst tightass. I suddenly remembered that Mira didn't even drink hard liquor, which, five years ago at least, had been an unforgivable sin in these circles.

Mira led us down the lawn to the shore, where the boys from Forensics were photographing a body sprawled against the rocks. The medical examiner was also on-site. I guessed they had been waiting for us for a while because everything was done. It struck me as stupid that they had all waited for me to look over the corpse before pulling it out of the water. I had no desire to see the carcass at all, to recognize it as Tommi, or to see what someone had done to him.

"How does it look?" I asked the medical examiner who stood nearby puffing on a thin cigar. At least a hundred pounds overweight, he despised me almost as much as I despised him. The difference was that I knew he was a real pro at his job, while he did not think as highly of me.

"Where's Kinnunen?" Salo asked suspiciously.

"Wherever he is, we can't stand around waiting for him," I replied antagonistically. "Let's get the ball rolling. What would you say about the cause of death?"

"Judging from his face, I'd say he died by drowning. But that depression in his skull looks interesting enough that I don't quite know what to think. I'll have to get him on the table." Salo spoke to the tips of Rane's shoes instead of to me.

"Is it possible he was whacked on the head and then dropped in the water?" Rane asked.

"Very possible. Whatever hit him certainly didn't *improve* his chances of survival. It looks strange, though. I'm curious to know what he was hit with."

"What about a rock?" Rane scanned the boulders on the shoreline. All sorts of smaller stones were strewn among them, some of which would fit nicely in a person's hand.

"Yeah, it'll certainly keep the boys busy if you put them to work checking every rock on this beach," said the ME with a snort.

I gave the paramedics permission to lift the body out of the water. They carefully turned it over. The face looked grotesquely familiar, the blond hair clotted with blood and salt. Even the bloating could not remove the expression of horror in the open eyes, which shone like blue warning lights, surrounded by the mottled violet skin of his face. Strands of seaweed adorned his white pullover windbreaker, and his shoeless legs, tanned as far up as I could see, were covered by a pair of jeans.

An image of the handsome Tommi from a few years before flashed painfully through my mind. Tommi was probably a couple of years older than I was, but still not quite thirty. I had seen younger dead bodies, but those had always been ravaged by booze or chemicals. I swallowed my tears and tried to clear my throat. Then I took a deep breath and started snapping instructions to the forensic investigators: Where could the dent in Tommi's head have come from? Could he have slipped off the dock? And so on. I knew my terse tone made me look jumpy, but there was nothing I could do to cover it up. Though we had seen a female defense minister muster the courage to cry in public, I still couldn't.

"Let's go find out what those folks in the house know," I said to Rane, turning toward the ornate villa. It was only then that I noticed the group sitting on the porch on the sea-facing side of the house. Though they must have heard my peevish outburst, none of them was looking in our direction. It was as though they were trying to block out the presence of the police altogether.

Upon closer inspection, the villa looked like a fake: maybe it was a reproduction of an older villa that had once stood on the lot. The paint had had a good twenty years to fade, but the house could not have been much older than I was.

The sun shone on the porch, and I cursed my hot jeans. As I expected, some of the seven people sitting on the porch looked familiar.

"Maria!" a clear, bright voice rang out in confusion. "Are you a policewoman now? Do you remember me? I'm Tuulia."

I remembered Tuulia well. She had been in our apartment frequently, and we had hung out together at the university café as well. I liked Tuulia, and I recalled that we'd had a similar sense of humor back then. She was prettier than I remembered, with the stately poise of a grown woman comfortable in her tall frame.

"I do." I couldn't bring myself to smile. "Yes...These days I'm Detective Maria Kallio. I work in the Violent Crime Unit. And this is Officer Lahtinen. Let's start by having you all introduce yourselves and tell us what you know about last night's events." I sounded ridiculous even to myself and didn't dare look anyone directly in the eye.

Apparently, Mira was a natural-born leader. She spoke in an even tone as though she were reading from a prepared statement. Maybe she really had planned what she would say in advance.

"My name is Mira Rasinkangas, and we're the Eastern Finland Student Association of Singers, or EFSAS. The company Tommi Peltonen works for has a summer event coming up, and they wanted music for it. They promised to pay well, and Tommi put together this double quartet to sing."

The group consisted of Tommi's quartet and four other singers who happened to be spending the summer in the city. Tommi's parents were off sailing at the moment, so their summerhouse had seemed like the perfect place to practice.

The eight singers had assembled the previous day, practiced for a couple of hours, and then moved on to the typical Finnish summer activities: sweating in the sauna and drinking. People had started to trickle off to sleep sometime after midnight; however, no one seemed very clear about Tommi's whereabouts. The last time anyone had seen him alive was around 2:00 a.m.

"I was surprised in the morning when I didn't see Tommi," Mira said. "But then Riku came up from the water, yelling that Tommi had drowned, and there he was...on the shore." Mira's voice trembled a bit.

"When you went to look at Peltonen, did you move the body?"

"I tried to check his pulse, but we didn't move him," replied a deep bass from the far end of the porch. "I'm Antti Sarkela, if you recall. I couldn't feel any pulse, and it was so obvious that he had drowned that it was pointless trying anything."

I remembered Antti too. I had been infatuated with him for nearly two weeks after he sat down next to me once on the tram and started up a conversation about the Henry Parland book I was reading. How many men knew who Henry Parland was? Then I had decided to forget Antti and shifted my attention to worshipping Henry, but ever since that conversation on the tram, I had found Antti both intriguing and irritating. He was very tall, with a narrow face and a large Aquiline nose, and I couldn't deny that I found him attractive. It was difficult to interpret the expression in his eyes at the moment, which seemed to convey a mix of sorrow and fear. I remembered that Antti and Tommi had been close friends.

"OK. This is my case now, which means that the interviews will happen in Pasila. For reasons relating to the investigation, I'd suggest that you all leave the house immediately. I'd like to start doing the interviews this evening, and I can offer a ride to anyone who needs one. I don't imagine there are any bus stops nearby. Before you leave, we'll also need your addresses and phone numbers, but that can wait. Rane, will you take notes? I'll start with you. Who are you?" I asked, turning to a small, young-looking man who was sitting near me. He looked like he might be sick at any moment.

"I'm Riku Lasinen," he replied in a high, clear tenor. "I'm twenty-three and I'm studying math and computer science at the university." The boy sounded like he was at a job interview.

"I'm Mira Rasinkangas," repeated the stout woman with the dark hair. "Twenty-six, history student."

"Pia Wahlroos," whispered a barely audible voice. I scanned its owner, who had large, brown eyes, auburn hair, and a slim figure. She wore a stylish linen sundress and a wedding band bearing some impressive rocks. I registered these details without managing to arrange them in any particular order in my mind. "I'm twenty-six, and I study Nordic languages."

"Sirkku Halonen, twenty-three. Chemistry. I'm Pia's sister, but she's married, which is why we have different last names." Sirkku was a faded, more run-of-the-mill duplicate of her thin, beautiful sister. Next to Sirkku sat a somewhat thickset man with bristly hair who held her hand reassuringly. Obviously a boyfriend.

"I'm Timo Huttunen, forestry. Twenty-five."

"Tuulia Rajala, twenty-nine. Deadbeat."

"Antti Sarkela. Math teaching assistant at the university. Twenty-nine. Although I really can't see what our ages have to do with anything." Rane uttered a disgusted snort—he had automatically started to record the word "although" and was grumbling at Sarkela as though it were his fault.

"Great. Get your things together so you can leave ASAP." As I set off down the path for the waterline to talk to the forensic technicians, I ran into the stretcher bearers on their way up. Tommi's next forwarding address would be the pathology lab.

When I returned to the house a short while later, Mira was emptying the refrigerator.

"By the way…where did each of you sleep?"

"Tommi's room is upstairs, off the landing. Riku and Antti slept on the other side of the hallway, in Tommi's brother's room. Timo and Sirkku were sleeping at the end of the hall, in Tommi's parents' bed, and Pia, Tuulia, and I were down here on the living room floor."

"So Tommi was the only one who was sleeping alone."

"I suppose. Although I don't think anyone slept much. It felt like there was always someone up doing something, people running to the bathroom, that sort of thing—and we saw Riku down here, even though there's another bathroom upstairs. I don't know about everyone else, but I only slept in fits and starts the last few hours. Tuulia has this god-awful snore, and no matter how hard I tried to wake her up, she just kept doing it."

"I'm sorry I kept you awake," Tuulia said, appearing suddenly in the kitchen. "I imagine Pia would have been awake anyway with her guilty conscience…" Tuulia glanced at the refrigerator. "So much for the bouillabaisse. Maria, you should join us for dinner once we're done with the third degree. A dinner in memory of Tommi…Even the tomato sauce is appropriately blood colored. It's a shame all we have is white wine."

"Give it a rest, Tuulia," Mira hissed, not noticing the trembling in the other woman's voice. I beat a hasty retreat and headed upstairs to a large landing where Riku was just folding up his sleeping bag. I looked out past the railing. A beautiful vista of the Baltic Sea opened out from the two-story foyer. Off the landing was a narrow hallway, at the end of which was a large bedroom, presumably Tommi's parents' room. The door was cracked and I could see a woman's legs on the bed. A man's hand was stroking them. Sirkku and Timo, I guessed.

The empty bedroom was Tommi's. It didn't seem to have changed much in the last ten years—it still looked like a teenager's room. Aqua-blue bedding, sailing posters on the walls, a couple of empty Cutty Sark whiskey bottles on the bookshelf, a few sailing books, a guitar. A sweater was draped on a chair, and a pair of shoes was crammed under the bed. On the night of his death, Tommi had been out barefoot—evidently he hadn't wanted to wake anyone. The bed was unmade, which suggested that wherever Tommi had gone off to, he had gotten some sleep first and probably expected to return to bed.

In the last room, I found Antti Sarkela lying on a narrow bed with his hands clasped behind his head. When he saw me, he jumped up like an army recruit confronted by his drill sergeant.

"Find any clues?" His voice was unmistakably antagonistic.

"Maybe. You slept in this room?"

"Yeah…"

"You know…or knew Tommi pretty well. Could you come with me to his room and see if anything is missing?"

Antti felt too big for Tommi's small room.

"I can't really tell," Antti said, peeking into the closet. "It's just the same clothes that are always here. Tommi kept a bunch

of his stuff here, so when we came out here yesterday, he just
had a small bag with him. That's it over there. It probably just
has some sheet music, some clean socks...Yeah, I think things in
here look just like they did before."

Antti's gaze landed on a beaten-up mixed-choir songbook
lying on the desk. It was open to Toivo Kuula's pathos-laden
"Drifting on the Tide." Even though I wasn't much of a fan of
rhyming poetry, I had always liked the Eino Leino poem from
which the song took its lyrics. Tommi had made copious notes
on the page. Antti averted his eyes, and I noticed that he was
biting his lip.

"Is this what you were practicing yesterday?" I asked, just to
fill the silence.

"Among other things. The client requested Finnish songs."

Tommi's wallet lay next to the music book, and I took possession of it. I had a strange feeling that I hadn't noticed everything the room was trying to tell me.

Soon after, we were ready to leave the villa. Forensics stayed
to look for any object that might qualify as a murder weapon,
and the shoreline was sealed off. A uniformed patrol stayed to
meet Tommi's parents, who were scheduled to arrive sometime
that evening.

I looked over the bewildered group of people I would be
interviewing. It was possible that some interloper from outside
the group could have witnessed Tommi's death, or could even
have been responsible for it. We couldn't rule out the possibility. There had been plenty of break-ins around the outskirts of
the city in recent months and Tommi may have surprised a thief
coming ashore in a boat. There were plenty of summer cabins
scattered on the islands, and most of them were unoccupied a
good deal of the year.

However, these seven people would be the focus of the investigation for the time being. At least one member of the choir had to know more than he or she was telling me, and it was possible that one of them had even killed Tommi. In that case, we weren't dealing with a hardened professional criminal, but a normal person whose guilt might soon become too much to bear, I thought optimistically.

Antti and Tuulia were down facing the shore yelling, and it seemed like they were trying to explain something to the uniformed officers.

"What's wrong?" I asked as I approached them to give the order to leave.

"Einstein. My cat," Antti answered. "No one has seen him for a couple of hours, and I can't leave without him."

"Do you think he's lost?" Tuulia asked, concerned.

"Of course not—he was born here! He's just out on one of his expeditions."

"How about you come back to look for your cat later," I said, sounding colder than I meant to. I told the officers who were staying on to keep their eyes out for the cat and to catch it if it turned up. They stared at me like I was a half-wit. "So we're chasing cats now too?" one of them muttered crossly.

Tommi's car would remain where it was until the technicians had a chance to take a preliminary look at it. The keys were in the ignition, so someone could easily drive it to the lab later. Pia Wahlroos's BMW had room for five choir members. There was no point in assigning an officer to their car to monitor them and make sure they didn't have a chance to agree on their alibis. They had already had plenty of time to do so before the police had arrived on the scene. I was willing to bet that Mira Rasinkangas and Antti Sarkela would be the only ones to accept a ride from the police—and I would have won. When I felt Antti's long legs pushing into the back of my seat, I shifted it forward. The contact irritated me.

"So what are you doing working as a cop, Maria?" Antti asked as we turned off the small forest road onto the pavement. "The last time I saw you, you were studying law."

"I went through the police academy before law school. There just happened to be a temporary opening."

"Have you solved a lot of these…murders?"

"Enough."

"Hey, man, don't go underestimating this girl's brains," Rane said sourly. This amused me. Rane's height complex had struck again. He was only just above the minimum police height himself and automatically reacted with hostility toward any man significantly taller than himself. Since he was defending me, I didn't bother pointing out to Rane that he'd just called me a "girl." The thin blue line.

"You were Jaana's roommate," Mira said, suddenly making the connection. "Now I remember…" From her tone, it sounded as though her memories of me weren't especially positive. Maybe it was that night we'd spent drinking together—when I made the mistake of opening my big, fat mouth about the pointlessness of choirs.

I would have to call Jaana in Germany. Since she had dated Tommi, she might be able to provide some important information. It was clear that Jaana knew most of the choir members mixed up in the murder, and it had only been a couple of years since the fateful Hessian tour.

No one spoke for the remainder of the trip back into the city. I wanted to get what I knew so far sorted out in my head before I began the interviews. Based on the ME's initial assessment,

Tommi had received a blow to the head diagonally from above and to the front with a blunt instrument. The possible killer was either considerably taller than Tommi—in which case Antti, who was in the car with me, was the only possibility—or Tommi had been sitting or kneeling when he was attacked. But he couldn't have been bent over, because then the blow would have come from a different angle.

Had Tommi arranged a meeting on the dock with someone he wanted to see in private? Or had he just gone outside and someone surprised him?

The only way I was going to get any clarity was through hard work, good questioning, and careful listening. The homicides I had solved until now had been simple: a drunk putting a knife in a drinking buddy's chest or a hatchet in his wife's head. But those had all been manslaughter. Was this my first murder?

2

Surges battering bow and keel

There was still no sign of Kinnunen at the station. The duty officer reported that the last time he had tried Kinnunen's apartment, he had reached my boss's new girlfriend. She had told him that Kinnunen was sitting on the esplanade on the patio of the Belle Époque Kappeli Café in the company of four pints. We had long since lost track of how many times we had been forced to cover for Kinnunen's dereliction of duty and no longer even bothered cursing him anymore. Rane and I just decided to get down to business without him so we wouldn't have to keep people hanging around the station all evening.

I decided to interview the choir members in alphabetical order since I couldn't come up with anything more sensible. I planned to ask the questions while Rane took notes. It was clear that he wasn't going to be much help with the case. He was already checking out in anticipation of a Monday morning with no alarm clock and the opportunity to purge his mind of all the cares of the world. But Rane would still hear what the witnesses had to say, and I'd be able to get at least a few initial impressions from him before he disappeared for his vacation. Over the last few months, I had found that despite his prejudices and occasional mean-spirited comments, Rane could be quite insightful.

Of course it ruffled his feathers to have a woman ten years his junior above him; he was a career officer who had worked his way up, unlike me, who had gone flitting from school to school.

Sirkku Halonen was up first. She was extremely agitated, so I started with some routine questions to calm her down. I'm not the maternal type, and I've never been good at comforting people who are hurt. I do better with hard cases than, say, little girls scared to death from being molested. Timo Huttunen tried to force his way into the room to protect his girlfriend, but I bundled him back out into the corridor.

Sirkku explained that she had known Tommi for about three years. She met him a couple of times before joining the choir, at parties thrown by Pia and her husband. She had been dating Timo for about a year. She thought Tommi was "really nice" and didn't have any idea who would have wanted to kill him.

"It looked like this was going to be such a fun weekend…I've got a summer job in the perfume department at Sokos downtown, and it's such a total grind all the time. I was really looking forward to this getaway."

It sounded like Sirkku felt worse about her lost weekend than the death of her friend.

At first it looked as though I wasn't going to get anything out of her. According to her, nothing in particular had happened on Saturday. They sang together for a while, and their voices were meshing really well. Then Antti and Tommi went to heat the sauna, while Riku played the piano—"Just think of someone having a piano at their summer cottage!"—and Timo and Sirkku sat on the deck drinking strawberry wine. Mira and Tuulia were inside preparing dinner for everyone.

"It was this really delicious ratatouille—though I thought there was a little too much garlic in it. Tuulia is a fabulous cook.

Then Timo and I went out in the rowboat while the rest of the group headed off to the sauna. We felt like being alone and didn't take our turn in the sauna until everyone else was done. I guess we came out around eleven o'clock."

When the lovebirds emerged from the sauna, the rest of the group was lounging around, drinking and listening to music downstairs in front of the fireplace. She recalled the mood at the time as relaxed.

"What time did you go to sleep? Did you go to bed before or after Tommi?"

"I guess we went to bed before him...I didn't look at the clock. Timo and I were sleeping upstairs in the big bedroom. I went to the bathroom once during the night, upstairs. I never went outside. Timo didn't either. He was asleep all night."

I wondered how Sirkku could know that if she had been asleep herself, though it was possible that they had been so tangled up in each other that the slightest movement would have woken her.

"Did Tommi seem normal to you yesterday?"

"Yes. He was in a good mood. He didn't even lose his temper with Pia during practice, though she was screwing up the whole time. Pia is a second soprano, and she was supposed to start the song solo, but she just couldn't get it. Tommi is always extra patient with Pia. I mean he was..."

Sirkku seemed to be suggesting that Pia had been included in the performance lineup for reasons other than her singing ability.

"To be honest, I think Pia and Tommi must have had something going on. Peter, Pia's husband, is off racing yachts in the US for almost six months. Isn't that a horribly long time? But Pia gets to go see him next month. Anyway, Tommi moved in on

Pia as soon as Peter left. Maybe I shouldn't be telling you this...
But Pia talked about it herself, and there probably isn't anything
wrong with mentioning it. I mean they go to movies and stuff
together. Luckily Peter is safely on the *Marlboro of Finland*, their
boat, I mean, because he certainly would have a reason to kill
Tommi. Well, no, not a reason to kill him, but he was pretty
jealous."

"So Tommi didn't have any shortage of women? What was
your relationship like with Tommi? Did you and Tommi ever
have...'something going on'?" I vaguely remembered that the
last time I had seen Jaana, she had griped about Tommi "lower-
ing his standards" and that he was "doing it with any little bitch
he could get into bed."

"Oh, well, just a little fling once in Germany, but nothing
serious." Sirkku did not appear to be ruffled by my direct question. Talking had clearly calmed her down, and now there was a
faintly proud edge to her voice. "Tommi and Jaana had already
broken up, but I know for a fact that Jaana's flirting with Franz
bugged Tommi. Tommi and I had a good time together, and I
hadn't even noticed Timo at that point. But it didn't last beyond
that trip, especially since I was going out with a guy named Jari
here at home."

"Was Timo jealous of Tommi?"

"About Germany? Nah, why would he be? There was nothing between us after we got back, and I would never cheat on
Timo."

Even though you cheated on your boyfriend at the time, I
thought with amusement. "Last night, when you went to the
bathroom, did you hear or see anyone else moving around?"

"The upstairs bathroom was right next to our room, so I
didn't have much time to see anything, especially since I was so

groggy and still a little drunk. And I fell right back asleep, though I did hear Tuulia snoring downstairs. I can't understand how Pia and Mira were able to sleep through that racket. Pia would have had a better chance of getting some sleep with Tommi, whatever else he might have wanted." Sirkku's expression turned guilty. "At some point after the sauna, I went upstairs and they were having some drama about Tommi asking Pia to sleep with him and her saying that she didn't want to. But that's all I heard."

"What woke you up in the middle of the night?"

"I had to pee, of course!" Sirkku's expression turned contemplative. "Well, I don't know...Maybe I heard some bang, but I'm not sure. I usually have to go the bathroom in the middle of the night if I've been drinking that late." Sirkku glanced at Rane and blushed.

I don't particularly like girlish flirting—maybe because I'm not any good at it myself. I let Sirkku go with a warning that I might need her again later in the week and asked her to send Timo in to see me.

"Why on earth is she advertising her sister's romance with Tommi? Does she think it has something to do with what happened?" I asked aloud, speaking half to myself and half to Rane. "In any case, we'll have to check whether the *Marlboro of Finland*—do you remember all the noise about cigarette ads again this summer?—anyway, to check whether it's in port right now somewhere and whether this Peter Wahlroos might have come to Finland for some reason in the middle of his race. I'd imagine that's pretty well impossible. Who knows though. Maybe the guy has hot Viking blood in his veins: if Penelope isn't up to fending them off, then Odysseus has to teach the suitors some manners."

I stopped mixing my myths as Timo Huttunen walked in. The thought of a vengeful husband hiding in muddy deck shoes in the bushes did not feel nearly as believable as Sirkku's hopeful

suggestion that the murderer was probably some random pas-
serby. I imagined they all hoped that.

Timo mostly seemed bored. With his blue-gray eyes, straw-
colored flattop, and sturdy frame, he brought to mind his name-
sake from Aleksis Kivi's *Seven Brothers*. At first glance, I would
never have guessed that he did anything art-related, at least not
classical music. He was the kind of guy you saw hanging out at
the pub next door to the gym, working on his third beer. His
opening line took me by surprise:

"I hope that neither of you was unkind to Sirkku. She is
completely devastated by what happened." The image of the
jock with the tankard crumbled in the face of his refined, almost
prim manner of speaking.

Timo explained that he was working at an agricultural
machinery dealership over the summer. He had been singing
with EFSAS for three years. His account of the events of the
previous night more or less matched Sirkku's version: sitting
around the table and on the deck, fooling around in the sauna
(he blushed with pride, and the beer tankard image flashed across
my mind again), sweet nothings whispered in front of the fireplace. Timo had slept like a log and not woken up when Sirkku
went to the bathroom, so he was unable to say how long she had
been away. Interestingly, Timo had his own theory about why
Tommi might have been murdered.

"I don't personally have anything against Tommi, but I had a
hard time watching his screwing around. I didn't like the way he
flirted with Pia. She's married, for God's sake. Antti didn't like it
either, and he said as much to Tommi."

"What do you mean?"

"Well, Peter—Pia's husband—was Tommi and Antti's old
buddy. Pia probably met Peter through them in the first place.

I went to take them a couple of beers in the sauna and couldn't help overhearing Antti saying to Tommi something along the lines of, 'Don't mess up your friend's life, he's got enough problems as it is.' Then Tommi said that she didn't seem to have anything against it. At that point, I turned around and went back inside because I didn't want to hear any more."

"So neither of them said explicitly that they were talking about Pia and Peter?"

"No, but who else could it have been about?" Timo's light blue eyes stared at me inquiringly. "Tommi was a pain when it came to women. He always had to hit on every girl he saw. I only got to know him better when he and Jaana broke up—you were Jaana's old roommate, right?—and since then he's constantly been on the prowl. Musically he can really, I mean *could* really, bring it; he was a good singer. Which he knew all too well himself. He was the leader of the group, after all."

There was clearly some bitterness in Timo's tone. Had Tommi criticized Timo's singing ability?

"He had a good degree, and I think he had just been promoted at work. I suppose he got paid pretty well too—at least that's the impression I got judging from his clothes and stuff... He had plenty to think about besides women, but somehow, I got the sense that they were what he mostly thought about."

I got the feeling that Timo was relieved to have Tommi out of the business of seducing other men's women.

Riku Lasinen, on the other hand, at first seemed genuinely grief-stricken. His eyes were so red that it was almost pathetic. Tommi had been one of his best friends. I thought about how I would feel if I woke up with a hangover, only to find my friend's corpse floating in the water. Riku had been singing in EFSAS for only a year, but he had spent several years in chamber choirs in Eastern Finland and Savonlinna.

"I hadn't ever been to Tommi's summerhouse before, and, damn, is it a swank place. Totally sweet. We went in Pia's car, and I drove 'cause I wanted to feel what it was like to be behind the wheel of a Bimmer. Timo and Sirkku were with us in the car. The others were ahead, and I wanted to pass Tommi, so I did a little rally move to get around him. That last dirt road was really fun to drive." Riku's strange, high voice was like that of an excited child. Judging from his breath, I deduced that he had fortified himself with a few pick-me-ups on the return trip to the city. Still, his enthusiasm over the car seemed inappropriate.

"Tommi was a good driver, but he scared the hell out of me a couple of times weaving across the road like a maniac—he had the girls screaming. Then when we got to the house, we started practicing. We sounded good as hell, and I was already getting my parts down. When we didn't feel like singing anymore, I sat down at the piano for a bit since the music for 'Lensky's Aria' was sitting there—do you know it?" Riku hummed the first few bars. I had never heard of Lensky before, but I concealed my ignorance by smiling lamely. Rane looked incensed. Apparently, I wasn't the only one who thought this experience should have sobered Riku up a bit more than it had.

"Then Tuulia came and told me not to play any sad songs, so I started going through this old volume of *Songs of Hope* that I found in the piano bench. Then I guess we ate and headed over to the sauna. Tommi and I went swimming and raced, and I won. By then, I was pretty drunk—Tommi had some real whiskey, Jack Daniel's, you know?"

I had had the pleasure of making the gentleman's acquaintance, a bit too intimately perhaps, on more than one occasion,

and now I recognized the smell on Riku's breath was Jack as
well.

"Tuulia and me danced a little, but the Bach on the CD we
were playing didn't really work for that. Then I guess I passed
out, and in the morning I didn't feel so hot."

Rane was tapping away furiously at his keyboard. I wondered whether he was trying to mimic Riku's eastern drawl.
Riku was in constant, nervous motion. Despite his blood-
shot eyes and two-day stubble, he was actually a very stylish young man. His slightly reddish hair—was that its real
color?—was cut in a trendy style, and his outfit looked like it
had been carefully coordinated, with his socks matching his
violet Burberry checked shirt and the frames of his glasses.
Short and slender, he looked even younger than he was,
almost like a boy.

Riku had found the body, and Mira had mentioned that
Riku had been wandering around downstairs during the night.
I asked him about this, and he flushed like he was guilty of
something.

"Yeah…I didn't even remember that. I was still pretty drunk,
I guess. It was sometime after midnight. I had gone to bed, but I
couldn't sleep, so I went to see what Tuulia was doing. She was
lying on her back snoring, and Mira was sitting on the bed staring at me, but Pia…she wasn't anywhere."

"You didn't see her upstairs either?"

"She must have been up there, with Tommi…Yeah, well,
see, when I was lying there trying to sleep, they were talking on
the landing upstairs and Tommi told Pia that she should come
sleep in his room. Pia said she wouldn't, that kissing and screwing were two different things. I guess you already know they
were fooling around…"

Though everyone appeared eager to share information about Pia and Tommi's relationship, Riku seemed to speak of it with a certain degree of admiration.

"And after that?"

"Nothing. I guess Pia went downstairs and then Antti came up to bed. When I still couldn't sleep, I waited for a while and then went to see Tuulia, but, as I said, she was sound asleep on her back snoring. I had one more whiskey to drown my sorrows and then I really did pass out."

"What time did you finally fall asleep?"

"Probably somewhere around three…"

"And Tommi was in his room then?"

"I don't know. The door was closed. And I don't know if Pia was in there or not."

"When you found Tommi in the water, was there anything significant about it?"

"Significant? Well, he was dead. That's significant. I can't say that I noticed anything; I didn't really want to look…And then my hangover hit, and I started puking."

"You didn't go back down to the water after that?"

"No. Mira and Antti went down there. Mira came back first, and then Antti, who said it was best not to go gawking and messing things up."

After Riku's torrent of words, Mira Rasinkangas's phlegmatic gravity was even more irritating. Mira clearly wanted to convey that she had no faith in my abilities as a police officer. This reminded me even more vividly of Mira's visits to our apartment and her way of treating me as a second-class citizen because I didn't play "real music." Punk bass didn't count. Then, during one of the usual evening gatherings after their practices, just out of spite I started criticizing one of the songs that made

up the foundation of the EFSAS repertoire. It was a lament about
wanting to return to Karelia, which the Russians took during
the war, and I had been listening to it through the wall for the
previous three hours. In reality my attitude toward classical
music wasn't nearly as negative as what I expressed at the time,
and no one but Mira had actually taken me seriously.

More than anything I was annoyed by my own reserve
toward Mira—a proper police officer should approach any
potential witness with the same neutral frame of mind.

"We arrived sometime around six," Mira began. "Riku
and Tommi were being stupid and driving recklessly on the
dirt roads—it was lucky we didn't end up in a ditch—and I
was feeling quite ill by the time we arrived, but of course we
had to practice. That was why we were there, to practice, even
though it seemed that some people had forgotten that. We did
manage to work quite productively for a couple of hours, but
then things started to slide and Riku started demanding beer
and so on."

"What else did you practice aside from the Toivo Kuula
piece?"

"We spent most of our time on that, since the second soprano
wasn't up to snuff—yet again—and Riku learns his parts so
appallingly slowly. Then we worked on some *Piae Cantiones* and
some easy Finnish folk songs."

"Who is the second soprano?"

"Well Pia, of course," Mira said with a snort, as though it
should be obvious. I remembered that Jaana had been a second soprano as well. She had described herself as a second-class
soprano, who couldn't sing high enough to be a real soprano or
low enough to be an alto.

"And after the practice ended?"

"Tuulia and I made food—as always, some do the work and some lie about—and then I washed the dishes before we went off to the sauna. Everything was just like normal. Riku was trying to sweet-talk Tuulia, which was maybe a little odd, but otherwise everything was more or less the same as any other night together after practice: sauna, talking, drinking. I don't usually drink more than two glasses, and I wasn't in a very social mood, so I went out to the boat dock for a little while and tried a few casts with a fishing pole that was out there. I caught a four-pound pike…if you can believe it. No one else could." Mira was clearly proud of her skill with a fishing pole. It was difficult for me to imagine her casting, but I could easily picture her killing what she caught. "After cleaning the pike, I was tired, so I was the first one to go to sleep, sometime around twelve."

"You were awake later that night though, because you saw Riku sneaking downstairs, right?"

"Tuulia was snoring to wake the dead, so Pia and I were up. Pia went to the bathroom, and then Riku appeared downstairs. I went to the bathroom as well and then tried to get Tuulia to turn onto her stomach so she would stop snoring, but I failed. Then I finally fell asleep."

"Where was Pia at that point? Had she come back?" I felt as though Mira was waiting for me to ask some truly stupid question. It was like I was sitting in front of a strict school teacher, one who knows that the upstanding-looking student before her is actually the class's worst lavatory smoker.

"I don't really know. I guess I thought she had gone somewhere with Riku. It would be best to ask her yourself.

"In the morning I was the first one to wake up, sometime after eight. I made coffee and went out to enjoy the beautiful summer morning. Around ten I put on some music to get the others up—we were supposed to be singing after all. Actually, I was a little surprised not to see Tommi anywhere, since it was his house. But you know how men are, always waiting for the women to make the coffee."

For once, Mira and I agreed.

"When Riku came yelling that Tommi was lying in the water, you and Antti rushed to the scene. Why?"

"What do you mean why? If somebody comes up to you yelling that somebody else is dead, then of course you go look. I guess the others were just sort of frozen in place, but in big groups, there are always a few people who know what to do."

"According to Antti, the two of you looked for a pulse and concluded from not finding one that Tommi was dead. Then you called the police before calling for an ambulance. Were you sure that Tommi was dead?"

"I didn't actually go very close to Tommi, and Antti acted almost like he didn't...like he wanted to shield me from seeing him. So I didn't see Tommi all that well, but I trusted what Antti said. As for who I called first, the number for the police happened to be listed before the one for the ambulance on the Peltonens' emergency list by the phone."

"Did you go back down to the water after you called the police?"

"No. Antti came back up, and then we just waited."

So Antti Sarkela would have had an opportunity to be alone with the body and destroy any evidence if necessary. Maybe it had been a traditional Finnish crime after all: two men in a drunken brawl. Over a bottle of vodka? Over a woman?

"Do you have any idea who would have wanted to kill Tommi Peltonen or why?"

"You'd be better off asking who wouldn't have had a reason to kill Tommi."

"Well, who wouldn't have, then?"

"I didn't have any reason to want him dead. I never had anything to do with him in that way. And I doubt Antti did either, since they were best friends. But the others...Sirkku had had a fling with Tommi in Germany, which ruined her relationship with her old boyfriend. Maybe Sirkku thought Tommi was serious about her—she's childish enough for that...and Timo has always been jealous of Tommi."

This seemed to be a topic Mira could get excited about.

"Pia may have gone further with Tommi than she wanted, and it was possible Tommi was threatening to tell Peter and break them up. And then we have Tuulia and Tommi. Now there's a strange relationship. Sometimes they're friends, sometimes they're dating. No one knows what Tuulia really thinks about Tommi. As for Riku, he just admired Tommi a little more than was good for him. He was dependent on Tommi in a strange way. And besides, Riku is completely infatuated with Tuulia at the moment, and Tommi had been teasing Riku about it. Tuulia was blatantly flirting with the poor boy, even though she could never take him seriously. I think Tuulia is definitely the best candidate for a murderer—no one else's nerves would have held out this long," Mira concluded.

No one else's but yours, I thought, and then curtly asked Mira to send Tuulia in as she left. I wished that my own brain would classify data as systematically as Mira's seemed to, but I just seemed to be getting more tangled up.

It was going to be more difficult to interview Tuulia than Mira because I had always liked Tuulia. We ran into each other occasionally in the university café and chatted whenever we crossed paths. Tuulia was unsure about the direction of her life in the same way that I was. She studied communications and sociology with limited success and then switched to theater at one point. Her latest thing was studying cultural history in Turku. She'd had all sorts of odd jobs over the years, and never seemed to feel any need to graduate or settle down.

"Hey, could Pia go next, after me? A bunch of us want to go back to our place to eat the leftovers from the villa and have a sort of memorial. Antti doesn't want to join us, so could he go last? You're going in alphabetical order, right?" Tuulia was obviously forcing herself to sound cheerful.

"OK. Are all the others still sitting out there waiting?"

"Yeah, no one really wants to go anywhere by themselves— or even with just one other person. Who knows who could be dangerous? Argh, it feels so strange. I've known Tommi for almost twenty years and now...We were in the same class with Antti all the way through high school."

"What are you up to these days?"

"I'm studying cultural history in Turku and taking a summer course that meets once a week. And I work as a playground monitor at a park a couple of days a week. The rest of the time I drink. So no, I still haven't turned respectable, even though I'm almost thirty." Tuulia smirked.

"What happened yesterday?" Though I wanted to, I couldn't acknowledge her smirk.

Tuulia's version was the same as the others—relaxed socializing, singing, a beautiful summer night. Mira had gone to bed first, followed shortly by Riku. Tuulia had been happy when he headed upstairs and passed out, since she had not been in the mood for flirting. Then Timo and Sirkku and the others had all gone to bed around the same time.

"I said good night to Tommi sometime after one, and that was it. In the morning I pounded on his door and told him coffee was ready, but he didn't answer. I opened the door, but he was gone. I guess I thought he'd gone for a swim—or maybe I didn't think anything of it."

"Why didn't you go down to the water to see what had happened to Tommi?"

"I don't have any interest in dead bodies. And for some reason I let myself think Riku was exaggerating. The little pest was still drunk even in the morning. Of course Mira ran down there because she couldn't contain her curiosity. She's always sticking her nose into everything. As for Antti...I wish he hadn't had to see it; he really liked Tommi." Tuulia buried her face in her hands for a moment, her blonde, bobbed hair falling over her forehead. I didn't have time to indulge her tears and continued my questioning.

"You've known Tommi for a pretty long time. Do you have any guesses about who might have hated him enough to kill him?"

"How should I know? Of course I keep trying to figure it out, but it's no use. There has to be a logical explanation though. The only person I can imagine doing anything that cold-blooded would be Mira, but I have no idea why she would do such a thing."

"Maybe she was secretly in love with Tommi?" I found it amusing that the women were blaming each other.

"It wasn't Tommi she was in love with! She's been stalking Antti ever since he and Sarianna broke up a couple of years ago. As you can imagine, she never confided anything to me, but everyone knows anyway. If I'm remembering this right, she basically threw herself in Tommi's lap at some party just to get Antti's attention, but of course it didn't work. Yesterday she waltzed in showing off that fish of hers—an interesting way to try to make an impression on a man, don't you think? It was a real bummer. For Mira, I mean. Antti definitely needs someone with a little more fire than that iceberg."

"What was your own relationship with Tommi like?"

"Oh, we had a great relationship. We were close and had a lot of fun together. We had a sort of mutually beneficial arrangement. We screwed when we felt like screwing and played each other's dates at cocktail parties when we needed to, and loaned each other money and stuff. It all worked great until yesterday. I'm sorry this had to happen to such a good friendship..." Tuulia was about to dissolve into tears again, but then clearly decided that a police interview was not the appropriate place for that sort of thing and made a desperate effort to shift back to her state of false cheerfulness.

"I really hope you can come up with some sort of motive for that bitch Mira. I wouldn't want any of the rest of us to turn out to be the one who did it." Tuulia tried to screw her face up into a smile, but didn't quite succeed.

"Why were you and Tommi still in EFSAS? Isn't it more of a student choir?"

"Well, I haven't exactly graduated yet," Tuulia said with a snort. "Maybe it's kids' stuff, but I like it, and besides, there's always someone to drink with after practice. Last fall I tried joining Cantiamo, but everybody was middle-aged, and they all had kids. Totally boring. I admit that EFSAS is probably just a way of drawing out my youth, an excuse to keep hanging around with twenty-somethings. Tommi just wanted to be the big man. In EFSAS he got all the solos, but in a better choir he wouldn't have stood out from the crowd so much. Antti is always trying

to leave, but so far we've been able to lure him back every time."
Tuulia stood up. "Do you have anything more for me or should I
ask Pia to come in?" Just as she was about to walk out, she turned
and added, "We should go out for drinks sometime when this is
all over."

Rane stared after Tuulia with disapproval. In Rane's world
a woman's place was at home making babies, and he loathed
Tuulia's type. He remarked dryly that we were not allowed to
be chummier with some people we were questioning than with
others. At least that was what they had taught him twenty years
ago at the academy.

I was forced to swallow my inappropriate retort because
Pia Wahlroos walked in at that moment without knocking. She
appeared more agitated than sad. She fiddled with her glossy
hair and nervously twisted her wedding ring, which looked too
big for her narrow finger—signs that she subconsciously wanted
to get rid of both the hair and the ring. I had read that in some
women's magazine. Of course, similar personality tests had said
that I was warmhearted and maternal.

Pia and Peter Wahlroos had been married for a little over a
year and a half. Peter was currently away sailing for six months,
and Pia wouldn't see him for another three weeks, when she
planned to travel to the States to meet him at the finish line. In
contrast to all the terrible things that everyone else had said, it
sounded to me as though she truly missed him.

"I let Riku drive my car to Villa Maisetta because I was feeling kind of anxious. I haven't heard anything from Peter in a few
days, and there have been such terrible storms that there haven't
even been any rankings for this leg of the race for a long time."

It appeared that she was more worried about her spouse than
Tommi's death.

"What was your relationship with Tommi Peltonen like?" Best to get straight to the point. Skirting around the issue wouldn't do anyone any good. At first Pia blushed, but then she lashed out almost violently.

"Oh, so the rumor mill has been hard at work! I've felt so lonely while Peter's been away, and we don't have enough money for me to be waiting in every port of call. Tommi is Peter's old friend, and Tommi's little brother, Henri, is also on the *Marlboro*. Of course Tommi and I have spent a lot of time together. Partly it's because of the messages we get from the yacht, but we've also gone out to eat and to the movies. But that's it! There hasn't been anything else to it, though none of them seem to believe it no matter how many times I tell them. Sirkku even told our mother that I supposedly went to bed with Tommi, which I most certainly did not!"

"Well, did Tommi try to get you to sleep with him? I'm sorry to have to ask, but this is part of the investigation, and I don't know yet what might be important," I said hurriedly and then immediately regretted apologizing for doing my job.

"Yes, he did try. The last time was yesterday. But I didn't want to."

"Do you think Tommi wanted to give the others the impression that there was more between you than there really was?"

"I don't know...Tommi wasn't as one-dimensional as he might have seemed on the surface. Sometimes I almost believed him when he said he'd fallen in love with me. But since I knew his reputation, I couldn't take him seriously. Yesterday was a little strange though. He said that he couldn't stand being alone anymore and that he just wanted to have me close to him. Of course I didn't believe that line—the last time he'd asked for that same 'closeness,' I ended up throwing him out of my house. But now...I don't know. Maybe he would still be alive if I'd given in."

I watched spellbound as movie-star tears rolled down Pia's cheeks. They did not smudge anything, did not make her nose run or her skin look mottled; somehow, they just belonged on her face.

"Do you remember exactly what Tommi said to you and when he said it?"

"We were on our way to bed. No one else was awake at that point except for Antti and Tuulia. Tommi asked me upstairs and, you know...we kissed and stuff, since I had been drinking more than normal, but Tommi got too intense, and I ended up saying something abrupt. Then it was weird because he started pleading with me. He whispered that he didn't want to be alone tonight because he was nervous. I told him that Riku and Antti were just on the other side of the hall."

"And then?"

"Tommi laughed a little strangely and said, 'Riku and Antti, now that really makes me feel safe.' I didn't know what he meant, but at that point I was irritated and went back downstairs."

"Do you have any idea why Tommi was nervous? Did he explain at all?"

"No. I just thought it was a new way of trying to get me in bed."

I let Pia leave and followed her out into the hallway for a moment. The entire group was still out there waiting; Timo and Sirkku sat wrapped around each other, and Riku lay with his head in Tuulia's lap. I asked them to stay in town for the next few days in case we needed to interview them again. They stood up and prepared to leave, uttering variations on, "Hey, we haven't been arrested yet" as they walked out. Only Antti

Sarkela remained. Maybe Antti had actually had enough time to fully comprehend the situation, because his lean face was pale and lined, looking much older than thirty. As he sat down across from me in the interrogation room, I began to imagine that he intended to admit to the murder. He looked that unhinged. However, he went on to answer my routine questions calmly enough. I still felt like I was plucking a bass with the top string tuned a third of an octave higher than normal though.

Antti had known Tommi basically his entire life—the two boys had played together before even starting elementary school. They had always been in the same class, and both had started out in the math department during their first year of college. After the army, Tommi had decided to switch to engineering. Antti had done civilian service in Rovaniemi instead of joining the army. After getting out, he had moved with Tommi into an apartment downtown. When serious girlfriends entered the picture, Antti moved somewhere else with Sarianna, and Jaana began to spend half her time at Tommi's place. I remembered quite well that she had never wanted to give up her own place though. Now Antti lived in a studio in Korso, out past the airport near the train line.

Antti had investigated the body superficially. He had done his civilian service as a hospital orderly, so he was used to doing basic triage and could tell when someone was dead.

"For the first time in a long time, we were really having fun. When we were driving out to the house on the East Highway, I thought Tommi was in a great mood. He was fooling around like when we were kids. On the news they said something about a drug bust, and he started playing mafia and racing with Riku, who he pretended had turned on the family, and Tuulia was right in on the game too. It felt like twenty years had suddenly fallen away. Tommi always liked playing pirates and that sort of thing when we went sailing as kids. Then we got to the house and started practicing. I thought it went really well. It was nice to be singing the same part with Tommi because he was so precise. He was the most musical one in the whole group."

Antti seemed to hesitate for a moment.

"Then, when we went to heat the sauna, I noticed that something was wrong. I thought it was because of Pia. I really couldn't tell you what Tommi truly wanted out of that relationship. We all go way back with Peter, and he's Tommi's little brother's best friend. I didn't approve of Tommi fooling around with Pia, and I told him so. But now, in retrospect, I don't think that was all Tommi was worried about."

"How did this worry express itself?"

"I don't know how to describe it. When you know someone really well, you can just sense their moods. A lot of times, Tommi started screwing around like a little kid when he was nervous. And he laid it on pretty thick during practice too, picking at Riku because he didn't know his parts and telling Mira over and over not to sing so loud."

"But you think he was more nervous than afraid?"

"Yes. Then that night, once we'd had a few drinks, everything seemed more normal again. We chatted about all the usual stuff, music and the upcoming performance and the choir's other projects. Mira went fishing and there was a little commotion when she hooked a pike and started screaming for someone to bring a net. It was a nice one—want to see?" Antti kicked his bag. "No one else wanted it, so I'm taking it home to my cat. That is, if he's willing to come live with humans again."

"You were sleeping near Tommi's room. Did you hear anything during the night?"

"I woke up when Riku snuck out to the bathroom in the middle of the night. I thought he had gone in there to puke, since he had drunk way too much again. I woke up one other time, when it was already light out. Some noise woke me up, and I've been racking my brain to figure out what it was—some bang anyway. We had the window open, and the birds were making a real racket. Maybe it was a door slamming. I really don't know."

"Who killed Tommi?"

"I don't know," Antti replied curtly. "But I'm glad that Peter is on the other side of the planet right now, because he would be entirely capable of murdering someone out of jealousy. He's really possessive."

"We'll be checking on his whereabouts. Now you're free to go look for your cat."

After Antti left I slumped down with my head in my hands. Rane was busily tapping away at his notes. I had hoped that the interviews would shed some light on whether this was an accident, manslaughter, or murder. Suicide felt like the least convincing possibility, but we still had to consider it.

We still had to talk to Tommi's parents and track down Henri Peltonen, Tommi's younger brother. We also had to arrange for a warrant so we could go search Tommi's apartment, and we had to interview his colleagues at work. I also needed to find out who his other friends were. None of the choir members had said anything about a permanent girlfriend, but he might still have had one—or more than one, given that this was Tommi we were talking about.

I was also going to have to look into Tommi's financial situation. He had a surprisingly expensive car for such a young man, especially one who probably still had student loans to pay off.

What kind of money was Tommi making at work? Maybe his murder had something to do with his job.

It was important that I not focus too much on the choir. Some members of the group had a life outside the choir. Tommi certainly did. I knew there wasn't any sense expecting to turn up much evidence in the first round of interviews, much less a direct confession tied nicely with a bow. But everyone had been so shockingly calm, as though it were the most normal thing in the world for a friend to die. It was possible that one of them was an exceptionally good actor. Or were they all innocent? But then, why would someone from outside the group choose a summerhouse buzzing with people as a site for a murder? It was unlikely there were even burglars prowling around during the vacation high season.

"If we assume that one of them murdered Peltonen, what would you say?" I asked Rane. He shrugged.

"Hey, listen, I'm perfectly happy that this isn't my headache. They're all strange birds, just look at the way none of them dares to break away from the others. But my favorite is definitely the round girl...Rasinkangas. She's a regular ice queen. Just like my mother-in-law. Definitely has the nerves to bash someone's brains in."

"But what's her motive?"

"Oh, you'll find it. That feisty girl, Tuulia Rajala, said that Rasinkangas threw herself in Peltonen's lap once. Maybe there were some unpleasant consequences that nobody knew about, and she's been plotting her revenge for who knows how long."

"It's too bad I won't be able to use your brilliant imagination on this case. This whole thing terrifies me. I knew Tommi, and I really can't be objective on this one."

"Take it easy. Use it to your advantage that you knew this Tommi guy and some of the rest of them. They seem to treat you as more of a friend than a cop. Maybe they won't take you quite as seriously, but in this case, that may not be a bad thing."

Over the summer Rane had witnessed other occasions when my role as a police officer hadn't been taken seriously. I was surprised to find that he was trying to buck me up.

"If I were you, I'd talk to that Rasinkangas again. She definitely knows more than she's telling. It looks like she's a little more of an outsider in the group and makes a habit of keeping tabs on other people's business. I'd also check out the kid, Lasinen. Maybe he was so drunk he doesn't even remember clocking Peltonen."

"OK, Uncle Rane. Have a good vacation."

After his pep talk, I genuinely meant that.

3

But what is man?
A restless will-o'-the-wisp, a restless will-o'-the-wisp

On Monday morning I looked at my reflection in the mirror and was satisfied with what I saw. My narrow, navy-blue uniform skirt and carefully pressed shirt were no-nonsense. I had pulled my hair back in a tight bun and applied dark makeup, which made me look older. Thankfully, I could use clothing, hairstyle, and makeup to adjust not only how people saw me but also how I acted. In my uniform, I was mature and businesslike, but in jeans and tennis shoes I always seemed to end up swearing and running places when I should be walking. As I applied a layer of lipstick, I felt as though I were painting on a mask in order to hide my true self—which was exactly what I wanted. At ten o'clock sharp I was meeting Tommi's father, Heikki Peltonen, who was some sort of engineer; before then, I needed to go over the results of the laboratory tests and the autopsy report.

Heikki Peltonen had called me late Sunday night. It struck me as ominous that the duty officer had given him my phone number instead of my boss's. The officer on guard duty at the summerhouse and Antti, who had returned to Vuosaari to look for his cat, told Heikki Peltonen what had happened. Tommi's mother, Maisa, went into shock, but Heikki Peltonen wanted

to meet me, the police officer investigating his son's death—he
was strictly avoiding the word "murder"—as soon as possible.
He seemed irritated that we sealed off the boat dock and were
looking for a possible murder weapon in the woods along the
shoreline. I knew that his abrupt manner was probably a reaction
to the traumatic news he'd just received. Grieving people often
behaved irrationally, and Heikki Peltonen belonged to a genera-
tion of men who had been raised to get along without tears no
matter what the situation.

The captain of the unit, the next person above me after
Kinnunen, called right after I got off the phone with Peltonen.
He explained briefly that Kinnunen would not be coming in to
work for the next couple of days because of a "stomach flu," and
that I would be responsible for the investigation into Tommi's
death for the time being. He ended the conversation by saying he
wanted to meet with me first thing in the morning.

I thought it might be necessary to have the divers take a look
underwater. Though the seawater would have washed away any
fingerprints, they might find the object that was used to strike
Tommi.

How Tommi had died remained unclear. I wondered why
I was automatically regarding this as a murder, when there was
still no evidence that that was the case. Although it could just be
manslaughter, I had a sense that the crime had been committed
in anger, so there would probably be fingerprints on the weapon.

After speaking with the captain, I had called the pathologist, Salo, who had confirmed that the actual cause of death was
drowning. The blow to the head had probably resulted in uncon-
sciousness, but it would not have been enough to kill anyone
outright. Tommi must either have fallen or been pushed into the
water, and then gotten water in his lungs. Salo was still not sure

whether the other contusions on Tommi's body were the result of a struggle or caused by the shore rocks, but he confirmed that at least one of the bruises on his cheek had been inflicted before he died. Tommi's blood-alcohol level was very high, so we couldn't rule out the possibility that he had somehow slipped, hit his head, and then fallen into the sea. But what would have tripped him on an empty dock when he was barefoot?

"The blow to the head occurred at three or four, assuming he ended up in the water immediately. There isn't any outside material in the wound, so we can assume that whatever he was struck with was something strong and solid."

"What do you mean?" I asked.

"Well, for example, it couldn't have been a crumbly rock. Given the nature of the edges of the wound, the object was blunt, but not perfectly smooth."

"How much force was needed for the blow?"

"That depends mostly on the weapon. Even a child could make a dent like this with something big and heavy. If all of your suspects are adults, I wouldn't rule anyone out."

There was nothing surprising or particularly enlightening in Salo's evaluation, and I had finally made it home a little after nine. I had had trouble falling asleep and felt like having a drink, but the only booze I had in the house was some mild, sickly sweet kiwi liqueur, a memento from a trip to Sweden six months before. I momentarily considered going out for a beer, but I was afraid I would backslide again, and that one would turn into two and two into three…I wasn't feeling especially sociable and would probably have taken out my frustrations on anyone who tried to sit down at my table, a constant annoyance at the corner pub.

Luckily, one of my old school friends called, and I spent half an hour gossiping with her about mutual friends and acquaintances. She was a regular newswire and always had some juicy story to tell. Some of her wilder tales even made murder seem run-of-the-mill. After that, I just gave up and went to sleep.

Now I tried to collect my thoughts as I stared out the tram window on my way to work. The tabloids hadn't come out yet, but I was nervous that at least one or the other of them would already have reporters on the case. Summer was almost halfway over, Finland had closed for business, and the newshounds had to start digging deeper for their shock stories. I could just picture the headlines—FEMALE DETECTIVE HEADS INVESTIGATION: MURDER STILL UNSOLVED—and wanted no part of the potential media frenzy.

The Pasila police station was already buzzing when I arrived. On my desk was an order from the captain to come report on the case. I put on my game face and marched into his office, which was hazy with cigar smoke. I couldn't stand tobacco smoke when I was sober, and I wasn't afraid to show as much to the captain. Let him smoke five cigars at once if he likes, just so long as he isn't poisoning me. With his big cigars and massive desk, he may have imagined himself as the hero of some American cop show. Did he have a bottle of booze in his drawer too?

I optimistically tried to wriggle out of the case by mentioning that I had known the deceased. It wasn't any use though, because there was no one else who could break away from what they were already doing and take it.

"Narcotics called asking for help the minute I walked in the door. Apparently, they've uncovered some big distribution ring and some of their boys made some premature arrests. So now they've got all these bit players who don't really know anything. We don't have anyone to send them either. Kinnunen is out for the whole week now—I just got the sick leave approval. And all of the older detectives are already overworked as it is... So, if you could just handle this..." The captain puckered his mouth around his cigar, looking uneasy. Kinnunen's alcoholism seemed to be a taboo subject with the more senior officers in the department.

"You're starting to have the routine down well enough. And Saarinen's sick leave will last at least through September, so there'll be plenty of work for you here. And if you get through this successfully, we might be able to start thinking about a permanent position...especially since it isn't like there's an overabundance of you women in this profession..." The captain drew these words out as though he didn't really want to let them out of his mouth.

"Well, we can revisit that later," I said noncommittally. I didn't want to promise anything. Though I wanted out of the department as soon as possible, I didn't want to irritate my boss any more than absolutely necessary at the moment.

"Your summerhouse victim's dad—Peltonen was his name?— is coming in to see you today, right? Be careful with him. He isn't just anybody—he's on the board of Neste Oil. And since his other son is in that yacht race they've been making all the fuss about, we could end up with the wrong kind of publicity." The captain's face was three shades grayer than usual. Normally, when people got worked up, they turned red, but my boss just grew steadily grayer until all real color had drained from his face.

I wondered how he already knew the Peltonens' resumes and took it as a sign that I was really in for it. It would have been easier for me to do my job if the captain didn't have such a fear of authority. I once had the unfortunate experience of looking on as the captain's concern for his own position interfered with the investigation of a rape allegation against a rising politician. The victim dropped the charges. Though rapes were usually foisted on the female officers, I hadn't been one of the main investigators in this case and felt lucky to have avoided it. I knew one of the officers who helped with the case, Detective Männikkö, relatively well, and his version of events made them sound like a soap opera. The victim was a middle-aged woman who, according to the tabloids, had several male friends. In the end someone had managed to sell the idea that the politician was the victim of a secret plot. The fledgling politician had played the part of the martyr, claiming that the woman had staged the whole thing to smear his reputation, and the tabloids wanted to believe him. Ever since, the captain's phobia of fancy titles had grown even worse.

"Karppanen just left on vacation too. So we've got a pretty big manpower shortage, but take Koivu as an assistant if you need him, and you can share Miettinen with Savukoski. Savukoski has that murder-robbery, but let's try to get this off the board fast. Virrankoski will be coming off vacation soon too."

The captain's phone rang just then, and I quickly slipped out of his office as he answered. I didn't want to think about continuing my temporary commission. Of course it would be an easy way to solve my problem of choosing a career, since I'd be able to put off the need to make a decision for another six months, but I had more pressing things to worry about just then.

My phone was ringing angrily when I got back to my office.

"It's Hiltunen, out in Vuosaari at the crime scene." I remembered the eager young cop with the blond hair from the day before. He sounded excited. "Um, I think I found the murder weapon."

"What!" Even I was surprised by the volume of my voice. "What did you find?"

"Well, it's, um, an ax with blood on it. It was over by the sauna building in the bushes. Should I bring it in to the station?"

"No, I'll send a photographer out. Do you have a partner with you? OK, once the pictures are done, leave him there and bring the ax in to the station. Leave the area where you found it as undisturbed as you can, and I'll try to come out there this afternoon."

An ax...That sounded simultaneously so revolting and so routine. Hiltunen seemed proud of himself. Hardly twenty years old, he was still just a baby. I hoped that he hadn't ruined all the fingerprints. If the blood was Tommi's, then we could start talking about murder. But what in heaven's name had an ax been doing down by the shore?

I tried to put in a quick call to Jaana in Kassel before Heikki Peltonen arrived, but the phone lines to Germany were jammed for some reason. I was lucky to find the number on the back of an old Christmas card, which I had saved only because the Santa Claus featured on it was extremely attractive and clad only in a beard and an elf hat. In years past I had assembled a rather comprehensive collection of pictures of handsome men on my wall, but in the end I grew tired of how formulaic they were. Most pictures of men that were meant to be erotic were quite boring once you'd looked at them for a while.

Heikki Peltonen was punctual. Based on our phone conversation, I had pictured him as a graying retired gentleman with a large midsection who went out for only the occasional leisurely Sunday yacht outing. In reality, Peltonen looked young to be Tommi's father. Though he had to be well past fifty, he still looked like he was in his forties, and his body looked graceful and flexible. His face shone with the tan common to those who spent their weekends sailing, and I saw that Tommi inherited his blond

Viking looks from his father. The fabric of his dark gray suit looked suspiciously like silk. Though I wasn't the type to go for older men, his handshake and the look in his eyes that followed it might have made me blush under different circumstances. I didn't have to worry about how to start the conversation because he took care of that for me.

"Miss— or is it Mrs.— Kallio, I very much hope that we can clear up the circumstances surrounding my son's death quickly. This kind of accident is sufficiently unpleasant even without being interviewed by the police. It is entirely too much to ask that my devastated wife answer questions of any sort. I also heard that Tommi's friends were all dragged down here and interrogated by the police last night."

"I'm sorry, but we have to explore every possibility. One of his friends may have been present when Tommi died."

"Are you saying that my son was murdered?"

"I'm not saying anything yet. But we have to take that possibility into account."

"Tommi's friends are upstanding, highly cultured young people. What reason would they have to kill anyone? If this is a case of murder, which I don't believe for a second, then it must have been someone from outside. There were a number of vacation home break-ins during the spring, and all sorts of bums have been camping out in the area."

It struck me as unlikely that even an amateur would have set out to rob summer cottages in the middle of a prime summer weekend, but I let Peltonen talk.

"And it may simply be that Tommi tripped. I'm sure they'd all been drinking too much, and sometimes the dock can be slippery."

"Yes…What did he hit his head on, then? The edge of the dock is so high above the surface of the water that it doesn't get wet, so if Tommi hit his head on it, we would still be able to see evidence of it. And the worn, rounded wooden edge of the dock wouldn't have left such a nasty mark. There aren't even any rocks next to the dock for him to have hit his head on; the nearest rocks are the ones he was floating against when he was found. We've even tested that scenario and established that it's impossible to hit those rocks falling off the dock."

The boys from Forensics had had a good laugh about that test, which had mainly consisted of floundering around in the water, but they had done it anyway.

Peltonen clearly wanted facts. Theories weren't going to sway him in the slightest. I was all too familiar with the fact that I was often the one who ended up sitting in the witness chair when I interviewed older, powerful men. I didn't even bother getting upset about their inquiries into my marital status or correcting their use of "Miss" with "Detective." Whatever. I was tired of trying to change every little thing about the world. I even used plastic grocery bags every once in a while and occasionally resorted to buying my morning yogurt in single-serving packages instead of the usual liter carton.

"My wife was also extremely upset that her fingerprints were taken, as though she were some sort of common criminal. You could at least have saved that indignity for a later time."

"Did they take your fingerprints yesterday? I'm sorry. That was an error."

Someone in Forensics had been rushing things. I had asked them to take the choir members' prints for safety's sake, but I hadn't said anything about the Peltonens. Now I tried to cover my embarrassment.

"You have another son, Henri Peltonen? And did I understand correctly that he is out of the country for a yachting competition in the United States?"

"Yes. Henri is the second trimmer on a maxi-class yacht named *Marlboro of Finland*. We don't know yet whether we want to notify him of this unhappy news on the boat or wait until the competition is over. This race is very important to him. Another of Tommi's acquaintances is also on the boat, Peter Wahlroos, whose wife, Pia, was also at Villa Maisetta, if I understand correctly. Hopefully this won't completely ruin the boys' race."

Again that reaction of focusing on trivialities, I thought.

I didn't get much information out of Peltonen, who seemed to have kept up with his oldest son's life at only the most superficial level. Tommi had visited his parents' home in Westend for dinner from time to time, and they had met up quite often at the villa, but he had had his own apartment and his own life for ages.

"It's true that Tommi may have had a few too many girlfriends and that we were starting to hope that he would settle down. Otherwise, he had his act together. He graduated from the Helsinki University of Technology with high marks, his apartment is paid for, he seemed to like his job at Finnish Metals Incorporated, and he loved music and sailing. Aside from his dealings with women, he lived a normal, quiet life. I can't understand why anyone would have killed him intentionally."

I noticed that the furrows beneath Heikki Peltonen's tan had deepened. He obviously wanted to make himself believe that his son's death had been an accident. Easier to endure the loss that way. If Tommi's death turned out to be murder, it would inevitably lead to painful questions and even more painful answers.

"What other friends did Tommi have aside from these choir members?"

"He didn't have very many other real friends, I don't think. He had colleagues from work and sailing acquaintances, of course, but I didn't really know the specifics of his life. Antti Sarkela might know."

"When did you last see Tommi? Did he seem like his normal self?"

"He called us Tuesday evening to confirm that the villa would be empty. It's been a little while since our last visit because my wife and I have been sailing on the coast of Sweden for the last three weeks. We didn't arrive home until Monday."

Peltonen paused to think. His brow wrinkled as he did so, and at that moment, he looked exactly like Tommi, who'd had the same habit.

"I don't know if this means anything, but a couple of months ago Tommi asked me what recourse there was for making a debtor take legal responsibility when there isn't any promissory note. When I asked for details, he was evasive. I got the impression that someone owed Tommi money and wasn't willing to pay, but it didn't seem like the sum was all that great—maybe around ten thousand marks."

"Thank you. That may be very important. And finally—and this is just a routine question—where were you anchored on Saturday night? We have to check everyone's whereabouts." I was waiting for an indignant protest, but Peltonen just looked resigned.

"Yes, I understand. We spent that night in a small guest marina a little west of Barösund, and in the morning we had coffee in a café nearby. Our friends Jarl and Brita Sundström were with us, so you can check our...hmm...alibis...with them. I can give you their telephone number."

Even though there was probably no point, I decided to follow up on this anyway. Trying to draw conclusions could be stimulating work in theory, but I had such scant material to work with at this point. I knew that I would also have to interview Maisa Peltonen once she had had time to recover.

After another attempt, I succeeded in getting through to Germany. A "Frau Schön" answered the telephone, and it took me a moment to realize that this was, in fact, Jaana.

"Hi, it's Maria Kallio, from Finland. How are you?"

"Maria! It's nice to hear your voice after so long. Are you coming this way for a visit? I'm on maternity leave right now with my little Michael. He's three months old. Just think, me with a baby! Sometimes I have absolutely no idea what to do with him."

"Well, I certainly wouldn't know what to do with a baby either. Unfortunately, I'm not coming to Germany. In fact, I'm calling on business. I'm working for the police department again, but it's a long story why. In any case, this is why I'm calling: Tommi, your old boyfriend Tommi Peltonen, has died, and he was probably killed."

Jaana's startled cries and sobs on the other end of the line made me realize that I could have delivered the news less indelicately. But Jaana eventually calmed down, and I was able to explain the general outline of the case.

"I really don't know why anyone would have murdered him," she said. "I mean, you remember how Tommi was, always going after different women. It was exhausting, and that's why I ended up leaving him. He just acted so infuriatingly superior if you ever accused him of being unfaithful or irresponsible. He just laughed in my face and said that he was only 'living life.' As if there were different rules for him than for me. He sure raised a big enough stink if I danced too close to someone at a choir retreat or something. Sometimes I felt like he didn't care at all about anyone else's feelings. But then at other times he could be perfectly lovely. He certainly didn't lack charm when he wanted something. But he was a risk taker. Once we were supposed to go out somewhere together and he showed up with his previous date…Hold on a sec, Michael's crying. I'm going to go give him his pacifier."

Jaana laid down the receiver. From farther off in the room came a child's whimpering and Jaana's tender cooing. It was surreal to hear those sounds coming from my old roommate's mouth. A few seconds later, the whimpering stopped.

"I imagine Tommi must have seduced some other man's girlfriend again," Jaana said with a sigh when she returned to the telephone. "He always needed all the girls' attention. Sometimes it felt like anyone would do."

"You basically knew everyone who was out at the villa, right? Do you know whether anyone might have had an old grudge against Tommi?"

"Yeah, I know all of them except for that Riku guy. Let's see. A grudge against Tommi…" Jaana hesitated before continuing.

"I'd say Sirkku Halonen probably held a grudge. After that trip to Germany, she ended things with her boyfriend because she and Tommi had had a fling. It was typical Tommi on display during that trip. I broke up with him just before we left, and then I met Franz…When we got back to Finland, Tommi tried to get me back and couldn't get it through his head that I had left my heart in Kassel. In any case, Sirkku didn't really get what was going on and kept badgering Tommi and accusing him of tricking her into breaking up with her boyfriend for no reason."

"Sirkku is dating Timo Huttunen now. Do you think that has any significance?"

"Huttunen? What a pompous ass. Nice-looking though. At least Sirkku hasn't lowered her standards. I don't know what

might be bottled up inside of Timo. He's so self-important. I
suppose he could be secretly jealous of all of Sirkku's exes."

At the end of the phone call, Jaana asked me to send her
regards to everyone, especially Tuulia. I promised to pass the
message along and asked her to call if she remembered anything
that might be important. Then I called the passport office to
have them verify that neither Jaana nor Franz Schön had been
in the country over the weekend. They couldn't give me any
information about Jaana immediately because she was still a
Finnish citizen, but no German national by the name of Franz
Schön had entered Finland, at least through the airports. I also
asked the passport office to check whether either of them had
exited Germany, even though suspecting the Schöns seemed
farfetched.

The *Marlboro of Finland* had been out on the Atlantic the
entire previous week. No member of the crew had set foot on
dry land, so both Peter Wahlroos and Henri Peltonen were out
of the picture—as I had assumed they would be.

I ate a rushed lunch in the police station cafeteria. Fortunately,
the tabloids still hadn't broadcast any crazy headlines about the
case. Apparently, a few reporters had been trying to contact me,
but the switchboard had been instructed to direct all calls to the
captain, who only stated that Detective Kallio was investigating the case. I knew that the papers would love to spin stories
about my gender—a female detective was news—and I wasn't
sure how I felt about that. On the one hand, my example could
give other girls the courage to enter less traditionally female professions; on the other, I didn't want any publicity about myself
as a police officer, especially since I didn't yet know whether I
actually wanted to be one. For the moment, the headlines were
filled with news about some Estonian prostitute thing: ESTONIAN

PROSTITUTE ROBS CLIENTS, screamed the *Ilta-Sanomat*, and the *Iltalehti* proclaimed, LUXURY WHORE TAKES MEN'S MONEY. Seemed like that was kind of the point of the exchange.

After cramming down my parmesan-crusted salmon, I headed back to my office. I heard my phone ringing as I walked down the hallway; a quick fifty-yard dash got me there in time to answer.

"It's Huikkanen from the lab. I've got this ax here if you're interested."

"Shoot."

"Judging from the salt on it, it looks like it was rinsed in seawater, but there's still some blood on it. Two kinds no less. We still haven't identified one of them—we might need to start taking blood samples from your suspects—but the other one is definitely Peltonen's. There's even a little piece of the back of his head on it, hair and skin and such. And dirt—where did that uniform dig this out of again?"

"But this is what struck Peltonen?"

"It looks that way. With the butt, thankfully."

"What's the other blood, then?" I asked.

"I'm not one hundred percent sure, but given that there was something that looked like scales on the ax too, I think the other blood probably came from a fish. I don't know what species."

Fish...Mira had caught a pike. Could she have finished it off with the ax?

"Were there fingerprints on the ax?"

"Loads of them. Looks like our murderer didn't bother washing the whole ax, but just rinsed the head, because there isn't any salt on the other end of the handle. There were two sets of prints on it: Sarkela's and Rasinkangas's."

"Wow. What positions?"

"Rasinkangas's prints are pretty interesting. They're actually only right-hand prints, and they're positioned in such a way that it would be impossible to strike the way you would normally lift an ax, with the blade toward the ground. In this position, you could strike with the butt, but you'd have to twist your wrist a bit awkwardly to do so."

"So the position sounds more like when you're moving an ax from one place to another." As I pictured the scene in my mind, I picked up a thick ruler and twisted my wrist, pretending I was wielding an ax. "Maybe she covered her hands for the actual act, but forgot afterward."

"Could be. Sarkela's prints are all over it, and it's clear that he held the ax in a variety of positions, including the classic wood-chopping one. He must have changed his grip several times. And that's all there was."

"Good. I was thinking I'd go out to the crime scene again today, but I have to handle a few other things first. I assume I'll get your report once it makes the rounds?"

I looked through my notebook for Mira's and Antti's phone numbers. Mira had a summer job at the city courthouse, which was close to the police station. Funny.

"Hi, this is Detective Kallio. I'd like to meet as soon as possible. Would two o'clock work?" Mira did not sound surprised by my call and replied with uncharacteristic meekness that she would try to take her coffee break around two. Antti was more difficult to reach at the university, but I finally got him on the line in the math department library.

"I make my own schedule, especially during the summer when there aren't any classes. I could be there at, say, three."

Antti didn't ask for any additional explanation either. I called the motor pool to reserve a car, because I still meant to head out later that afternoon to investigate the dock and the site where the ax was found. Though an honest confession would be welcome, I doubted I would be arresting either Mira or Antti today. I was tired just thinking about it all.

Mira arrived precisely on time. Although nothing about her behavior indicated sorrow, her black skirt and white blouse looked like mourning garb. She could just as easily have been visiting the bank to make a withdrawal from a fat checking account as in a police station for an official interview.

"Did you have a good send-off party last night?" I asked brutally. I wanted to provoke her to express some kind of emotion. Any emotion.

"It did us all good." Still no feeling.

"In what way?"

"It was clear that no one wanted to go home alone—except for Antti, though of course we tried to get him to join us. It did us good to talk and think about what happened."

"Well, what conclusion did you come to?"

"That it must have been an accident. Hopefully. We're certain that Tommi didn't kill himself. He liked himself entirely too much to do anything like that. But could someone really have killed him? Though Tommi could certainly be irritating, that seems a little too farfetched. But we all understand, of course, that we will all be treated as potential killers until you solve the case. Sirkku was particularly hysterical about that."

"Were you blaming each other?"

"Some of us suspected Antti and thought his reserve was a sign of a guilty conscience, but we don't all agree on that. Riku claimed he was positive he heard Antti going into Tommi's room during the night, but Riku was so drunk there was no way he could have heard anything. If someone did murder Tommi, my nominee is still Tuulia. Her fits of rage can be...appalling."

"I still don't know yet whether we're talking about murder, but we've found an ax with Tommi's blood on it. It had your fingerprints on it too. How do you explain that?"

A bewildered expression appeared on Mira's face, but it quickly changed to amusement.

"Is that why you wanted me here? Yes, I handled that ax a couple of times. Someone had left it in the middle of the sauna building porch, and I moved it to the side so no one would trip on it. And then later in the evening, I caught that big pike. I yelled for someone to bring me something to bash its head with. Antti brought the ax from the sauna and killed it. I imagine that in all the excitement we left it on the dock." Mira snorted. "If I were going to kill a person, I would have the sense to use gloves. They talk about them in every single mystery novel ever written." She paused for a moment, then continued.

"Who else's fingerprints have you found on it? Antti's, of course. He chopped the wood for the sauna, since none of the other boys could be bothered to make the effort. Antti said he likes chopping wood, and you can tell just from his biceps," she said, suddenly blushing.

I remembered what Tuulia had said about Mira's interest in Antti, and somehow it made her seem more human. She didn't have poor taste in men, I thought, but then I sighed with disappointment. There was a reasonable explanation for everything. Of course, it was possible that Mira wasn't telling the whole truth. Antti could have used the ax after chopping the wood as well, and he would have had the strength and coordination for a blow like this. And besides, the blow had come from above, and Antti was the only one who was tall enough to have struck him from this angle if Tommi had been standing. If Tommi had been seated, though, height would be irrelevant. Mira's obvious need to protect Antti was a little amusing. At least she didn't seem to be trying to hide her infatuation.

"Did you have anything else? My coffee break doesn't last forever, but I'm so close to the station that you can have me run by every day if you need me to," Mira said brusquely, as though regretting her earlier loquacity.

After Mira had gone, I cursed my stupidity when I realized that I could have at least offered her a cup of coffee in exchange for taking up her break time. On the other hand, an interview over coffee mugs would have felt like a gab session, and I was afraid of creating such congenial situations while working on this case.

While Mira had been calm, Antti at least looked like he was sad. Though it was possible he always wore black jeans and a black T-shirt, his pale face and red-rimmed eyes made it look like more than that. I wondered about the reason for the red eyes—insomnia, drinking, or crying—or perhaps a combination of all three?

"Hi—what was your rank again? Detective? Any results yet in the investigation?" he asked in a tired voice as he slumped down in the chair across from me.

"Yes. We found the murder weapon, and it has your finger-prints on it," I stated grimly. Antti's hostility irritated me much more than Mira's had, and I became even more irritated as I realized I was irritated at all. Back in the day, Tommi had been nice to look at, but Antti had been nice to talk to. Antti wasn't bad looking either, especially since I had always thought that men with large mouths and Roman noses were sexy. A cross between Mick Jagger and Dustin Hoffman would have been my ideal. I checked out the biceps Mira had mentioned, trying to maintain an indifferent expression as I did so. The black T-shirt covered some undeniably nicely shaped arms.

"What the hell? Do you really mean Tommi was murdered?" Antti was unable to conceal his alarm.

"It's starting to look that way."

"What murder weapon are you talking about?"

"An ax someone tried to conceal under the sauna. Laboratory tests show that it's the murder weapon."

"Oh, that ax." A hint of a smile appeared on Antti's lips. "I split at least half a cord of wood with that ax. The Peltonens only have one usable ax. Typical for that family—they have at least four different bark scrapers, but only one decent ax. Anyone could tell you about it—about the firewood chopping, that is, not bark scrapers. If you need any more evidence, just look at these blisters on my palms." Antti spread his hands out on the desk, palms up, so I had no choice but to look at them and see the blisters on his long-fingered hands.

"I'm getting pretty decrepit if I get blisters from a little job like that. So anyway, of course my fingerprints are on the ax."

"And later in the evening you used it to kill."

"What the hell are you talking about?"

"You murdered a fish in cold blood." Antti's tense expression relaxed as he laughed, which seemed to do him good. My words made me want to laugh too, but I mentally kicked myself in the shin.

"Well, I guess I did. There wasn't anything else for it, though I admit I would rather have let the fish go. Obviously, we left the ax on the dock and...oh damn it to hell!"

"Did you find your cat?"

"Einstein? He was asleep on the sauna roof when I went back to Vuosaari. He always ends up there in the afternoon when we're at the villa, because the sun is so warm right there. Einstein was born under that sauna. He's a kitten from the Peltonens' old cat."

Talking about the cat seemed to thaw him out a bit, but I had to get back to business.

"How much did you owe Tommi?" I asked.

"Owe Tommi? What the hell are you talking about? I didn't owe Tommi anything. Why do you think that?"

"Who owed Tommi money?"

"Tuulia probably owed him some, but I doubt it could have been very much. Riku's finances have been pretty messed up for as long as I've known him, and I think Tommi had loaned him quite a bit. Riku doesn't have any common sense when it comes to money. He spends it all on champagne for pretty girls in restaurants and stuff like that. Tommi always acted a little like Riku's older brother and probably wanted to help him out."

"OK. We'll have to find out. You mentioned Tommi and Pia's relationship when we talked yesterday. What was it like?"

A look of vexation passed over Antti's face.

"If I only knew. It was usually easy to see what role each of Tommi's women played for him. He never had more than two serious girlfriends, Jaana and a girl named Minna, who he went out with in high school. The others..." Antti spread his hands wide. "Pia was sort of a different case. Tommi didn't talk to me much about it, possibly because he knew how I felt about it. Maybe Tommi really was in love for the first time in his life. I'll probably never know."

"Maybe not. Has anything occurred to you since we last spoke that might help with the investigation?"

"No. The whole thing is still just as senseless to me as before, I'm afraid. I spent all last night thinking about old friends like Pia and Tuulia and trying to decide if one of them could have killed my best friend. And now you tell me Tommi was definitely murdered. Do you get what's going to happen here? We're all going to start spying on each other and turning against one another just to save our own skins. I'm already feeling like I need to hurry and come up with a murderer for you before you arrest me.

"And then there's EFSAS..." Antti paused for a moment. "We call our choir director 'Hopeless,' although that might be a better description of the whole choir at this point. Hopponen is his real name. He called me today. Mira told him about what happened: best bass singer dead, paying gig canceled, bad press for the choir, and to top it all off, one of the other core members probably a murderer...Although I'm sure he'd prefer to twist things to have it be Tommi who made that hole in his own head."

"Who do you think did it?"

"That's for you to find out, Miss Detective. The funeral will probably be within a couple of weeks. Don't arrest anyone before then. We'll need as many of our singers there as possible." Antti buried his head in his hands and then shook himself as if to chase away his own bad thoughts. "It would be best for Maisa...for Tommi's mother, that they bury him as soon as possible. She isn't mentally stable as it is, and I'm afraid all of this will crush her once and for all. This is a terrible thing for her."

Since my return to the force, I had investigated a dozen or so homicides, all of which had turned out to be manslaughter of one type or another, mostly crimes of passion. They had always been terrible for someone, not just for the victim and perpetrator but for their friends and family as well. They caused insecurity, self-accusation, fear, and doubt. Though I had always tried to keep my emotions in check, I couldn't help but feel them. Now I felt even worse. I wished there were a switch in my head I could flip to turn off all my feelings, leaving only a robotic crime-solving machine.

"About the ax again…How did you leave it after you finished off the fish?"

"I rinsed the worst of the scales off the blade and then probably left it on the right side of the dock. It would have been right there for anyone to pick up. If I had just taken it back to the sauna…"

"Don't start what if-ing." It came out more as a command than friendly encouragement. I muttered a quick farewell and then kicked him out of the office. I was in a hurry since there were so many things I needed to check on-site. But one thing had become clear: this was probably premeditated murder, not manslaughter. Anyone could have remembered that the ax was down on the dock and lured Tommi there. But unless the murderer was Mira or Antti, we were missing a set of fingerprints. And the perpetrator of a premeditated murder might also have had time to plan how to throw off the police.

4

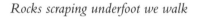

Rocks scraping underfoot we walk

It was surprisingly calm on the East Highway for late afternoon traffic. I was driving a faded gray Russian Lada that belonged to the department, and listening in as the boys from Forensics traded stories over the seats. I had gotten them to drop what they were doing and come with me because I thought I would probably be able to lift the restrictions on the Peltonens' villa after this visit.

There was a speed trap on the Vuosaari Bridge. I was driving significantly over the sixty kilometers per hour speed limit, but I calmly zipped past the baby-faced traffic cop. It felt like an eternity since I had done my stint in Traffic, as though I had been a completely different person six years ago.

Being in Violent Crime was easier in the sense that my current work didn't generally cause moral dilemmas. There was always sense in chasing down rapists and killers. As a patrol officer, however, I had felt like a nitpicker lying in wait for speeders—which hadn't been as big a problem then—arresting drunks, and handing out tickets to old ladies riding their bicycles without headlights.

Then I received the transfer to Vice that I wanted. I imagined I could save the world, but the only thing I'd felt was complete helplessness. One woman's goodwill couldn't do anything to combat the revolving doors of institutionalization and drug abuse. The underage prostitutes and abused children were the hardest. In school, I guess I had upheld this image of myself as a kind of Mother Teresa of law enforcement, but in reality, I couldn't do a thing for anyone. I reacted too strongly to everything happening around me, and I didn't realize until afterward that I was just too young to endure the constant chaos of crime I had been submerged in. My departure to study law was an escape, a desperate attempt to make some sense of the system in which I found myself spiraling downward.

And now I was back at square one, as a police officer. I remembered the captain's comment earlier that morning that my placement could continue after September if I wanted. The person who actually held my position, Saarinen, was on an extended sick leave with a bad back. Rane claimed it was more of a psychosomatic problem: Saarinen was bored with his work and tired of covering for Kinnunen's drinking and fixing Kinnunen's mistakes, so he was putting off returning to work for as long as possible.

In a lot of ways, continuing on would be the easy answer. I still wasn't interested in going back to school, and I didn't have the energy to contemplate changing professions yet again. I had piled up enough student debt already. Of course it didn't make any sense to leave my degree unfinished with just a thesis and a couple of big tests left, but I lacked the necessary motivation.

They were dissecting the Narcotics Unit's latest clown act in the backseat. If the impatient cops had waited just another week to start making arrests, they would have collared a good chunk of the capital's newest properly organized drug ring. As it was, all they had netted were a few hash dealers who didn't know much of anything about the ring's organization.

I sneered along with the technicians as they made their jabs. I knew I didn't want to be a drug cop. Their work had grown a great deal more dangerous in recent years. Lately, the Violent Crime and Narcotics Units had been liaising a lot, since a good number of homicides had been turning out to be internal score-settling between the drug gangs. The work was completely different from my police academy days when all you had needed to know to work Narcotics was how to arrest and interrogate the odd pot smoker.

The sea appeared for the first time along the road. A cat bounded after a bird in a field full of yellow tansies along the side of the highway. I rolled the car window down all the way.

The Peltonens' summer home looked just as idyllic as before. The patrol officer guarding the place was on the lawn reading the *Helsingin Sanomat* newspaper with his shirt off. He was surprised to see us. He was also clearly vexed when I explained that we probably didn't need anyone to keep watch anymore.

"Were you here when the Peltonens came back?"

"Yeah, one of the choir singers came back just before them too. Apparently, you had given him permission to come get his cat. He told them about their son. The old lady almost had a seizure and wouldn't stop screaming until the man rammed some sort of tranquilizers down her throat. But luckily they left quickly and took the dude and his cat with them. By the way, did you hear Forensics found a little blood down on the end of the dock? They sent it back to the lab. Maybe it's the murderer's. Or it could have dripped off the ax."

"Really? Good." I turned my face away—the images of the ax dripping blood and Tommi's smashed skull covered in gore turned my stomach.

I went over to the sauna building by the water in hopes of discovering something new where the ax had been found. The Peltonens' ten-meter sailboat was gleaming on the water, anchored to a nearby buoy. The family certainly wasn't lacking money. A villa in Vuosaari, an apartment in Westend. If I remembered correctly, there was also a log cabin in Lapland near one of the resorts. Jaana had gone skiing up there with Tommi a couple of times. A snippet of conversation sprung to mind from several years earlier.

"Sometimes it bugs me that he's such an effing silver-spoon brat," Jaana had huffed after another fight. "He's so used to getting whatever he wants. I just can't stand it anymore. If he wants to sleep with some other woman, then he just goes ahead and does it and doesn't give a damn how I feel. If he wants to take me to Stockholm for the weekend, then his dad picks up the tab. But then he's so freaking nice and smart and handsome when he wants to be. Sometimes it makes me afraid…It's almost like there's something cold inside him that he's always trying to hide, but sometimes it comes through by accident."

I could picture Jaana's legs, tanned from sailing, her anguished sea-blue eyes, a bottle of beer—which was always available from my part of the refrigerator in the apartment—in her hand.

"I can't always understand his logic. He tells me I don't own him, and of course I don't, but then he tries to own me. He enjoys having power over me. He wants to own people, to control them. With sex, with flirting, with lending them money and so on. He's exactly the kind of guy who's so damn nice until you get to know him."

Almost immediately after that conversation, Tommi had shown up to make peace, and Jaana had relented—all too easily, in my opinion. Tommi had known how to make people forgive him—sometimes the peace offering consisted of flowers, other times it was champagne.

But this time Tommi had failed. He had made someone so angry that their only solution had been the ultimate one.

The heather was already blooming behind the sauna, and some late cow-wheat poked through the blueberry bushes here and there. There was no actual foundation under the sauna, just an empty space in which you could have stuffed all sorts of things. I wondered how Hiltunen had thought of looking under here and found the ax, which, based on the photographs I had seen, looked like it had been carefully placed there rather than thrown under. Studying the spot in person made me none the wiser.

So someone had left the house, clocked Tommi with the ax that had been left on the dock, and then gone to the trouble of coming all the way up to the sauna to hide it. Why? Why had he, or she, rinsed the ax instead of throwing it into the sea to hide it? If the murderer had been some outsider coming from the water, you would have expected him to at least take the ax along and dump it out somewhere in deep water. That the murderer had hidden the ax under the sauna seemed to suggest that one of the choir members staying in the house had, in fact, killed Tommi.

Had the murderer come to the sauna to get cleaned up? But no blood should have sprayed out from a wound like that. Were the fingerprints they had found on the ax any use as evidence? Both Antti and Mira had given credible explanations for them. But how had the murderer handled the ax, then? No glove fibers had stuck on the smooth ax handle, and gloves would definitely indicate planning. I crawled under the building to look for a hidden pair of gloves and cut my wrist on some glass shards. I crawled out rump-first, swearing, back into the bright light of day.

Gulls screeched on the shore, and a water bird that looked like a great crested grebe was swimming farther out. Would this house remain the Peltonens' idyllic retreat, or would Tommi's body always be floating next to the dock? On dark autumn nights it would rise from the sea...

I thought of my own parents. If any of their children were killed at their beloved summer cabin, I doubted they would ever set foot there again. My mother had called me the night before to ask how I was doing. She thought it was awful that my job was solving homicides, and she sounded worried. My parents had been terribly disappointed when I entered the police academy. They thought there were much more appropriate uses for my intellect, like, say, studying Finnish or some other language. Something more fitting for a girl. Though I had always been the "boy" in the family (there were three girls altogether, which my parents clearly viewed as some sort of failure), they had still imagined I would end up in a "softer" profession. Though it had nothing to do with either of their fields—my father taught math and chemistry, and my mother English— they would have been perfectly satisfied with law school. One of my sisters was studying German and Swedish and was married to a chemist, and the other was studying English and dating a mathematician. I was the oddity of the family, both with regard to my profession and the lack of a man in my life. My mother, who thought any idiot was better than no man at all, was clearly becoming quite concerned about it. For now, things were less tense than usual though, because I had convinced my parents I was back on the force only to help pay for the rest of my law degree.

I walked upstairs to study Tommi's room again. On the desk, someone had placed a picture of an energetic-looking Tommi on the deck of a sailboat. Next to it was a half-burned candle. Otherwise, everything was as it had been when I last saw it.

Then I noticed that an expensive watch—presumably Tommi's—had also appeared on the desk. Where had that come from? The watch was ticking obstinately. I picked it up, admiring its beautiful hands. The hour and minute hands were made of gold and slightly curved, and the second hand was silver. The bronze alarm hand was set for three thirty. Strange time to wake up, I thought. Who would want to wake up at three thirty? Unless…unless Tommi had wanted to meet someone from the party in secret and arranged a meeting for three thirty in the morning. Or maybe this other person had wanted to meet Tommi—to murder him.

As I drove back toward Pasila and the station, I realized that I had successfully reconstructed in my mind how the crime must have happened, but that still didn't help much. The perpetrator remained faceless and sexless.

Who did I still need to interview? Tommi had been the assistant director of EFSAS, so the choir director, Hopponen, might be able to tell me something about him. And maybe the other members of the choir would have something to add. Maybe it would be useful to drop in on one of their practices.

Where to go from here? I thought I should probably pay Riku a visit as soon as possible, because his debts could constitute some sort of a motive. The thought of a scared, drunk Riku hitting someone over the head with an ax seemed plausible enough.

5

One born to pleasure and another born to pain

Riku lived in the heart of one of the roughest working-class neighborhoods in the city. The windows of his building faced a notorious liquor store, and the sounds of clattering trams and disheveled bums' colorful commentary filled the street. I watched as one staggered in front of a tram coming from the east, saved only by the driver's sudden braking. I was glad once again not to be in uniform, because if I had been, I would have had to intervene. As it was, I just continued on my way and let passersby gawk at the quarrel unfolding between the driver and the wino.

Finding the correct back door was difficult because a single brick wall spanned several buildings. After a couple of tries, I located the last name Lasinen on a resident directory and climbed the stairs to the fourth floor. I was happy to note that the climb didn't leave me panting. I rang the doorbell and switched on the small voice recorder in my purse when I heard steps inside. Recording our conversation wasn't legal, but I didn't have any intention of using the tape as actual evidence. Our meeting could not be considered an official interview, as that would have required the presence of a second police officer as a witness. I simply wanted to chat with Riku, as off the record as possible.

Riku looked surprised to see me, but not frantic. With the redness in his eyes gone and his stubble shaved off, he barely looked like an adult.

Riku's apartment was a caricature of the quintessential bachelor pad. The cramped entryway opened onto a spacious room with a loft built over the kitchenette. The apartment was comfortably and stylishly decorated, but cluttered in the extreme. Ashtrays and rumpled clothes everywhere, orange peels on the floor, and empty beer bottles in the corner. Despite my high tolerance for clutter, even I thought it looked filthy.

Riku made room for me on a black leather armchair by haphazardly tossing a couple of Benetton shirts on the floor. He sat down across from me on the unmade bed and lit a cigarette. After a moment's hesitation, he offered me one too. I declined. I smoke only when I'm drunk.

"Sorry it's a bit of a mess here, but I haven't had time to clean much because I've been so busy." He sighed. "And I really should be leaving soon. We play *kyykkä* on Mondays during the summer at the Kaisaniemi field since we don't have rehearsals that night."

"*Kyykkä*? What the—? No, never mind. Don't explain," I said, silencing his enthusiastic attempt to reply. "Let's handle the official business first. Last night when you were all together at dinner, you said you thought you heard Antti in Tommi's room on Saturday night. But you didn't say anything about that to me during our interview. So which is it? Did you hear something?"

"Well, see…I don't really know. I dunno if I was dreaming or what, but I just thought somebody was over in Tommi's room and I kinda thought it was Antti."

In reality I wasn't nearly as interested in what Riku may or may not have heard as I was in his finances. Maybe he had just cooked up a way to blame Antti when the others started to suspect him. Did that mean Riku was guilty? I lost patience with pussyfooting around and got to the point.

"How much did you owe Tommi?"

Riku's expression went from relaxed to frightened in the blink of an eye.

"It was somewhere around one thousand, right? And of course you didn't have a red cent to pay him back with. Then Tommi started getting difficult when he didn't get his money. You must have had a pretty bad run-in over it; am I right?"

"Yeah, but that was on Thursday..." Riku stammered, tamping out his old cigarette in an overflowing ashtray and lighting another. Apparently, I had guessed right, but I wasn't sure how to get Riku to keep talking.

"I have your bank statements," I lied smoothly. "But it would still be best if you told me about the state of your finances yourself."

Riku took a few nervous drags on his cigarette, stood up, opened the window—which let in air so full of dust and exhaust fumes that it wasn't much fresher than the tobacco smoke in the room—and then sat back down, defeated.

"Well, see, I owed him almost two grand," Riku said. "But he promised he wouldn't tell anybody! Who snitched? Or did you search his place and find the IOU? He fuckin' made me sign one. Couldn't even trust a friend..."

The search warrant had not come yet, but I hoped to have it the following day. Riku didn't need to know that though, so I just nodded.

"I've needed money for all kinds of stuff lately. Nobody can live on these goddamn student grants and there just aren't any jobs. I borrowed a little from him just before Christmas, when I was out of cash, but I paid him right back when I got my spring semester money. But then I ran out again. And I couldn't ask for money at home 'cause they'd just pester me, saying things like, 'Why you gotta travel and how much you been drinkin' and why you got them weird clothes, ain't regular jeans good enough for you like everybody else…' Tommi was real decent—he loaned me the money and said I didn't even need to pay interest. But he wanted that promissory note. And I'm working now, as a pizza delivery driver. Boring, but I wanna go to Nice in August…"

"But on Thursday, Tommi demanded that you pay him back immediately or there would be trouble, right?"

"Yeah…He called me at work and met me there and we came back here. I wondered why we couldn't go to a bar, but he said he wanted to talk alone. He said he needed a pile of money 'cause he had to buy a new car, even though I couldn't see what was wrong with the old one. And when I said I didn't have any, he threatened to tell the police that…" Riku swallowed.

"That what?"

"Well, that I owed him money! I didn't know he'd be so goddamn unfair!" Riku punched a cushion angrily.

"Was two grand enough reason to kill a friend?"

Riku's expression turned horrified and he jumped up off the bed.

"I didn't kill him! He was totally normal on Friday and didn't say a word about any of it. So I thought it was all fine, that he'd just panicked a bit or something. But then when we were racing the cars on the way out there, I was kinda afraid 'cause it was like he really did want to run me off the road…I don't know. Maybe he was trying to threaten me. But I didn't kill him, Maria. I'm not like that. You gotta believe me!" His puppy dog face looked at me with the expression a small creature wears when it is attacked by a larger, far more powerful animal. But I couldn't relent.

"Tommi's death was convenient for you though," I said cruelly. I couldn't bring myself to be nice to Riku because he reminded me far too much of Pete. Those same puppy dog eyes, the same careless spending. Pete was an ex-boyfriend. I had never bothered keeping track of the money I loaned him, but he probably squandered half of my salary in the watering holes of this very neighborhood the first year I was on the force. Then he left to do his civilian service, instead of going into the army, and decided that he couldn't actually go out with a cop because I represented the established social order. I cried for a couple of weeks, then mostly just mourned my lost money.

Riku had made his way over to the window again, as if trying to escape. Though he might be guilty, his motive struck me as pretty weak.

"Do you even remember what happened Saturday night?"

"Oh, so you think I killed Tommi and don't remember? Don't make me laugh. Are you going to arrest me?"

Riku's voice had risen to a shrill falsetto, and the hand holding his cigarette shook uncontrollably. His attempt at playing man-of-the-world had completely fallen apart.

"If I had any evidence, you would already be in a holding cell in Pasila, but we'll let it be for now," I said antagonistically. "Tell me about the other people who owed Tommi money."

Riku walked over to the kitchenette and opened the pantry, which seemed to contain mostly bottles. "I need a shot of whiskey," he muttered to himself. "Do you want one, or are you on duty?"

"Just a little," I said, even though I knew I shouldn't. However, I thought that having a drink together might make him feel more inclined to confide in me. Evidently shots came in drinking glasses in this apartment.

"Actually, I don't know who else owed Tommi money, although he did have more money than anybody else I know. He had already graduated and had a good job. I guess all of us probably borrowed from him every now and then—like if we were in a bar and we ran out of money, we just got Tommi to pull out his Visa card. Tuulia said something once about how much she owed Tommi, but she sounded like she meant it in the sense of being thankful. Maybe Tommi helped her get a job or something like that. And I think he and Timo probably had some dealings."

"What kind?"

"I don't know exactly. Ask Timo yourself." Riku had a cagey look about him that made me think he knew more than he wanted to tell. "If you ask me, Mira is the murderer," Riku said, pouring himself more whiskey. I still hadn't gotten past the first sip, although Riku's Ballantine's was decent.

"Based on what?"

"Well, because the rest of us are so strung out, but she's just so damn calm. Like she knows something. But I don't have any idea why she would have wanted to kill Tommi. It's Antti she's stuck on."

There it was again: Mira's infatuation with Antti. I couldn't stand the thought of having to ask either one of them about their love lives.

"How is all this whiskey going to affect your game play?"

"We always bring beer. It doesn't affect *kyykkä* throwing, and I doubt we'll play much anyway. I guess you don't know much about the sport. We'll probably just plan what we're going to sing at Tommi's funeral, which is happening next Saturday. Did you know that?"

"Yeah…" Forensics and the pathologists had just finished investigating Tommi's body and released it to the family. I still hadn't received all of the fiber analysis.

"I don't think I could sing at a friend's funeral," I said.

"I think it's terrible too. We'll see how it goes. You could come to the funeral and arrest whoever doesn't cry—but then it would be Mira for sure."

Riku had relaxed after realizing that I didn't intend to drag him to Pasila after all. I sipped slowly at my whiskey, savoring the feeling of relaxation that flowed through me. I hadn't noticed how tense and keyed up I'd been all day. I suddenly longed for a walk in the fresh air, which was usually a good way for me to clear my thoughts.

Riku started to get ready to leave and asked me to wait for him to change his clothes so we could go together. He'd already figured out that I didn't have a police car with me. A third whiskey had completely loosened him up, and he began telling me familiar-sounding choir gossip, mostly talking up his own singing ability and berating the others', the other tenors in particular. Back when I lived with Jaana, I had observed how eager the singers were to criticize each other's abilities. As I listened to Riku, I got the feeling that EFSAS was a veritable breeding ground for jealousy. Hard to believe someone would murder a friend just for singing a little off-key though, I thought, as Riku complained about Timo.

On the tram, Riku suggested that I come and get better acquainted with the finer points of the game of *kyykkä*, but I wasn't interested. After Riku jumped off at the Kaisaniemi stop, I continued on to Eira, where I set off for a stroll along the shoreline. There wasn't much to praise in Helsinki's beaches, but the sea was always the sea. I was born inland, but for some reason I've always enjoyed being near open water. For a moment, I found myself wishing I weren't walking alone, that there was someone with whom I could have laughed at the crows cawing irritably at each other and admired that little elephant-shaped cloud, but the thought passed quickly.

A sailboat bobbing on the horizon brought my thoughts back around to Tommi. I knew I should have a talk with Pia Wahlroos pretty soon; she might know something about Tommi's love life. I didn't quite know what to make of Pia, but I sensed that she belonged high on my list of possible killers. As did Riku, despite his assurances to the contrary. I had a hard time placing Timo and Sirkku anywhere but at the bottom of the list, because a fling a couple of years earlier seemed like an insufficient motive for either of them. It was hard for me to imagine Sirkku hitting anyone with an ax anyway. Maybe I should switch my focus to the way Tommi was killed. Thinking about the killer's method felt like an important line of inquiry.

The murderer had clearly wanted to be rid of Tommi quickly. So it was likely that the killer was either enraged or afraid. Who was capable of really losing his temper? Probably Antti, as well as Timo. Of the women, Sirkku was the excitable type, but it was easier imagining her crying coquettishly and beating Tommi on the chest with her neatly manicured fists than doing something genuinely violent.

And Mira? I knew a lot of extremely calm people who rarely lost their cool, but who, when they did, unleashed their wrath like all hell had broken loose. What could Tommi have done to make Mira that angry? I could imagine Tuulia could really bite your head off too, but for some reason it was hard for me to picture her striking anyone. Tuulia would definitely opt for poison.

What if Tommi had assaulted Pia? Maybe he'd come on to her while he was drunk and Pia couldn't see any way to break free of him other than grabbing the ax and walloping him. Oh, if only this case could turn out to be self-defense! I suddenly felt terrible that I might be sending someone to prison for years and years, even though that was where a successful conclusion to the case would inevitably lead.

Coming back to police work had been one of my most idiotic ideas. I thought back to the announcement in *Policeman* (although I always felt like boycotting the magazine because of the irritating name) about the temporary post I was filling. I suppose I had gotten the job because I was a woman, which, of course, was what everyone thought. At times I wished I were ten years older and had a family. Early on in my career, some of the boys had asked me out on dates. It had been the same when we were at the academy. When I never took any of them up on their offers, it naturally caused all kinds of rumors. "She's good looking, but she doesn't have a boyfriend. She must be a lesbian. Why else would she have wanted to do men's work?" I had heard that phrase more times than I could count.

Why did I need to explain myself to my colleagues? I had a love life—albeit not a very active one—but time was slipping away, and there were plenty of guys who chose the highway when they heard I was a cop. Lately I had been so busy that I had forgotten sex even existed. I wanted to do my job well, and there was a lot for me to learn in the Violent Crime Unit. When things ended with Pete, I thought I would never fall in love again. About a year later, Harri, an avid botanist and ornithologist, had entered the picture, but his most exciting trait had unfortunately been that he could identify every plant and bird in Finland—and could teach me to do the same. Harri wasn't much of a match for me in any other ways either. He was entirely too nice, soft, and empathetic, and I had treated him badly. Fortunately, he had finally gotten tired of me bossing him around.

No, I didn't want to be dependent on anyone. I was beginning to be so set in my routines that I couldn't imagine sharing
them with anyone else. I wanted to eat my breakfast without
anyone stealing my newspaper or talking to me before I drank
my coffee. I wanted to watch chick flicks on TV without anyone
commenting on how stupid they were or being surprised when
I cried at the happy ending. I wanted to lounge in the bathtub
at two in the morning eating chocolate and drinking whiskey
if I felt like it. I sometimes wanted a sympathetic ear for my
dark monologues…I had thought about getting a cat. A cat and
I would be relatively little trouble to each other. A cat might be
possible despite my long work hours. A man would be much
more problematic. Making love from time to time would be
nice, but I had been getting along just fine without sex for a long
time already. Maybe my libido just wasn't very strong.

Lost in thought, I had arrived at Ratakatu, where a loud
greeting from a police academy comrade who had ended up
in the Finnish Security Intelligence Service snapped me back
to reality. I realized I'd been thinking more about myself than
about Tommi, which irked me. It was possible that we would
find the answer to Tommi's death in his apartment, and I hoped
that the search warrant would come through tomorrow. It was
terrible how a person became public property when he was murdered. First, open the body, evaluate the state of its inner work-
ings, inspect what he ate last. Then rummage through the rest
of the life—home, relationships, finances, friends. Invading the
private lives of both the victim and the suspects. I was peeping
into their lives too, but I only knew how to read some of the
signs on display.

6

But within each heart the tick of a clock

When I came to work on Tuesday morning, the search warrant was waiting on my desk. Next to it was a confirmation that neither Jaana nor Franz Schön had entered the country during the past week. Koivu had called the phone numbers provided by Heikki Peltonen and confirmed the movements of the *Maisetta* with the Peltonens' sailing companions. The proprietor of the Barösund service station also remembered them well, because Heikki Peltonen had demanded a refund for a package of sausages he claimed were bad. During the night, I hadn't been able to come up with any possible reason for the Peltonens to have murdered their own son, so they were probably out of the running now. We might still uncover some unknown perpetrator or perpetrators, but for the time being, the only remaining suspects were the choir. If I was going to find the truth, it would only be by dragging it out of these seven people.

When I called the lab to inquire about the results of the blood analysis, the forensic chemist was obviously pissed about something.

"Oh, it's you, dollface. This blood stain of yours from the dock might be *really* important."

"Oh, how so?" I asked, ignoring the sarcastic tone.

"It was really strange blood. If I hadn't had that ax, I would have been totally up a creek. Which is to say"—he paused—"it's the same blood from the pike," he continued dryly.

"So it isn't Peltonen's?" I asked, even though what I felt like doing was slamming the receiver down in the little pissant's ear. He grumbled cynically for another minute about the time he'd wasted on this irrelevant analysis before I got rid of him.

If Tommi's blood wasn't on the dock, he must have fallen straight into the water from the force of the blow. Sounded pretty cold-blooded. Maybe the killer hadn't even hung around long enough to see what had become of his victim. I felt like vomiting. As luck would have it, the captain stuck his head into my office at that very moment, his ever-present cigar hanging from the corner of his mouth. Before I had a chance to say anything, he barged in and started smoking up the place. I could feel the vein in my forehead starting to throb.

"Well, have you solved Peltonen's son's case yet?" the captain asked, glancing at my breasts in my slightly too tight blouse. It had been the only one of my shirts that was clean and relatively unwrinkled, so I had had to wear it even though the third button was always on the verge of popping open.

"Did Daddy Peltonen call to lean on you?" I asked before I had a chance to consider my words. The captain snorted, and cigar smoke wafted threateningly toward my cluttered desk.

Before he had a chance to answer, I continued, "I'm just leaving with Koivu now to go search Tommi Peltonen's apartment. Maybe we'll turn something up. And listen, could you please not smoke in my office? I can't stand cigar smoke."

Now the captain's superficial temporal vein started throbbing, but he nevertheless backed out the door with his cigar. As he was leaving, he turned back to look at me and said, "When you women are given a chance to do demanding jobs, you also have to show that you're capable of something other than bellyaching about extraneous details." With that, he slammed the door.

The door opened again almost immediately, and Koivu made his way in. "What did the old man just say to you?" Koivu asked, eyes wide. "Did I hear that right?"

"Yeah. The little shit got angry when I asked him not to smoke in my office."

"You didn't!" Koivu burst out laughing.

"You bet your ass I did!"

"You have no idea how many people have wanted to say that to him. Do I dare go anywhere with you when you've got your hackles up like this? By the way, he told me to tell you that the Mustikkamaa case can wait for now until this one is solved."

Before Tommi's murder, I had been working on two stabbings that had taken place during the Midsummer's Eve parties on Mustikkamaa Island. One of them was already more or less cleared up—the same night, we had picked up the victim's drinking buddy, who, once he had recovered from the worst of his intoxication, had, to his dismay, remembered killing his friend at the end of an argument over a bottle of vodka that had run dry. We would probably never solve the other case, because the other party to this second midnight knife fight had been the famous "anonymous assailant." All of the eyewitnesses to the incident had been so drunk that the descriptions of the man varied significantly. The victim in the case, whom we had been calling Mustikkamaa Number Two, had lived but lost one of his kidneys in the scuffle. After Tommi's murder, there would undoubtedly be something else the boss considered more important. Wino showdowns were an all-too-common occurrence in our unit.

I was happy to have Koivu's help. He was the best cutup in my section and the sharpest as well. It sickened me to invade Tommi's home, but I felt no need to justify my reactions to Koivu.

"Nice-looking place," Koivu said as we stepped into the living room of Tommi's one-bedroom apartment. Situated at the end of Iso Roobertinkatu, the building commanded prime views of Sinebrychoff Park. The main room was sparsely decorated, furnished with only a lounging sofa, a piano, and a good number of books and records. The bedroom had a wide double bed, with a handsome seven-branched candelabra on the nightstand. Making love by its light must have been romantic. I wondered whether the candelabra had been in the apartment back when Jaana had spent her nights here.

On the small entry table was a telephone. A red message light blinked on the answering machine. My heart skipped a beat—there might be something on the tape. Luckily, it was a familiar model.

There were two messages. The first had obviously been from a pay phone because the clink of coins dropping in interrupted the message periodically. "It's Tiina. The plans are ruined now. You're a cheap man. I can't trust you. Come to my place on Sunday." Cheap man? I thought in confusion. The second message was even stranger. "M here. Sunday night. I'm taking off tomorrow. Call me now." The caller was a man, his voice hoarse and withering. I removed the answering machine cassette to take with me. Tommi obviously wouldn't be needing it anymore.

The notepad on the phone table was the kind you tore pages out of, so there was only one message on it: "No Tuulia Monday!" In addition to the exclamation point, it was underlined. Have to remember to ask Tuulia what that meant, though it probably referred to something trivial like a canceled squash match.

Koivu had started inspecting the music shelf. "Almost all classical," he said, disappointed. "There's a little Beatles and some Queen, but a whole bunch from some guy named Bach. Isn't that a white wine? Really good stereo too—there's gotta be twenty thousand marks of gear sitting here. And this TV and video setup looks pretty new too. What did this guy do for a living?"

"Geological engineer. We'll go drop in on his work tomorrow."

"I guess they pay pretty well then, wherever he works. He wasn't just a techie either. Look how many books the guy had."

"Yeah...and not just book club garbage either," I said, scanning the collection. Instead of mainstream hardcover bestsellers, the shelves were filled with classics in English and French: Joyce, Proust, T.S. Eliot, Baudelaire. It was hard imagining Tommi reading *Odysseus*, but maybe there had been more to him that I had thought.

Tommi's kitchenette was decorated in neutral colors and very clean. In the refrigerator, I found milk, cheese, a few Beck's Dark, and a bowl of fruit. A dry loaf of bread sat on the table. Spices and baking supplies were in short supply: Tommi evidently hadn't been much of a chef. The upper cupboard was full of the classic Arabia and Iittala dishware found in so many Finnish homes. The contents of the lower cupboard confused me though: It was filled to capacity with clear, unlabeled bottles. Each was filled to the top with clear liquid, with an herb sprig resting in the bottom. I opened one, took a sniff, and then took a tentative taste. It was some kind of strong, burning liquor with a hint of anise.

"Koivu, come over here. I have an official assignment for you." I extended the bottle to him. Koivu took a more generous swig than I had and then grinned in astonishment.

"Moonshine," he said. "And some weird flavoring. A little like anise. Strong as all hell. Is there much of it?"

"There must be thirty liters at least. Does this apartment have a cellar or attic storage locker? Will you call the super and ask? We might find a still."

Koivu went to look for the building superintendent's number, and I moved on to riffling through Tommi's desk. The upper drawer contained a pile of old bankbooks, account statements, stock certificates, and other financial papers, which I decided to take back to the station. The next drawer was full of old pocket calendars and some letters. Those would go also. The bottom drawer held a copy of Tommi's master's thesis in engineering geology and a couple of photo albums.

"There's no basement in this building, but there is an attic. I'm going to go see if any of Peltonen's keys fit the door." Koivu was clearly eager to find the distilling equipment.

I opened one of the photo albums at random, and the first picture I saw was of Jaana, grinning at the camera with a carrot in her hand, in the narrow kitchen of our old student apartment. I flipped through the album, which was filled with the usual family snapshots: Tommi as a child, sailing in a dinghy. Tommi casting a fishing line from the same dock where he had just died. Tommi and his brother climbing up to a tree house. Elementary school class pictures, in which I recognized Antti and Tuulia. The three of them always seemed to wear the same expressions: Tommi grinned comically at the camera, Tuulia smiled sensually, and Antti looked thin and sullen. Pictures of a school hike in Lapland, pictures of Tommi with a graduation cap on his head and a bouquet of roses in his hand. The same pictures all of us had.

The newer album contained mostly choir pictures and photos from a few friends' weddings. Tommi must not have been a particularly enthusiastic photographer, or else he had used slides more than prints. There weren't any slide boxes on the shelves though. Just then, Koivu came hustling back. He was panting.

"Guess what. Up in that attic storage cage there must be at least a hundred liters of that same hooch. I didn't see any still equipment anywhere though, so he must have kept that somewhere else. But Peltonen was running a regular moonshine factory!"

"Wow. We'll have to put a good lock on that storage door. Would you mind checking the bedroom for anything interesting?"

"We could confiscate a couple of bottles for ourselves. No one would ever notice," Koivu said with a wink. "It's lucky Kinnunen isn't here. He'd probably go totally off his rocker." Then he went off to attack Tommi's clothes closet. "Some awfully nice-looking silk shirts in here. I think I could handle having a couple of these. They look a little small though." Koivu rummaged through the pockets of Tommi's clothes with an amusing eagerness. What did he think he was looking for? Weapons? Drugs? Meanwhile, I was thinking about where the distilling setup might be and why Tommi had been making all that alcohol. And who were Tiina and M?

"There isn't anything fun here but a decent collection of porn magazines," Koivu said, emerging from the bedroom dangling open a *Playboy* centerfold. "Why aren't women who look like this interested in me? Why do I always just get good girls with brown hair?"

"Because you're blond and you look like a nice guy. If you tried to look like a tiger instead of a teddy bear, then maybe you'd have better luck. Should we maybe take possession of those porn magazines? It probably wouldn't do Tommi's mother any good to see them here." With any of my other colleagues, looking at pornographic magazines would have felt like sexual harassment, but Koivu had always treated me like a big sister, someone with whom he could honestly wonder at the facts of life.

We knocked on walls and furniture, looking for any possible hiding places, though I felt ridiculous even as we did it. We didn't find anything of interest aside from the financial documents, letters, and calendars. And of course the moonshine.

On the way home, Koivu bought a copy of one of the afternoon tabloids. The domestic news contained a brief mention of a death in Vuosaari, but they called it an accident and simply stated that the police were continuing their investigation. Maybe the board of Neste Oil had handed down an order to the captain to keep a low profile. If so, that was fine by me.

We stopped by a local fast-food joint for burgers, and I bought a chocolate milkshake as a pick-me-up, which Koivu looked at with an expression that said "women," as if men didn't like chocolate too. He intended to continue on to Kaarela to work an assault case he and Savukoski were on. I planned to head back to the office to go through Tommi's papers. I mulled over what we should do with the moonshine. Impound it as evidence? But of what? Obviously Tommi had been selling bootleg liquor. Could that have given rise to some disagreement that led to his death? I could already see the headlines: BOOTLEGGER BUTCHERED AT VUOSAARI VILLA.

A pile of messages lay on my desk. After making it through those, I dove into Tommi's papers. The room still reeked of cigar smoke, so I opened the window and stared for a moment at the cement wall of the building across the way. I was tired and didn't feel like starting anything. But I forced myself back into my chair, put my feet up on the desk, and tried to pretend I was Philip Marlowe.

The postcards Tommi had kept consisted entirely of innocent messages from friends and relatives. Many of them were from Henri and Peter on yachting trips, the newest from only a couple of weeks earlier. I found myself wondering why Tommi had decided to save these cards in particular. I usually tossed all of mine in the garbage.

Reading the few letters Tommi had saved felt like voyeurism. Henri and Peter had written wonderful descriptions of their sailing journey around the world a couple of years before. I got so absorbed in them that I momentarily forgot what I was supposed to be doing. Tuulia's letters were also travelogues, from a trip to the United States she had taken a few years back. They were warm, funny, and personal, and I laughed out loud at Tuulia's accounts of her mishaps. I wished that someone would write me letters like this. Tuulia and Tommi had clearly trusted each other a great deal.

Antti had written several letters from Lapland over the course of a couple of summers. They revealed that Antti's ex-girlfriend Sarianna had been a veterinary intern in Lapland, and that Antti had been up there, once to do forestry work (I recalled his biceps again) and once on leave to write his thesis. He had written fastidious descriptions of the landscapes, the books he had been reading, and his ideas for his thesis, which were Greek to me—category theory had never been my strongest subject.

Only two of the letters were of real interest. One of them was from Pia, dated about two months earlier.

"Tommi," it began simply. "Since you never believe what I say, I hope you will believe my words when I write them. I have told you over and over that I don't want to be anything more than friends with you. I don't love you. I love Peter." I got the impression from the letter that Tommi had truly fallen in love with Pia and tried to lure her into some sort of affair with him, but that Pia hadn't wanted to betray Peter. Something had happened between them though, because Pia wrote: "I know you know how to make the truth look ugly. I believe you will tell Peter if you think it will benefit you."

Blackmail? Sounded interesting. I would have to question Pia more closely about that. Or maybe her gossipy sister could shed more light on Pia and Tommi's relationship.

Reading Antti's most recent letter almost nauseated me. Why the hell had I chosen a profession in which I had to dig around in other people's business? But that was precisely what I had wanted when I was a kid—to intercede in others' affairs, to help them—even the ones who didn't want my help.

"Tommi. Sometimes I have to put my thoughts down on paper to work them out. It helps me to try to formulate them in a way that other people can understand them too. Sometimes it feels like you know me better than I know myself, so that's why I'm writing to you."

Enormously despondent and personal, Antti's letter was either a cry for help or some kind of request for advice. It was dated about a year earlier, after Antti had broken up with Sarianna and started to wrestle with his dissertation. My impression of Antti was that he was a calm individual, but he was clearly desperate when he wrote this letter.

From the perspective of the investigation, the letter contained one section of interest: "You asked me why I don't go ahead and screw Mira, since it would be so easy for me. But it wouldn't be easy for me. I think it was wrong of you to play around with Mira, even though she knew what she was doing. Mira isn't stupid. I've never understood your relationships with women. Sometimes I wish I could be as frivolous as you are, treating women like objects. Everything might be easier then. Screw around all you want, but goddamn it, don't hurt Tuulia."

I was starting to get dizzy. Had there been something more serious going on between Tuulia and Tommi after all? I couldn't believe that Tuulia the realist would suddenly have fallen in love with Tommi, whom she knew so well. But how did I know what people really felt? I only pretended I did.

Pia, Tuulia—and Mira. Tommi "playing around" with Mira? Mira allowing it? Obviously my preconceptions about these people were way off. I wished I kept a bottle in my bottom drawer, like Marlowe did, to help refresh my mind. I could probably have found one in Kinnunen's filing cabinet, but I settled for a cup of weak hot cocoa from the vending machine down the hall. Even I couldn't stand to drink the coffee from that vending machine.

Tommi seemed to be tangled up in the love life of every one of my female suspects. Sirkku in Germany, Pia this spring, Tuulia a year ago, and Mira before that…It was a good thing the whole choir hadn't been practicing in Vuosaari. How many more girls had Tommi burned with his philandering?

I moved on to Tommi's other papers. The topmost item was an envelope containing a financial statement and audit report for EFSAS. Tommi had evidently been one of the auditors. Riku was the choir treasurer, Timo the chairman, and Sirkku the secretary. Of course. They were exactly the kind of people who became chairmen and secretaries.

Tommi had settled the final payment on his mortgage in May, which I thought was astonishing. Over the past couple of years he had been making consistent early principal payments, in relatively large amounts. Maybe he had received an advance on his inheritance from his father. I made a note to call Heikki Peltonen to ask about his son's finances again and to confirm the date and time of the funeral.

Tommi had carefully saved all of his account statements, as well as his tax returns. He even had copies of all of his tax deduction receipts from the previous year. If only I were this meticulous with my own finances! I wondered how on earth this guy had been getting by, since virtually all of his salary income had been going toward paying off his apartment. Granted, that salary was twice as large as my own, but still, paying off a two-hundred-and-fifty-thousand-mark loan in three years was quite an achievement. I thought of his sleek car and noted that there wasn't any mention of a car loan anywhere, not even a lease agreement. I found a copy of his car insurance policy, which listed the value of the vehicle at a little over twenty thousand.

Beads of sweat formed on my forehead when I started inspecting Tommi's bank statements. In addition to his regular salary payments, there were occasional, surprisingly large personal deposits to his checking account. One certificate of deposit for ten grand had matured the previous Christmas.

I went to the restroom, washed my face, and fetched another cup of hot chocolate. The phone interrupted me a couple of times, but when I finally finished slogging through Tommi's financials, I was both confused and satisfied.

Based on the papers I had gone through, it was clear as day that Tommi had been receiving generous sums from a source other than his regular day job. I doubted he could have earned that kind of money just selling moonshine. Or, if he had, then he had been producing it on a truly colossal scale. Money, liquor, and women. Those were the marks left by Tommi's life. The combination somehow felt familiar, like a rock song come to life.

The bank card charges in the account statements indicated that Tommi had spent a lot of time eating and drinking in restaurants. It was clear that he had often footed the bill at the bar EFSAS frequented, but he had also visited pickup joints like the Hesperia Club, where most of the single girls were for sale, with surprising regularity. I hadn't imagined that Tommi would need to buy companionship, but what did I know? Maybe he liked it that way.

"Up and at 'em!" Koivu shouted from the door, waking me from my reverie.

"Oh, hi. How was Kaarela?"

"Boring. And now I'm supposed to go to Malmi to meet some gypsy dudes who got stabbed. Have they called you up there?" Koivu flopped down in the chair across from me, shoved three pieces of sugar-free gum in his mouth, then pushed the rest of the packet over to me.

"Thanks. No, I didn't get an invite to that particular party. Maybe it's Miettinen's thing."

"Anything interesting in Peltonen's papers?"

"Loads. Koivu, have you ever been to the meat market at the Hesperia?"

"Nah, I don't have that kind of money."

"Well, you're going there tonight with Tommi's picture. Or do you have something else going on? I'll talk to the boss about the overtime. Ask around with the professional-looking girls whether they knew Tommi, and emphasize that it's about a murder. You know, like on TV."

Koivu looked excited. Today was going to be one of those days he could tell his pals about at soccer practice later.

"It's better that you go than me," I continued.

"Yeah, since you probably don't own any high heels or fishnet stockings."

"By the way, I think you still have those porn magazines…"

"I need to get up to Malmi," Koivu said suddenly, rushing to the door. "I'll come through here on my way back, and we can talk about this evening," he said from the door, blushing.

Was Koivu the right man to go to the Hesperia Club after all? Poor kid might get his wallet emptied by one of the veterans there. I spent a moment being astonished at my maternal attitude toward Koivu, but then my phone rang, and I got the call to head up to Malmi too.

7

Which when it stops, 'tis time for death to reign

On Wednesday morning, August felt like October. With the wind howling outside, I would have preferred not to get up at all. The previous night in Malmi had been complete chaos. Two Roma families had been settling scores the old-fashioned way, resulting in one corpse and three wounded. Koivu and I spent the whole evening driving back and forth between the Malmi and Meilahti clinics trying to figure out who had stabbed whom.

I finally let an exhausted Koivu go home sometime after 9:00 p.m. I decided that it would be wiser to visit the nightclub after we investigated Tommi's company. It was possible that the bank charges were just from corporate events, though if that were the case, would Tommi have paid with his own credit card?

After arriving at work, I called the captain on the phone and told him what had transpired in Malmi. At ten, Koivu and I headed off toward Espoo. I had done my makeup more carefully than usual and wore a clean, loose-fitting blouse with my uniform skirt. Though I would have preferred to fall straight into bed in the company of Lord Peter Wimsey, I had heroically done laundry the previous night, wishing the entire time that I had my own Bunter to care for my clothing.

Koivu drove the rattletrap Black Maria, which the motor pool had given us because all of the patrol cars were either out or being serviced. The van's radio relayed intermittent, choppy messages as we chatted about the incident in Malmi. With too many cases to investigate at once and not enough time to do anything properly, it was easy to feel a bit schizophrenic in this job.

I had arranged to meet with the head of Tommi's department through a secretary. The secretary had simply referred to "Dr. Marjamäki," and it seems that I'm not an enlightened enough feminist, because I automatically assumed that the head of the international joint projects division of a large mining and metallurgy company would be a man. It wasn't until the division head stood up from behind her desk to greet us that I realized that Dr. Marjamäki was a woman, Doctor of Geological Engineering Marja Mäki.

"Detective Kallio and Officer Koivu from the Helsinki PD Violent Crime Unit," I said from the door in my most official tone of voice.

In her nicely tailored black skirt suit, gray silk blouse, and high-quality flats, the trim Dr. Mäki was a professional woman straight from the pages of a women's magazine. Subdued makeup and jewelry that matched her suit rounded out the overall impression. Her voice was cultured and low, almost masculine. I immediately felt like I hadn't pressed my blouse well enough and remembered that I hadn't polished my shoes.

Mäki asked her secretary to bring coffee. She drank herbal tea herself and didn't even touch the crisp-looking Danishes the secretary placed before us. I managed to crumble most of my own on my skirt.

"Mr. Peltonen had a good handle on his field and was a pleasant coworker," Mäki began. "He was with us for four years. We took him on during his thesis work and were so pleased with his work that we offered him a permanent position. He had exceptionally broad linguistic abilities—in addition to Finnish, he spoke English, French, Russian, Estonian, and German."

"Who did he usually work with?"

"He generally handled relationships with our foreign joint ventures. It was rather independent work. I was his closest superior, and he shared a secretary with Mr. Roivas, one of our economists. Lately Peltonen had mostly been working on a joint Finnish-Estonian project. We're trying to develop more environmentally friendly technology for Estonia's oil shale mines," Mäki explained, as though she thought for a moment that I was a reporter.

"What sort of a person did he seem like to you?"

"He was an extremely pleasant young man," Mäki said firmly. "Charming. Funny." Suddenly her voice faltered, and her controlled outer shell shattered. She buried her face in her hands, and we heard stifled sobs from behind them. Koivu and I glanced at each other, disconcerted. Dr. Marja Mäki did not strike me as the sort of person I could go over and pat consolingly on the shoulder.

When Mäki finally raised her face, I saw that her mascara had run, turning the thin lines under her eyes into dark furrows.

"I'm sorry," she said. "This has been a terrible shock for all of us. Tommi...It feels so horribly empty here without him." She burst into tears again, no longer bothering to conceal them.

"What if we were to go to Tommi's office and go through his things?" I suggested tactfully.

In the midst of her tears, Mäki called in her secretary, who led us to Tommi's office and promised to send his secretary in to see us.

Tommi's office was small and surprisingly dull. The furnishings consisted of a desk with a connected computer table, a bookshelf, a chair, and an uncomfortable-looking sofa. Tommi must have handled consultations with groups larger than a few people elsewhere. One wall was decorated with an enormous world map, which was stuck with blue and red pins.

"She sure was broken up," Koivu said as he studied the map.

"It's about time someone was sad about Tommi's death. I've been surprised that these choir people have been so calm. What do the pins mean?"

"Joint Venture Status, June thirteen," Koivu read from the edge of the map. "I wonder if it bothered him to handle Estonia, since they have mines in China and South America. I guess workers' rights aren't high on their priority list."

The binders and books on the shelves were all work related. The desk drawers were almost empty, and the top one was locked.

"Koivu, do you still have those keys with you? Let's see if one of them fits this lock."

As Koivu dug the keys out of his bag, I opened the unlocked roll-front cabinet on the other side of the desk.

"Well, would you look at that! Recognize this?" I lifted the liter bottle of clear liquid onto the desk. About half of the contents remained. I sniffed carefully.

"Same stuff?"

I handed the bottle to Koivu, who took a taste and grinned. Had Tommi kept a bottle in his cabinet to cheer himself up when he had to work overtime? I also found two shot glasses in the cabinet—one of which had muted red lipstick on the rim—along with a white shirt that was still in the packaging and black socks, obviously for emergency situations.

One of the keys did, in fact, fit the lock of the upper drawer. To our disappointment, all we found were the standard work-related letters, receipts, and bills. I collected them to go through later anyway. While I was shifting the stack of paper into my briefcase, a picture fell out. It was of Pia, smiling on the deck of a sailboat.

I heard a knock at the door, and a frail-looking woman in her fifties walked in. She introduced herself as Tommi's secretary, Mrs. Laakkonen. She too was deeply shocked by Tommi's death, but she didn't try to hide it. She just continued answering my questions as the tears rolled down her cheeks.

Tommi had been a nice boss. Demanding and precise, but nice. Yes, he had been forced to do a lot of entertaining, going out to restaurants and nightclubs. He had several company credit cards for those occasions. He kept his papers in irreproachably good order, and all the receipts were certain to be in his files.

"Did you ever have to organize Peltonen's personal schedule, for example, arranging meetings with his friends?"

Mrs. Laakkonen smiled.

"Theoretically that wasn't part of my job. But I suppose you could say that some of the people he asked me to arrange meetings with were more friends than business associates. That was quite rare though," she rushed to add, as if afraid to speak ill of the dead.

"Do you remember any of the names of those people? And please, don't hold anything back—everything is important in a murder investigation." The word murder brought on another torrent of tears, and I cursed my stupidity.

"Tuulia Rajala…and someone named Mrs. Wahlgren."

"Wahlroos? Pia Wahlroos?"

"Yes, I suppose it was Wahlroos. And he also called a Tiina quite often. There were a few other women as well who didn't seem to have anything to do with work."

"Do you have this Tiina's phone number?" I asked, remembering the message on Tommi's machine.

"I doubt it. It was understandable that girls would call Tommi. He was such a handsome young man…"

Laakkonen had no information about whether Tommi had been involved with any of his colleagues outside of work time. Koivu and I interviewed a few more of Tommi's coworkers and the building's main receptionist. Everyone I spoke to was subdued. It was clear that Tommi's death had been a shock to all of them—and I didn't learn anything new from of any of them.

Koivu, however, met a rather chatty economist.

"This Jantunen made all sorts of insinuations. He claimed that Peltonen and Mäki had some sort of liaison going on and that Peltonen was always off in Estonia chasing tail."

"Mäki and Tommi? Wow! Well, of course. I should have guessed the minute I saw that Tommi's boss was a woman. Was there someone in particular in Tallinn?"

I requested that they put Jantunen on the intercom, but he wasn't willing to say anything more. It seemed that the gab session with Koivu had been secret guy stuff. Again. Maybe Jantunen was just afraid of spreading rumors about his boss.

We finally went back to talk to the division head again. Dr. Mäki had calmed down by then. She had wiped away the smeared mascara and applied some lipstick. It looked unpleasantly similar to the shade I'd seen on the shot glass in Tommi's office cabinet. Was there something to Jantunen's story? Had

Tommi had a relationship with his boss too? How was I going to fish out the truth on this one?

"You worked closely with Tommi, right? Is there anything you could tell us about Peltonen's private life?"

"Well, he had his choir hobby. Wasn't he at a rehearsal retreat last weekend when he…when he…I gathered he spent a lot of time with the other choir members."

I remembered that EFSAS had been practicing for Tommi's company's summer party. What if Marja Mäki had known the practice schedule and come to check who Tommi was spending the weekend with out of jealousy?

"Where were you last Saturday night?"

Mäki stared at me, and I saw fear spread from her eyes to the rest of her face.

"What do you mean? I was in Paris."

"Alone? With your husband?"

"With my oldest daughter. My husband was here at home… in Vuosaari." Mäki burst into tears again. Nevertheless, I continued to pepper her with questions, and her answers painted a clearer picture.

Mäki and Peltonen had had a relationship, mostly on Tommi's office sofa after late nights working overtime and in hotel rooms on work trips.

"I don't think we were in love though," Mäki said with a sniffle. "It was more a mutually beneficial arrangement. We got along well."

Mutually beneficial arrangement. Tuulia had used the same words.

"In what sense was it a mutually beneficial arrangement? Did you maybe give Tommi money?"

Mäki flushed with rage.

"You listen here, missy," she hissed. "I may be a worn-out old hag in your eyes, but I didn't have to pay a manwhore. Tommi wanted sex, and so did I. Neither of us was paying for it."

Mäki had been under the impression that her husband didn't know about the affair. Just before she got home from Paris on Monday morning, a call had come in from the office. Her spouse had told her the terrible news when she walked in the door.

"Martti said first thing, 'That gigolo of yours is dead now.' And the children were standing right there listening!"

Apparently Martti Mäki had known about the relationship for some time. Marja Mäki clearly feared that her husband had killed Tommi. He claimed to have been home alone Saturday night, because the youngest of the two Mäki daughters had been away at riding camp.

"You understand, of course, that I'll have to interview your husband. Where can I find him?"

"That may be difficult...He left yesterday evening to go play golf in the Algarve in Portugal for a week."

My mind was swirling as we drove back toward Pasila. Koivu whistled thoughtfully next to me.

"He was a pretty intense dude," he observed to himself. "We haven't met a single woman yet that he left in peace. Except maybe the secretary."

"You can bet he charmed her too. Damn it to hell! I wish Martti Mäki hadn't snuck out of the country. If he's the murderer, he sure isn't ever coming back now. But how would he have known that Tommi was in Vuosaari too? I'm not going to be able to get an international arrest warrant with such flimsy evidence. I'm hungry. Should we go grab something vegetarian? Eating some rabbit food might help get my brain going."

I didn't make it home until after eight. I verified Martti Mäki's whereabouts and left him a message to call me back. I figured I didn't have anything to lose.

The thing that puzzled me most was why Dr. Mäki had so willingly told us about her relationship with Tommi and her suspicions regarding her husband. Despite her grief, she seemed like a person who kept everything under tight control. Did she hope that her husband had murdered Tommi? Or did she want something else? I sensed that perhaps Tommi's death was being used as a pawn in a game of marital chess, something I definitely didn't want to get mixed up in.

I spent the rest of the night sorting out Tommi's papers. He had kept his work and private calendars surprisingly well separated. His work calendar contained only work information: meetings, phone call reminders, airplane arrival times, and so forth. Lately there had been several discussions with a business called Mattinen Consulting, which seemed to have some connection to the Estonia project. I couldn't find the company in the phone book, so I made a note to ask Dr. Mäki about it.

The private calendars contained exclusively personal business: choir rehearsals and gigs, meetings with girls, squash times, and the like. The name Tiina appeared now and then, but no more often than any of the other women's names. The other names that came up repeatedly were Helvi and Merike. Had Tommi been playing boy toy for other wealthy women as well? Was that why he had gone to that nightclub? The calendar was also teeming with strange abbreviations like T. 10:00 H. I wondered whether T. could be Tuulia, whether H. meant home. What had really been going on between them?

I was perplexed that I couldn't find any sort of address book among Tommi's belongings, neither in the bag at the villa where we had found the calendar nor in Tommi's apartment. There hadn't been a list of numbers on the phone table in his apartment or in his office. Were we supposed to believe that he kept all of these different women's phone numbers in his head? Could one of them have come to the summerhouse at night and killed Tommi out of jealousy? But then how would Tommi have known to meet her on the dock? And would she have come by boat? I could feel a headache creeping up the back of my skull. I had been thinking intently for half an hour with my shoulders hunched over.

I decided that a good jog would be a better headache cure than ibuprofen. I was just digging my running pants out from the bottom of the laundry bin—they still had one more run in them—when the doorbell rang. Probably Jehovah's Witnesses or the TV license inspector. I could send the J Dubs on their way by explaining that I was Orthodox, which was a lie, but the television license inspector would be more of a problem. I had bought an ancient black-and-white TV with a screen about the size of a sheet of paper at a police auction a couple of years before, and for some reason I just hadn't ever gotten around to paying the public broadcasting support tax. However, I also knew that I didn't have any obligation to let a license inspector in.

I peeked through the peephole like an old lady and was delighted to see that it was Tuulia outside.

"What's up, Master Detective? I was just one street away visiting my cousin and thought I'd come by and ask how the investigation is going."

"Come on in," I said, genuinely happy to see her. I decided to ignore whether Tuulia's story was true. Maybe I didn't need to go for a run so badly after all.

"Riku was foaming at the mouth on Monday, saying that you almost arrested him. Is he number one in the rankings?" Tuulia asked as she hung her denim jacket on a hook.

"Well, no. I had a couple of things I had to clear up with him. My rankings are still in flux at the moment, but I can't really tell you anything more than that. I've interviewed others aside from Riku. Haven't the rumors gotten around yet?"

"Well, yeah. Antti and Mira were there too. We went over to the student association to practice the songs for the funeral. Terrible rehearsal. Hopeless, I mean Hopponen, our choir director, was a wreck. It was like we—I mean the ones who were at the villa—and everybody else were two completely different groups. Sirkku lost it in the end and started screaming that she hadn't killed anyone so stop staring."

"Interesting."

"The worst thing was we all lost it when Hopponen told us that Tommi's mother wants to hear Sibelius's 'Song of My Heart.' Nothing came of it since everyone went to pieces— except Mira, who just charged on with the alto part as if nothing had happened. Of course we want to sing whatever the family wants at our friend's funeral, and as well as we can, but hell... even Hopponen fell apart."

"Everyone who was at the villa is coming to sing?"

"If someone didn't come, we'd just assume they were the murderer. Damn it, Mira pisses me off! She doesn't even sing. She just shouts. Do you know what my cousin asked me after our spring concert? 'Who was that soloist?' She honestly thought that Mira was a soloist since her voice was so much louder than the rest of the group. I could almost kill her sometimes...I mean, figuratively speaking, you know," Tuulia added uncomfortably.

I didn't really feel like talking about work and changed the topic of conversation for a minute before turning to the matter of the calendar entries.

"Would you have had a date with Tommi the night before last if he had still been alive?" I asked suddenly. It was probably best to get through the official business first so that we could relax.

"How so?"

"Tommi wrote NO TUULIA MONDAY! in all caps on the notepad by his phone."

Tuulia seemed to be thinking hard. "No, that was...We had arranged to go to Theater in the Park, but then I decided I wasn't interested because everyone who had seen the show had totally ripped it to shreds, so I asked Tommi to cancel the tickets. I'd already forgotten the whole thing."

"According to Tommi's calendar, you two had quite a lot of dates. Were you playing squash or something?" I picked up the calendar, but Tuulia snatched it away from me, surprisingly covetous, and started to flip through it before I could stop her.

"Oh, you mean these Ts? Those don't have anything to do with me. I wonder what *T* could mean. Tommi always had all kinds of crazy coding systems. In school a black square on his calendar meant that he had been drinking that day and a heart meant he had gotten...And you can bet he scattered more of both around than was really true. Sometimes he was a little childish. This is probably some woman."

"Do you know anything about any of these other people? Who is Tiina? Or Merike?" I took the calendar from Tuulia and started to read the names aloud to her. Tuulia could explain who many of them were: choir members, relatives, coworkers. There were only a couple of names I mentioned that Tuulia couldn't identify.

"Do you know anything about Tommi's secondary income?"

Tuulia looked dumbfounded. She didn't have a clue about any side jobs, but after thinking for a moment, she remembered something.

"I think they were some sort of temporary gigs. Sometimes he talked about some sort of consulting work, and he seemed to know a lot about certain specific laws. Maybe he was doing something off the books, dodging taxes."

I mentioned that Tommi had been receiving additional income regularly.

"Do you know anything about a trust fund or anything like that?"

"Yeah! That must be it!" Tuulia said excitedly. "They're all high-finance types, so they probably pay out their inheritances ahead of time to avoid the taxes. Tommi's parents have so much money they don't know what to do with it. I doubt that Heikki would admit it to you if you asked him though. Henri's going to have money pouring down on him now. It's a good thing he's off in the States—aren't people usually killed for money?" Tuulia paused for a moment. "Hey, I like your apartment just fine, but is there any beer here? I had a pretty intense squash match this morning and now I'm starting to feel it."

My refrigerator contained the dregs of a liter carton of yogurt, a container of processed cheese spread, and that bottle of kiwi liqueur. The rest of my food reserves consisted of a package of coffee, half a loaf of rye bread, and three desiccated apples. Trips to the grocery store had been few and far between lately.

"Nothing? Really? Well, let's head down to Elite, then. Or does some professional code of conduct say you can't?"

I thought about my jog and remembered what they had taught us in the academy about cops staying neutral. I figured a couple of beers would work as a neck relaxant just as well as running.

"Yeah, sure, but on one condition."

"Yeah?"

"That we not talk about the case. We can talk about any-thing else—music, politics, books, even reindeer herding—but not my work. I'm just going to get more and more mixed up if I keep churning this over in my mind all the time."

"Are you mixed up? You poor dear," Tuulia said with a grin. "Well, hey, so am I. It'll probably do us both good to think about something other than Tommi for a while."

I washed the makeup off my face, applied a fresh coat, let my hair down, and was suddenly very thirsty. Thirsty for beer, thirsty for laughter, thirsty for friendship. I didn't have the energy or the desire to think about professional ethics. Maybe going drinking with Tuulia was wrong for me the cop, but it was definitely right for me the person.

And we had fun. Tuulia was in rare form and regaled me with stories about all her escapades and mishaps. Her cheerful, anarchistic approach to life sometimes made me feel like I was already dead and in the grave. Tuulia's tales of summer hitchhik-ing trips, screwing around at rock festivals with sixteen-year-old boys who suffered from virgin complexes, and swimming in the Tapiola fountain pond in downtown Espoo made me envious. Some might have said that Tuulia didn't want to grow up, but I thought it was more like she didn't want to dry up.

"I don't want to be on any set track: graduate—buy an apartment—pay a mortgage—get a husband—make babies. Be respectable. I want to be irresponsible and do exactly what I feel like for my whole life," she explained and then tipped half a glass of beer down her throat so that part of it ran down her jaw onto her neck. She laughed and wiped it off with the back of her hand. Her open-neck blouse emphasized her clavicles, and her neck rose high and proud from between them. She wore gold half-moons in her ears, and a similar ring with sparkling gems adorned her finger. Pretty kitsch.

"What are you thinking about, Maria?"

"How much fun it is to talk to a sensible woman. I'm surrounded by way too many men at work. For some reason the only women I can really understand are the vagabonds, I mean the kinds of women who haven't settled into any traditional roles."

"You seem pretty lonely. Jaana said sometimes that you were kind of a hermit."

"I just can't stand putting myself out there. People are OK, even men, but playing the dating game just makes me gag."

"Do you have someone special? I mean a man?"

"No. I've had a few who've hung around for a while. Pete drank all my money away. The second one, the bird guy, was a total emotional cripple, and then the most recent was this one study partner in law school who couldn't stand that I got better grades than he did. That's it in a nutshell. And I don't have it in me to just go in search of some man because I'm supposed to have one. I'm too interested in my own comfort to put up with just anyone. I don't think that all men are idiots, but there haven't been many bright spots lately. Do you have somebody?"

"Not for ages. Tommi was…" Tuulia bit her lip, and I suddenly remembered Antti's appeal in his letter not to hurt Tuulia. "Sorry for mentioning the taboo subject, but Tommi was…special in a way. A kindred spirit. Fucking infuriating sometimes." She paused. "Barkeep! More of the same! You want another one too, don't you, Maria?"

"I wouldn't mind a third." I noticed that Tuulia was choking back tears, and I started to talk about the latest Aki Kaurismäki film, which I had seen the previous week. From there, we started debating men's and women's roles, criticizing the government, and laughing until our sides ached. A couple of smug-looking guys tried to join us, but Tuulia wrapped her arm around my shoulder and said crossly that our own company was quite enough. We chuckled at the abrupt change in their expressions.

As we stood at the tram stop, I realized I was drunk. Tuulia said that she couldn't walk to the railway station to catch her bus, so I had promised to wait for the tram with her. The evening air was cool, and Tuulia pulled her hands up into the overly long sleeves of her sweatshirt.

"I have really bad circulation; my hands are always cold."

"Do you remember playing clapping games to stay warm at recess when you were a kid? How about we try that?" We started slapping hands, slowly and stiffly at first, but then the old knack came back and we were clapping hands faster and faster, ignoring people's quizzical looks and giggling like ten-year-olds.

"You have really warm hands," Tuulia said. "Warm hands, cold heart. Is it true?"

"According to that logic, you have a warm heart. Is that true?" I tossed back.

We hugged each other before the streetcar carried Tuulia away. As I walked home, I thought about when I had last touched a person like that, in a way that brought me pleasure.

8

Drifting on the tide, along this endless road we glide
No man, not one, may know

I was tied up with the Malmi stabbings for the rest of the week. One more victim came in on Friday when the youngest son of one of the Roma families stabbed a first cousin of the other family. I was trying to understand their perspective on things, but that would have required a better understanding of Roma culture than I had, and I simply didn't have time to delve into it right then.

I tried to contact Hopponen, the choir director, several times and finally reached him on Monday.

"I'm still on summer vacation. I only came back to the city to rehearse for the funeral, and I'm in a bit of a rush. I have a lot to get done before tonight," Hopponen explained.

"This is a murder investigation," I said, trying to force some authority into my voice.

"Yes, of course I want to help. Could you maybe come to the student association tonight when we take our rehearsal break? Around seven thirty?"

That was fine with me. It would give me a chance to meet some of the other members of the choir and ask them about Tommi.

Martti Mäki had called me on Thursday. After a moment of
hesitation, he had told me that he hadn't been home at all on the
night of the murder. When I asked whether anyone could cor-
roborate that, he was flummoxed.

"Well, see...I don't know the woman's name." She had been
a chance acquaintance he made at the Kaivohuone Club in the
park. Mäki had spent the entire night with her at Hotel Vaakuna.
I arranged to meet him immediately after he returned to Finland
on Tuesday. Perhaps I was naive to trust him, but I didn't have
any choice. Why would Mäki have bothered hiding the ax under
the sauna? While Koivu was doing his rounds of the downtown
nightclubs, he might as well stop by the Kaivohuone Club with
a photograph of Mäki.

I left Pasila a little before seven. The previous night I had
been up until midnight interrogating one of the assailants in
the knifings. I was tired, and my head felt empty. I wished I had
someone waiting for me at home with a hot bath drawn and a
cold beer. Or even just a purring cat. I hoped that my meeting
with Hopponen at the rehearsal wouldn't take long. I needed to
clean up, do some laundry, and sleep more than six hours.

As I rode the tram downtown, I thought about Koivu's experience at the Hesperia Club. At first the bartender on shift had
said he remembered Tommi well, but then he suddenly claimed
that he hadn't had time to pay attention to what he was up to.
Koivu said that chatting up the women had been even more
difficult. None of them had been willing to admit to knowing Tommi, though Koivu easily detected the recognition that
flashed in some of their eyes when he showed them Tommi's
photograph. Maybe Koivu had been too soft.

The choir practiced in the Eastern Finland Student
Association's space on Liisankatu. Their singing carried from

an open window all the way down to the street. I recognized Kuula's tune: "Drifting on the Tide." That was what they had been rehearsing at Vuosaari too. Did EFSAS intend to perform that at Tommi's funeral?

The elevator was out of service, so I had to climb the stairs to the fifth floor. The singing was even louder in the hallway, breaking off from time to time, and then starting over from the beginning. Didn't the neighbors ever get upset?

The door was locked, so I rang the bell. After a long wait, Mira came to open the door. She did a double take when she saw me.

"Hello. I came to meet your choir director," I explained.

"Our break is in about ten minutes," Mira replied and then marched back into the practice room. I was a little early, and Hopponen didn't seem to be in any hurry to stop for their break, so I had a chance to observe the rehearsal for close to half an hour. I had an excellent vantage point from the side door of the large room and could see not only the whole choir but also their conductor sweating it out in front of them.

The choir's autumn season had not begun yet, so only a couple dozen singers were present. There were decidedly fewer men than women, and only one tenor aside from Riku and Timo. Despite the relatively small number in the group, the hall felt crowded. Even with one of the windows open, the air was stifling.

Hopponen, or Hopeless as they called him, led the choir from a platform that stood about a foot above the ground. He was short, fat, and bald, with the exception of a few long wisps of hair around the sides and back of his head, and he had a white goatee that waggled when he moved. Hopponen's baton work was strange to say the least—at least to my untrained eye, it was impossible to tell what time the song was in, let alone what was the downbeat. As he conducted, he hummed various parts, seemingly at random, like Glenn Gould. His shirt was too short and kept coming untucked from his loose jeans. Every now and then, he pushed it back in with one hand. Apparently, the ladies in the choir made a habit of checking to make sure Hopponen's hair was combed, that his tuning fork was in his pocket, and that his fly was zipped before performances. I wondered whether perhaps he was trying to use absentmindedness to bolster his image as an artist.

"Shut it, tenors!" Hopponen suddenly bellowed. "Can't you read music? That's the bass solo!"

I saw Timo's cheeks flush with embarrassment. Riku stood next to him grinning maliciously.

"Take it from the top; there was a lot of sloppiness all through there. Sopranos and altos, clear break between the dotted eighth notes and triplets at the beginning of the second page. And basses, don't lag! From the beginning! Second soprano, may I have that D?"

Hopponen received at least two different versions of the requested note. The other voices sighed in exasperation. The same spectacle had obviously played out all too often before.

"The higher version is correct," Hopponen observed dryly before motioning to the second sopranos to begin. At first there wasn't a peep. Then someone began, very uncertainly, and a voice rose from the alto row to back up the second sopranos. General chaos ensued.

"Be quiet, Mira, you're just messing it up!" Pia shouted, surprisingly sternly.

"What exactly is so hard about this beginning?" Hopponen asked, scratching his bald head.

"We don't dare start when everyone is just waiting for us to screw up," explained a plump, harried-looking redhead next to Pia.

"I can sing with them until the second alto starts," Mira suggested and received several furious complaints in reply. It took awhile for Hopponen to get the situation under control.

"It sounds stupid if you sing with the second sopranos from over there on the other side. Tuulia, could you sing the first measure with them?" Hopponen finally suggested.

This solution seemed to work, and the song finally gained momentum. As I really started listening, I realized that the piece was truly touching, almost like it was written for Tommi's funeral: "Drifting on the tide, along this endless road we glide, no man, not one, its length may know."

The choir began to improve. I was standing closest to the altos, and Mira's voice often overpowered the others. Tuulia's soloist story was probably more than simple malice. Mira just charged on through the song, singing in the same unhesitating *forte* throughout. I wondered whether the person singing next to Mira was deaf in one ear. Closer to the middle of the alto row, Sirkku swayed in time to the music as she sang, which made her look idiotic.

Behind the altos sat the tenors. Timo sang with his nose in his sheet music and never even glanced at Hopponen. Riku's expression was one of concentration. When he sang, he looked less childlike than usual. My eyes moved along the back row to Antti, who was just belting out in his low bass, "All, all shall fade away." For a moment I thought I could detect tears in his eyes.

"Thank you!" Hopponen yelled midline. "Thank you means shut your trap!" he continued, when some of the group failed to stop singing. "All shall fade away, page three, line three. There are two Fs there. What might that mean?"

I could see many irritated looks in the ranks. This scene had also obviously been repeated often.

"*Fortissimo*," came a general muttering.

"If you know what it means, then why isn't anyone but the second altos doing it?"

"But they always sing *fortissimo*," I heard Tuulia huff. She grinned at me as she said it, and I couldn't help but grin back. The smile warmed me, making me forget the claustrophobic atmosphere.

"And tenors, your high Gs are always flat. Every one of you should be able to hit it."

I saw Riku glance at Timo again.

"Sopranos, a bit bolder through the whole thing, and basses, you're just a smidgen behind. Pick it up! Page three. Basses, your first entry, please."

I continued looking at Tuulia. She had quickly regained a serious expression. Tuulia's singing sounded both beautiful and effortless. Jaana had said that Tuulia was naturally a very high soprano, who didn't even have trouble hitting the occasional B above the staff.

Pia seemed to be troubled though. She had stopped singing, and I could see tears running down her face. The plump redhead offered her a handkerchief.

The choir sang the song one more time, without interruption this time. They were finally starting to sound rather melodious. Then Hopponen declared that it was time for a break, and I started weaving my way through the benches toward him. He disappeared in a flash into a back room. I accidentally knocked someone's music onto the floor. When I picked it up, I saw that its owner had improved Leino's poem: "One is born to treasure and another has no brain, but within each heart the tick of a clock. When it stops 'tis time for this choir to give me pain."

At the part "No man, not one, its length may know" he had drawn a vulgar picture. Next to the line "A new dawn yet will break" was a crudely sketched sun passing gas. And this wasn't even the engineering school choir.

I bumped into Antti, who was breaking pieces off of a large head of cauliflower and shoving them in his mouth.

"Hi, Maria. Want some?" He extended the cauliflower to me.

"No thanks. Where did Hopponen disappear to?"

Antti pointed toward the back room, where Hopponen was currently explaining something to Timo. I walked over and interrupted them with a loud greeting.

"Hello…" Hopponen replied uncertainly. "Would you like to join the choir?"

"No. Detective Maria Kallio of the Helsinki Police Violent Crime Unit."

Hopponen glanced at me, looking confused, and then took my outstretched hand. Foiled by my jeans again. Maybe I should consider making the uniform skirt and bun a permanent look.

"Oh, yes, I almost forgot about you." Hopponen shooed Timo away, closing the door after him.

"What exactly is it you wanted to know?" he asked, twiddling his goatee.

"Tommi Peltonen was the assistant choir director, right? What duties did that entail?"

"The assistant director doesn't do all that much. Sometimes we split the choir in two, and Tommi practiced with one half while I took the others. In theory, the assistant director leads

the choir if the director isn't around, but I try never to miss performances or rehearsals."

"Was Tommi the assistant director the entire time he was in
the choir?"

"I don't remember things like that. I can't be expected to
keep track of which year each person joined the choir. Tommi
was with us for a long time though, probably close to ten years."

"Isn't this supposed to be a student choir? Tommi had already
graduated and was a bit old for it."

"Student choir is a flexible concept. We're happy to keep
good singers on even after they leave school. And Tommi
seemed to enjoy being involved." Hopponen smiled lecherously.
"And I'm sure he didn't mind the crop of new young girls who
show up every year."

"So Tommi was popular with the girls in the choir?" I asked,
as if I hadn't heard anything about it before.

"Oh, yes, Tommi had girls to spare." The smile flashed
again, then disappeared. Maybe Hopponen thought it unseemly
to talk of the dead in such a jocular manner.

"To spare? What do you mean?"

Hopponen pushed his shirttails into his pants, looking
abashed, and refused to elaborate. When I asked whether I could
interview a few of the choir members during the rehearsal, he
grew irritated.

"This is our last practice before the funeral, and the whole
choir is in their typical summer shape."

I had to remind him once again that this was a murder investigation before he agreed. Then he glanced at his watch and saw
that the break had already gone on far too long.

The choir members had broken up into small groups and
spread themselves around the various student association rooms.

It looked to me like the ones who hadn't been at Vuosaari were in a standoff with those who had been there. Only Riku was chatting amiably in the smoking room with one of the altos. Glued to Timo's side, Sirkku stared at me fearfully from the sofa in the entryway.

When Hopponen declared that the break was over, Timo climbed onto the conductor's platform. He waited—to no avail—for the group to settle down and finally yelled in frustration, "Listen up for a minute! We need to go over Saturday's schedule. The funeral will be at Temppeliaukio Church at two o'clock. We'll meet at one so we have time to get warmed up and go through the program one more time."

"What hymns will they be singing?" Mira asked.

"They didn't know yet," Hopponen said, breaking in. "Mr. Peltonen promised to notify me tomorrow, and I'll call Timo so he can start circulating the words. It would be good for everyone to scan through them a little beforehand."

"After the funeral, there will be a short memorial at the Laulumiehet Restaurant," Timo continued. "We've been asked to come and sing one or two songs. They are Chorale 62 from the *St. Matthew's Passion* and Genetz's 'Land of Peace,' and that's what we'll practice for the remainder of our rehearsal. Any questions?"

"What clothes?" Pia asked.

"Sunday best. No choir costumes," Timo answered.

"The same clothes you would normally wear to a friend's funeral," Hopponen added. "Dark suits for the men."

"So no flowery dresses or too much makeup for the women," Mira said sternly.

"Did you want to say something?" Timo asked me next, stepping down off the platform to make room for me. I bounced up, and for a moment I had an urge to start waving my arms around like Hopponen. With some effort I controlled myself.

"Good evening. I'm Detective Maria Kallio from the Helsinki PD Violent Crime Unit. I'm investigating Tommi Peltonen's death. I'm hoping that if any of you knows anything that might shed light on the case, you'll come forward now. I'll be back in that smoking room, and I'd like each of you to come have a chat with me before you leave this evening."

"What about the ones who have already talked to you?" Mira asked antagonistically.

"No need, unless you have something new to tell me, and I don't ask for you specifically. Here on the board is a telephone number where you can reach me later if something comes to mind." I jumped down off the platform and motioned for the short alto sitting next to Mira to follow me. I refrained from asking her whether her hearing was still normal in her left ear.

Unfortunately, I didn't learn anything noteworthy from the other choir members. Antti, Tuulia, Riku, and Pia seemed to have known Tommi best. A couple of the women implied that they'd been involved with Tommi at one point or another, but it seemed that it had been quite some time since all of that.

Anu, the plump, redheaded second soprano, was the first one to have anything of real interest to tell me.

"The last time I saw Tommi, we were playing *kyykkä* and then we went for beers at the Three Liisas. The ladies' room there was small, so we had to line up outside. The pay phone was right next to us, and while I waited in line, I could see that Tommi was having a fight with somebody on the phone."

"About what?"

"Money, I think. He said, 'one fifth now, but that's all there is.' When he noticed me, he said, 'Listen, Emma, I can't talk now,' and hung up the phone. Then he snapped at me, something along the lines of what the fuck was I doing eavesdropping. I guess it was something important."

"So Tommi was speaking with a woman?"

"That's the impression I got."

"Does the name Emma mean anything to you? Maybe an old choir member or someone else Tommi might have mentioned?"

"No, I can't think of anyone by that name."

There hadn't been any mention of an Emma in Tommi's calendars either.

"Which of you were playing *kyykkä* that day and who went to the bar?"

A sly look crept over her face. She must have understood what I was getting at.

"All the regulars. If I'm remembering correctly, then it was everyone who was out at the summerhouse. Oh, no, except for Antti. That was why Mira looked so disappointed. She went home after the game and didn't come to the Liisas. But there's no way she could have made it home in time for me to overhear her on the phone with Tommi, since she lives so far away."

No one else had anything enlightening to say. I felt like chatting with Tuulia just for fun, but I couldn't come up with any excuse for calling her in. It may have been that I was just feeling shy, like I had revealed too much about my inner self when we'd been out together the other night.

I could feel the previous night's interrogations in my temples and my arms and legs. I listened a little while longer as the choir practiced the familiar Bach chorale, and hummed along a bit with the sopranos.

Where had Tommi sat? He had been a first bass, so that would have put him in the middle of the back row. Did the bass part sound different without Tommi?

So Tommi had been talking about money with some woman. Had he been in debt to someone? Was that the secret behind the expensive car and the other luxury gadgets? Was that woman why he had demanded his money back from Riku?

"Do you think someone else is going to die soon too? Do we need a police guard during rehearsals?" Antti asked as he appeared in the hallway and marched toward the phone. From what I heard of the beginning of the call, I concluded he was calling the Peltonens to inquire into the details of the funeral arrangements. I stuck my tongue out at the back of his black T-shirt and slammed the door on my way out.

What a pain in the ass, I thought as I ran down the stairs. First he offers me cauliflower, and then he taunts me. The whole lot of them are crazy. People generally think of singing as a per- fectly decent hobby, but based on the rehearsal I had just seen, it mostly brought out people's bitchiness. No doubt every person in the choir had experienced moments of wanting to do away with their neighbor or the conductor. Maybe someone had just gotten fed up with Tommi criticizing their singing...

I bumped into a couple of law school friends in Kaisaniemi Park on their way to dinner and drinks near the train station. After a bit of persuasion on their part, I decided to join them. After all, I could always clean my apartment tomorrow, and there would be plenty of time for sleep when I retired.

9

Sea and sky and land—all, all shall fade away

Work remained chaotic. For the rest of the week, it felt like half the city had decided to start abusing their families. After dealing with five domestic violence cases in three days—one dead elderly mother, two beaten wives, one drunk husband pushed off a balcony, and one little brother with his foot shot off by his father's hunting rifle—I was ready to swear off ever getting married or having children. I only had time to think about Tommi's case intermittently, but when I finally got a chance to do another read-through of his papers, I found I had only more questions.

Though it was not imperative that I be there for the investigation, I wanted to be present for Tommi's funeral. Tommi's father had told me about the funeral arrangements when I called him to inquire further into Tommi's finances. Although Heikki Peltonen had denied any illegal prepayment of an advance on Tommi's inheritance, I didn't fully trust him. The family's doctor had forbidden anyone from questioning Tommi's mother so far. I knew that I could get permission if I needed to, but I didn't want to pressure her.

The forensic technicians didn't find anything worthwhile in Tommi's car. It was covered with several people's fingerprints, some unidentified, but none of them raised any flags in our database. There were no bloodstains, and nothing was stashed in there. As far as I was concerned, the impound could release the car to the Peltonens.

On the day of the funeral, I walked to Temppeliaukio Church from home. My old black dress was tight across my shoulders. My parents bought it for me for my high school graduation, but I hadn't been lifting weights back then. Black stockings covered my unshaven leg hair. I hadn't bought any flowers, because Tommi didn't need them, and the living might take a dim view of a police officer bringing them. Besides, I wanted to concentrate on the other people with flowers, to see whether Merike, Emma, Tiina, or this M person might be among them. I had no intention of invading the private memorial service that was to take place after the funeral.

The day was cloudy and it looked like it might start raining at any moment. Perfect funeral weather. There was no thunder, just a resigned, almost thirsty anticipation of rain. The groundsels growing on the slopes of the bedrock into which the subterranean church was built looked like they were yearning for moisture after several weeks of drought.

I slipped unnoticed into a corner of the balcony. I thought about the last time I had been in a church—it had been my friend Annikka's wedding the previous winter. Churches always felt foreign to me, and I didn't know how to act in them. I always felt clumsy and loud, and the priests' sermons never succeeded in getting through to me. Religion was something I thought about only rarely, mostly because I didn't want to. Now, however, I tried to think about where Tommi had truly gone. Around the station there were rumors that, twenty years ago, one of the most effective cops in the VCU had regularly visited a spiritualist to move homicide cases forward.

Apparently, it had worked pretty well. I had a hard time believing in anything like that, but what did I know? I suppose anything could be possible—maybe Tommi was in the place believers called heaven. Or was his place in hell?

Maybe every person's heaven was different. I imagined Tommi cavorting with voluptuous female angels, then realized that was an inappropriate thought in a church—no one had noticed me smiling to myself at a funeral, had they? On the other hand, perhaps Tommi had simply ceased to exist. Completely. The dark tone of Antti's letter came back to me. He certainly didn't think there was a Tommi anymore, in any sense. The only thing that came after death was a black, irrevocable finality.

I looked down from the balcony. The church was only sparsely filled. The choir sat in their places in front of the mourners, almost facing me directly. A simple oak casket rested before the altar. It would soon burn along with Tommi. Heikki Peltonen sat in the first row, and the woman in the mourning veil hunched against him was obviously Tommi's mother. How many tranquilizers had been stuffed into Mrs. Peltonen before the funeral?

All of my suspects were in the group preparing to sing. Pia and Tuulia were on the right edge of the soprano row. Pia, whose eyes were already red, was dressed in an elegant black gown though the fabric looked almost inappropriately fancy for a funeral. Tuulia wore a slim, black sweaterdress that made her hair and face look whiter than normal. Sirkku sat with her head bowed, holding Timo's hand behind her. Mira was scanning the crowd, and her eyes flashed with obvious hostility when they fell on me.

The men sat in the back row; Riku was barely visible behind the altos, and Antti's head rose above the others in the back corner. His black suit trousers were too short, revealing a band of slender shin above his black socks. Antti had pulled his shoulder-length hair back in a ponytail with a black scrunchie.

Hopponen sat at the organ. I saw his hands shaking and found myself fearing for the members of the choir, for Tommi's mother, for myself. I feared the anguish behind those red eyes, that it would flood out of control, and that the orderly singing would turn to weeping and wailing. I feared that someone would cry to the heavens "Who?" and "Why?"—questions I still did not know how to answer. Maybe Tommi had the easiest time of it. After all, it was over for him.

Hopponen played the first chords of the opening hymn. I had always enjoyed singing, so I picked up a hymnal and joined in. Hymn 613, first and second verses. From the beginning of the first verse, I began to wonder at the choice of song, and the words of the second seemed even more apropos of the situation, perhaps too much so: "Neither magnificence nor majesty, neither youth nor skill may save, when thrown open is the grave. The moment of departure shall come, and all shall meet that reward. But when and how knoweth only the Lord." I found my voice shaking. It must have been because I hadn't sung in so long.

After the congregational hymn, it was the choir's turn to sing. I recognized the "Lacrimosa" from Mozart's *Requiem*. Its strains were haunting and cruel, as were the dark, menacing words: "Lacrimosa dies illa, qua resurget ex favilla, judicandus homo reus. Huic ergo parce, Deus." Tears when man rises in his guilt for judgment…Had Tommi been evil? He toyed with people, yes, but evil? Would God, if there was a God, forgive him? I couldn't take my eyes off the choir. I could pick out Riku's fluting tenor and Mira's splendid, dark alto. Maybe the most beautiful thing about her was her voice. The basses thundered the low notes, and the sopranos climbed higher and higher, their voices never faltering. A light flush appeared on Tuulia's pale face as she sang.

The prayers and Bible readings washed right past me. The priest, a young man with an appropriately solemn demeanor, directed his words toward Tommi's parents. I noticed Pia digging a handkerchief out of her purse and remembered that I needed to interview her soon. Sirkku grabbed Timo's hand again. I still hadn't been able to come up with a sufficient motive for those two. I could imagine Timo accidentally killing Tommi in a rage if he had been making fun of Sirkku. Timo seemed like the kind of guy who thought it was a man's duty to retaliate against any insults directed at his woman. No one had ever defended me like that, but I didn't want that kind of man in my life. On the contrary, I remembered punching a drunken idiot who had shouted that Harri the birdman was a long-haired queer while we were standing in line at a hot dog stand.

But would Timo and Tommi have had any reason to meet secretly at night? What if the letter *T* on the calendar did mean Timo? And what if we found the distilling equipment in one of the love birds' apartments? The priest stopped talking. Hopponen walked discreetly from the organ to stand in front of the choir, and the men stood to sing. "Grove of Tuoni, grove of night! There thy bed of sand is light, thither my child now I lead..." They had evidently decided to sing the men's version, because the women simply couldn't stand to sing it. There were only six men, and Riku and Antti appeared to be alone at the outer edges of the vocal range.

Tommi's mother began to cry, and a surge of weeping swept like a wave back through the rows of friends and family, drawing the women in the choir along with it. Tuulia didn't even try to hold back her tears, and I would have liked to go and comfort

her. Pia hid behind her dark, bobbed hair, and a girl I didn't
know blew her nose so loudly that I could hear it all the way
up in the gallery. Hopponen led on with a trembling hand, his
goatee shaking. Only Mira sat, calm and expressionless, the grief
all around her having no effect on her whatsoever. I wondered
how much of her placidity was an act. Or had Mira truly hated
Tommi so much that she was actually rejoicing over his death?
If so, why?

I admired the boys' self-control. It's true that society doesn't
give men permission to turn hysterical with grief. But how
were they able to sing amid the general weeping, with Tommi's
mother practically howling despite all the sedatives? Riku's first
tenor was light and beautiful. When he sang, his shrill speaking
voice turned ethereal, like it was an instrument of the divine.
The intermediate voices were a bit rough in places, and the first
bass's cheek twitched dangerously. Antti sang in his astonish-
ingly low voice straight to Tommi's mother, as though wanting
to assure her with his eyes that Aleksis Kivi's words were indeed
true: "Far from hatred, far from strife..." After the song ended,
I tasted blood in my mouth. I had bit my sun-chapped lower lip
until it cracked.

Fortunately, the funeral homily snapped me back to reality. It made me angry to hear the priest dance around the way
Tommi had died. Admittedly, it was a difficult subject since the
case had yet to be solved, and it was likely that the murderer was
present in the chapel. According to the priest, however, God
had, in his infinite wisdom, decided to allow Tommi to "pass
from among us." I hated euphemistic language about death.
There was no way the priest would have spoken that way if he
had seen Tommi's body. That was the sort of image that kept a
person up at night.

The choir stood again to sing "Drifting on the Tide." The sopranos' first words trembled slightly, and Pia looked seriously distressed. This was the song they had been practicing in such a carefree way at the villa. How different it must have felt to them now. "All, all shall fade away," thundered the basses. "That spring will come again and a new dawn yet will break," the choir sang optimistically a moment later. "Or have they lied?" came the doubtful basses once again. One thing was certain: spring would never come again for Tommi.

Next came the laying of the wreaths. I fanned my indignation by thinking about all of those beautiful flowers that would bring no joy to the person lying in the casket. Tommi's mother barely had the strength to stand next to the coffin for a moment, even supported by her husband. The relatives followed, then came Tommi's coworkers. Tommi's secretary carried the wreath, and Marja Mäki read a vapid message of sympathy in a confident voice.

Finally Hopponen and the first bass with the twitching cheek lowered the choir's wreath onto the casket. I noticed that none of Tommi's friends—Riku, Antti, Tuulia, or even the choir chairman, Timo—had qualified for the job.

As far as I could tell, almost everyone present in the church had taken a turn at the casket, but no flowers had been left by the women or by the man named M mentioned in Tommi's calendar. Heikki Peltonen had told me that the family wanted a small service, and there hadn't been an obituary in the paper.

I had probably come to the funeral for nothing.

It had also been pointless to think that the murderer might crack during the funeral. My foul mood worsened as I watched every one of my suspects looking so righteous singing the Lord's Prayer. "Thy will be done"—did the murderer really think that?

According to Christian ethics, the murderer would get caught. An eye for an eye and a tooth for a tooth—God, how I wanted to catch Tommi's killer! Did I want revenge? Did I want to succeed? Did I want to mete out justice?

But did I have it in me to throw the first stone?

In the early days of my career on the police force, I had involved myself emotionally in every case I investigated. I had felt empathy toward the victim, but I also wanted to understand the criminal. Was I back at that same level of involvement again? I didn't want that. I didn't want to start projecting my own sense of morality on every case, weighing the blameworthiness of the acts against the proportionality of the punishment. By going from being a person who made arrests to being one who determined the punishments, I hoped to have the opportunity to dispense real justice. A police officer was supposed to arrest the brats who scribbled graffiti on cement office building walls and the stupid college kids who sampled a joint—but a judge could assess the justice of a given punishment. Was I really capable of taking on that responsibility?

Hopponen returned to the organ and began to play Handel's "Largo." The funeral party sat in their pews, waiting for the immediate family to leave first. Tommi's father lifted his wife carefully by the arm. Maisa Peltonen stood on slightly shaky legs and then suddenly began shouting over the organ.

"You monster! You murdered my son, whoever you are! How dare you stand here in a church! How dare you sing at Tommi's casket! How..." Her voice dissolved into halting sobs, and Tommi's father turned his wife's head toward his chest as if to quiet her. Hopponen fumbled through the rest of "Largo" on the organ, while the rest of the party stared uncomfortably at the ceiling or the floor. The choir members looked anywhere but at each other. Timo was beet red and held Sirkku's hand tightly. She had shoved her knuckles in her mouth as if to stifle her own cries. Pia had buried her face in a handkerchief. Riku's face twitched. Only Mira remained calm.

The rest of the mourners only began to leave once Tommi's parents had exited the church. The memorial was likely to be fraught. The flower-strewn coffin remained in its place at the altar, to be burned in silence.

I tried to slink away without being noticed, but Antti was faster than I was. He ran after me outside and grabbed me painfully by the arm.

"Damn it, you've got to do something fast!" Antti hissed at me, his eyes narrowed like a cat preparing to pounce. "Maisa is at the end of her rope. She's promising to get revenge, to murder us all. She won't be able to stand this much longer."

"Well, confess then!" I hissed back, shocked by my own words and at least as angry as he was. Antti let go of my arm and stared at me in horror.

"Listen, you're on totally the wrong track! If you really suspect me then it's no wonder nothing's happening!"

"You could at least be a little more cooperative."

"So it all comes down to *my* willingness to cooperate?"

The other members of the choir had surrounded us. I recalled the old blindfold game in which one person spins in the middle of the group with her eyes covered and then has to guess who her finger is pointing at. Could I use that technique to reveal the murderer?

"Antti, let's do a quick run-through before the memorial," Hopponen said. The clouds had darkened while we were in the church, and a few tentative drops of rain landed on my forehead.

"I've told you already that I'm not coming. This was my last time singing with EFSAS. And besides, I'm in the middle of a conversation with Nancy Drew here."

"Antti. We need you," Mira said in a commanding voice.

"Come on; let him be." Tuulia started dragging the rest of them away. A moment later, Antti and I were alone in front of the entrance to the church. Only Mira glanced back at us.

"I'm really not interested in coffee and sweet rolls or reminiscing about Tommi's childhood," Antti said to me as though to explain himself. Then he set off down the street, clearly expecting me to follow.

"How did you get it into your head that I killed Tommi?" he asked when I caught up to him.

"That was just a gamble."

"Have you tried that technique on the others? No results, eh?"

"No, I haven't. But try to get it through your head that I really *do* want to figure out who the murderer is, and I've been doing the best I can. But I'm not some kind of fucking superwoman who just solves murders—snap—like that. I need help, not shouting. I don't know who's guilty yet, but I have some ideas. There are all sorts of things we have to check out, but it all takes time. If you don't trust that I can get the job done, then don't. But I still have to try to trust myself."

Antti kicked a crushed beer can with the tip of his scuffed shoes and said, "I'm sorry. I just got worked up in the funeral… But I agree with Maisa: Someone in there is a first-class hypocrite. If only I…if only I knew which things were significant and which weren't." He looked embarrassed.

"It would be best for you just to tell me everything and then let me decide what matters. Don't you go trying to play private detective. And don't go telling the person you suspect that you and only you know something incriminating. You'd find yourself hanging out with Tommi again—wherever he is now."

I told him my image of heaven, in which Tommi was living it up with angels that looked like *Playboy* centerfolds. For the second time since Tommi's death, I saw Antti laugh. The tension in his face relaxed for a moment, and the furrows in his cheeks melted into laugh lines.

"It's a nice thought, but I can't make myself believe in any kind of heaven. To me Tommi just doesn't exist anymore. Period. But not completely, not yet. Despite everything, he was my best friend."

"Despite what everything?"

"Well, we had slightly different values—and lifestyles—the last few years. I could never understand all of his exploits. He had to live every day like it was his last." Antti snorted at the figure of speech he'd used. "Maybe he sensed that he wouldn't be hanging around long. He always claimed he would die of AIDS or liver cancer. But like that hymn says, only the Lord knows how we'll leave here."

I wondered what Antti would say if he knew I had read his letter. My attempt to treat people with a professional distance was failing with Antti now too. We had come to the corner of the cross street that led to my apartment, and the rain had begun to come down in earnest. I wasn't in the mood to get wet.

"Should we go to Elite to wait out the rain?" Antti asked.

"Actually, I live in that green building over there. If you aren't in a hurry, I could make you a cup of coffee. I don't have any sweet rolls though."

"Too bad. I could go for some rolls now," Antti said with a smirk. "I guess I could try to tell you more about Tommi. Maybe that will help somehow."

We climbed up to the third floor. I apologized for the mess, though my flat was actually in a remarkably tidy state. It irked me that I immediately started playing the part of a woman for Antti instead of that of a police officer. I made the coffee and put some bread on the table. Thankfully, I had finally found time to visit the grocery store the day before. In the meantime, Antti inspected my bookshelves and plucked at the electric bass standing in the corner.

"On Sunday, you said you've known Tommi your whole life."

"Since elementary school. Just like Tuulia. They were both pretty brave when they were kids. I was the one who was always a little dull and overly cautious, but I read all the adventure books and had good ideas for games. Tommi was a natural leader and organizer. And a showman. He was always a little cold, using people, doing anything to get what he wanted. But you could get along with him if you didn't give in to him."

Antti clearly hoped that talking about him would get Tommi out of his system. I let Antti talk without interruption as he reminisced about the choir, about sailing outings with Tommi's brother and Peter Wahlroos, about incidents that had taken place when they lived together. As I listened, I mentally recorded the picture of Tommi that Antti was sketching: free with money, into conquest and control with women, greedy for power, adventurous, cheerful, selfish.

"Did you have any differences of opinion about his actions, for example with women? Did he ever try to get between you and Sarianna?"

"Yeah, he tried making a pass at Sarianna, but she made it clear there wasn't any point. No," Antti continued, as if heading off the question that was on my lips, "we didn't stop dating because of Tommi. We just didn't have anything in common anymore. So much for my motive. That *is* what you thought, right?"

I tried to stop myself from blushing. Despite the relaxed atmosphere, our conversation felt a bit like an interrogation. For some reason, it made me sad that Antti regarded me only as an interrogator, that he didn't consider confiding in me to be a sign of friendship.

"What about the other women who were already spoken for, like Tommi's boss?"

Antti smirked and shoved a big piece of bread in his mouth.

"Oh, so you know about that. There was no way Tommi could keep his hands off a classy woman like that, and apparently she couldn't keep her hands off him either. I got the impression that it was even-steven on both sides."

"How straight was Tommi being with Pia?"

"I think Tommi was probably more in love with her than he knew himself. I imagine her unavailability played a part in it; it was rare for Tommi not to get what he wanted easily. Pia was a challenge."

"Did something happen between them that Tommi could have used to blackmail Pia with later?"

"Blackmail?" Antti looked flabbergasted.

"There was a lot of extra money in Tommi's bank account lately. What if some of it came from the Wahlrooses?"

"Oh, come on. He wasn't an extortionist...or, what do I know?" Antti stared contemplatively into the bottom of his coffee cup. I poured him the last drops from the pot while he made himself a third open-faced cheese sandwich.

"I imagine he had his ways of making money—under the table?" I prompted tentatively.

"How should I know! This is starting to feel an awful lot like a grilling."

"You're free to leave if you don't feel like answering," I said coldly.

"Sorry. But this is hard. You are a police officer after all."

"I am. And I want to ask you some questions. Were Timo and Tommi friends? Or Tommi and Sirkku?"

"Well, there was something between Sirkku and Tommi once, on a trip to Germany a long time ago. They weren't friends, but they could get along. Timo's a bit stiff; he wasn't a fan of Tommi's style."

"Tommi and Mira?"

"Once."

I tried to conceal the interest this bit of information piqued in me.

"Mira's desperate attempt to make me jealous," Antti continued. "I don't loathe Mira the way Tuulia does, but her constant fawning over me has been a nuisance. I'm just not interested in her in that way."

"There's never been anything between you?" I hated my own curiosity, but I wanted to know, even though it didn't have anything to do with Tommi's murder.

"Well, no. I don't make a habit of going to bed with girls out of pity. So no motive for me there either. I wasn't jealous of who Mira was with. I was just angry at Tommi about his tactics."

"What tactics?"

"You can ask Mira about that. I've already said too much about her business."

Antti looked out the window and must have noticed that the rain had stopped. I could see all too clearly the dark shadows under his eyes and the movement of his mouth, as though he had started to say something but then stopped short. It bothered me that all I could get out of him were evasive hints. Maybe I should arrest him for concealing evidence, but I didn't want him to hate me. I obviously had a problem: I wanted to solve the murder, but I didn't want any of my suspects to be the murderer.

"You were one of the EFSAS auditors. Did you ever see last year's accounts?"

"Tommi handled them and said everything was in order. So I just signed my name on the report. Why?"

"Well, look at this." I brought the account ledgers over from my desk and looked for the receipts I wanted. It took Antti, the mathematician, only a moment to find the irregularities.

"You mean that Riku…"

"Evidently."

"Oh, that goddamn little idiot! Listen, I have to go. My parents are coming by my place tonight to get Einstein and take him out to the country. It's a bit dull for him in my apartment, and my parents have a cabin in Inkoo where he gets to hunt mice."

At the door, Antti turned and said quickly, "You ordered me not to play private detective. But don't you turn this into a game either. We have a hard time treating you like a real police officer, and not all of us even expect you to solve anything. Whoever killed Tommi might be unpredictable. You ought to be careful too."

Before I had a chance to reply, he was gone. A few moments later, I saw his dark figure striding up the street, hands in his pockets.

I felt miserable and restless. I had thrashed my muscles in the weight room the day before, so vigorous exercise wasn't an option. Wine would only make me feel more blue. The only alternative was work. I had plenty of questions, but I wanted to start by talking to Mira. She might already be home from the memorial service.

I traded my funeral clothes for jeans and sneakers, and grabbed a tape recorder and a few of Tommi's papers. Though it was a bit of a trip out to her place, I didn't want to call ahead to make sure Mira was home. Surprise was the best strategy. I started walking toward the bus stop, wondering along the way whether Antti had wanted to warn me that he was the one I should be afraid of.

10

How shall the soul be saved from woe?

Mira was home. Apparently she had just walked in, because she hadn't yet had time to change out of her dress clothes into something more comfortable. She held a half-eaten apple in her hand.

"Do I have to let you in?" she asked inhospitably.

"No. We can go downtown to the station too."

Without saying a word, Mira moved aside and let me into the narrow entry hall.

I took off my denim jacket and hung it on the crowded coatrack.

The apartment was quiet. It being Saturday night, Mira's roommates had probably gone into the city to party. On the phone table was a list of cleaning chores. No doubt Mira watched it like a hawk.

"Let's go up to my room."

I climbed the stairs up to the second floor, where there was a comfortable-looking kitchen and two small bedrooms. Mira's room was dominated by a piano. A white, crocheted lace coverlet was spread over the bed, and the shelves were full of history books. A bright red, half-finished sweater lay on the armchair, and I found myself wondering whether Mira was knitting it for herself. So far I had only ever seen her in dark clothing. Like

other heavyset women, she probably trusted them to have a slim-
ming effect. Perhaps she was thinking of changing styles. Mira
snatched the sweater off the chair and motioned me to sit there.
Then she sat down on the bed with her knitting and started
click-clacking away unnervingly with the needles.

"How official is this interrogation?"

"Unofficially official," I said and turned on the recorder in
my bag. If Mira told me something enlightening, I'd have to
rethink my strategy when I got back to Pasila, but I would worry
about that then.

"We've spoken twice now, but on neither occasion did you tell
me the most important thing about your relationship with Tommi.
He paid for your abortion last spring at the Women's Clinic. I'm
guessing because he was the child's father. Am I wrong?"

I had been confused at first when I saw the Women's Clinic
bed charge bill mixed in with Tommi's tax deduction receipts.
There had been no patient name, but there was a date from the
spring of the previous year. Tommi's old calendar had contained
an entry that read M WC 18-19 on the day before the payment
date. Some notes on the page had included the abortion department's phone number. The reference in Antti's letter to Tommi's
"playing" with Mira fit my theory too.

Rage burned in Mira's eyes. I had clearly hit the mark.

"Of course you had to dig that out! How many people have
you told about it so far? I thought that hospitals were confidential."

"There was a copy of the bill in Tommi's papers."

"The fact that Tommi paid for the abortion doesn't necessarily mean he was the father."

"So you were such good friends with him that you told him
about your abortion and asked him to lend you the money even
though you didn't tell anyone else?"

Mira clutched the red sweater in her hands and then angrily hurled it into the corner. I saw that her hands were trembling. Next to her head, above the headboard, was a large photograph from some EFSAS concert of Mira, Tommi, Antti, Tuulia, and a few others singing in dreadful blue performance gowns. Maybe Mira wanted to see Antti's picture every night before she fell asleep. Why the hell had I thought working would improve my mood?

"Do you want to hear my theory about how it all happened? You were sitting up one night with the choir like you always do. You were upset because you felt like Antti never paid any attention to you"—at this point my courage almost failed me, since this really and truly was none of my business—"and Tommi didn't have anyone keeping him company that night. You decided to show Antti what he was missing, and, uncharacteristically, you started flirting with Tommi. But the game went further than you meant it to. Of course you understood that Tommi knew exactly why you were suddenly interested in him. Your infatuation with Antti was no secret. And maybe Tommi even wanted to taunt Antti, to show him how easy it was to have you. What I don't understand is how you were both so stupid that you managed to get pregnant."

Mira burst into a strange, jerky laugh that sounded like a cross between sobbing and giggling. Gradually, her laughter morphed into an odd hiccupping, through which she explained:

"It was classic tragicomedy! The great lover's condom broke. Do you know why Tommi kept his mouth shut about the whole thing? It would have hurt his reputation if his women had found out he didn't even know how to use a rubber!" Mira grimaced poisonously and stopped laughing. "You seem to know my business even better than I do. It was Antti's birthday, in February, in his apartment in Korso. I was wearing mascara for the first time in my life, and I didn't realize how strong the punch was. I danced with Antti—he still asked me to dance back then—but he was as aloof as ever. Then Tommi cut in, took me from Antti, and started kissing me. For once I just let myself go, and I ended up at Tommi's place."

"And you got pregnant?"

"On the very first try. Like in the old movies where an innocent country girl comes to the city to work as a maid and gets seduced. Maybe I should forget school, get married, and start making babies."

"Is that what Tommi said?"

"No way. At first I thought I wouldn't tell him at all, but... it would have been his child. And it was Tommi's fault, so I thought it was only fair that he at least pay half."

"What did he say?" I was guessing that Mira had never told anyone about the abortion and that the only other person who knew about it was now dead. We were using each other—I was abusing her need to talk and she was taking advantage of my official position. A police officer is like a priest in that she is bound to discretion. Mira knew that I would never tell anyone what I heard if it didn't have a direct impact on the investigation.

"He was shocked, of course, almost more shocked than I was. Then he tried to turn it into a joke and said he hadn't ever been a daddy before. 'You aren't going to be one now either,' I said and told him I intended to have an abortion. He was relieved and told me that he would pay all the expenses, because he had so much more money than I did. Why wouldn't I have let him pay? But he couldn't buy away the shame. He didn't have to go through any medical examinations or tell his life story to a social worker. He didn't have to lie with his legs spread on a table to have his uterus scraped out or have the nurses snap at him when he said the anesthetic wasn't working. Yes, sometimes I wanted revenge...He made me a murderer either way."

Mira snorted at my dismayed expression. "I didn't kill Tommi. My parents belong to the Christian League, and they raised me to think abortion is murder. If they knew what I had done, they would probably disown me. I don't regret it though. What would have become of the child? Tommi and I couldn't get married. We detested each other! Those two weeks before the abortion were the worst weeks of my life. I felt like I was tied to Tommi because there was someone growing inside me who was both part of him and myself. I was throwing up all the time. It was like my body was trying to get the creature out, but it just didn't want to come. Have you ever had an abortion? Although I guess I have no right to ask."

"No. I mean no, I haven't had an abortion. I've been poisoning myself with pills for years." It's true that Mira didn't have any right to ask, and I didn't have any obligation to answer, but for some reason I wanted to.

"Did Tommi threaten to tell your parents? Or did he threaten to tell Antti? Maybe he teased you about Antti and said he'd tell him all the dirty details about what you did together, or maybe he mocked you for being in love with Antti. That was why you hated Tommi."

"I didn't hate him. It was more like contempt. He teased me about Antti, and I teased him back about his clumsiness, which he was ashamed of. He wouldn't have wanted to tell anyone about me. But what right did he have to mock my...my love. How is that anyone's business? How is it your business? Do you think I like having everyone know I'm hopelessly in love with Antti? In love! You're the first person I've said that to out loud." Mira started laughing her strange laugh again. It felt wrong.

"'Poor Mira, so ugly and so serious, how can she possibly think she could ever snag someone like Antti?' That's what they all think, including you. And Antti is kind to me. If he were mean, it would be easier not to care. Sometimes I hate myself. I hate this humiliation. Love is so much more destructive than hate. If Tommi had done something to Antti, I could have killed him..." Mira broke into sobs, and she cried hideously, gasping, her face swelling and turning red hidden behind her hands.

I bent forward and touched her on the shoulder, but she shook me off like a maggot. "Go away," she croaked through her fingers. "Go ask Tuulia why I didn't hear her snoring at five in the morning when I got up for a drink of water. Or go ask Timo how much a bottle of moonshine costs." Mira's sobbing grew even more hysterical. "Piss off!"

I left. I grabbed my jacket from the coatrack and started tramping through the rain toward the bus stop. What could I have said to Mira? She didn't want my words; I couldn't do anything for her. Not for Mira, and probably not for any of the others either.

I decided to follow Mira's suggestion and go look for Timo. Sirkku lived in Haaga, which was more or less on the way back into town, and they might be there together. The bus was just pulling up to the stop, and I ran to catch it. I felt some satisfaction that I had likely correctly guessed the identity of the person responsible for making the moonshine.

At Sirkku's apartment, I found only a roommate, who said that Sirkku hadn't even dropped by for the past few days. I headed downtown to Timo's address, which was near the cathedral, but no one answered there either. As I stood in the stairwell admiring the elegant art nouveau paintings on the walls, I thought about what to do next.

I was sure Riku wouldn't be home on a Saturday night, so I walked over to Kaisaniemi and jumped on the tram, which took me to Lauttasaari Island. I might as well try Pia too.

The Wahlrooses' end row house was easy to find. Although I had no complaints about my own apartment, I still felt a slight twinge of envy. The west-facing windows of the building opened onto the bay, and a few sailing yachts and a couple of muscle boats bobbed at the nearby dock. Given that they essentially had sea access from their backyard, I guessed that one of the boats was probably theirs. I had never gone sailing, but it looked fun. Jaana had gone out with Tommi a few times, but had complained that she hadn't been able to do anything except try not to be sick.

Light shone from the windows on the side of the house. I rang the doorbell, and after a moment, Pia's voice came from somewhere. "Who's there?" I was confused for a moment because I had only ever seen an intercom on an apartment building.

"Maria Kallio, from the police."

"Wait just a moment. I'll come open the door." The moment lasted a couple of minutes, and then Pia appeared in a thick, cream-colored dressing gown, with a matching towel covering her hair. She smelled like luxury skin cream, for which I had neither the resources nor the nose.

"I was in the bath," she said brusquely.

"I'm sorry to interrupt, but I have a few questions for you."

"At this time of night on a Saturday?"

"This is a murder investigation. But would some other time work better for you?" Pia seemed to think for a moment, then motioned me in.

"So you didn't arrest Antti?" she asked, looking disappointed as I took off my muddy tennis shoes. My department-store denim jacket looked like an orphan among the Wahlrooses' couture.

"I couldn't find any reason to. Was the memorial service nice?"

"Tommi's mother didn't come, if that's what you mean. The mood was still a bit uncomfortable though. We sang a couple of pieces and then left because we felt like everybody was staring. Sirkku and I thought the whole fuss would finally be over if you arrested Antti. Not that I would wish any harm on Antti, or anyone for that matter, but this business is starting to get on my nerves...And I absolutely have to be able to fly to San Francisco in two weeks—that's the finish line for Peter's race. I can go, right?"

It hadn't even occurred to me that anyone might leave the country. Did I need to confiscate all of my suspects' passports?

"Hopefully the case will be over by then. Finding a resolution as quickly as possible is in my best interest too." There was something about Pia that made me more stiff than usual.

"Would you like some tea? I always have a cup of chamomile tea after my herb bath. It's very relaxing."

I realized I hadn't eaten anything since breakfast except for a slice of bread and cheese with Antti. Tea sounded nice. Pia ushered me into the living room and then disappeared into the kitchen.

After Mira's student apartment, with its standard furnishings, and my own flea-market-decorated home, the Wahlrooses' living room looked lavish. The view of the sea was undeniably impressive. The blue-and-beige furniture formed cozy enclaves where one could hole up to read or listen to music. Small, unusual objects adorned the shelves and tables, obviously keepsakes acquired around the world. The only thing that bothered me was the sterility created by all the tidiness. There were no half-read books lying around or newspapers folded open to the television schedule on a coffee table. It was like an interior decorator had just finished with it.

The ceramic teacups Pia brought were the same shade as the sofa slipcovers. Alongside the tea, she served delicious buttery scones, presumably straight from the microwave. I was so hungry that I took one before Pia even had a chance to offer me any. If this had been a movie, Pia would have been the murderer and the scones would have been poisoned. As the poison paralyzed me, she would confess her crime and then push me off the dock into the sea. If this were a movie, the hero would show up at the last second to save me. But this was reality, and I could take care of myself.

"Very good," I mumbled, my mouth full of pastry.

"Peter made them. They're from the freezer. He's an excellent chef. In fact, he cooks on the *Marlboro* too."

"Did you meet Peter through Tommi?" I discreetly clicked the recorder on again in my pocket.

"Tommi and Henri were Peter's sailing friends. Antti sailed with them sometimes too. When Tommi turned twenty-five, he organized a big party out at the Peltonens' villa and invited the choir and his other friends. That's where we met."

"Love at first sight?"

"In a way. I had heard of Peter before, since he was in the papers a lot during that last big maxi-boat race."

"Were you and Tommi romantically involved prior to that?"

"No! He was dating Jaana at the time. In the beginning, we spent a lot of time together as a group. It was the Peltonen boys and their girlfriends, Antti and Sarianna, and us. Henri and Peter have a boat together, that one there." Pia pointed to the most beautiful sailboat moored down at the dock. "It sleeps eight comfortably." "How do you have money for all this?" I asked before I had time to think.

Pia looked taken aback for a moment, but then she replied, somewhat mockingly, "I don't. Peter does. It's money he inherited. Stocks. Have you ever heard of a company called Kymi Timber? Peter's grandfather sold it five years ago, when it was still a thriving business. Peter is the only grandchild."

"What does Peter do for a living?"

"He's an economist with KOP Bank on the securities side, but he hasn't worked for almost a year. He's actually a professional yachtsman these days."

"He must be away sailing a lot. Don't you get lonely?" I was trying to disguise my desire for information in false friendship, but I imagined that Pia probably saw through it.

"Yes. He's been away a great deal this year. He will have been gone half the summer for this one race. And I don't want to fly from one port of call to another. Traveling alone is so dreadfully boring, and there are the time changes to deal with and everything. I'd rather be home and try to get my thesis done, but it is wretched. I'm sorry that Peter has to travel so much, but he's got all these sponsorship agreements he's obligated to fulfill these days."

"Tommi was probably good company for you, then. What was really going on between you two? A lot of people keep dropping hints about your relationship being more than a friendship."

"That's all it was, at least as far as I was concerned!" Pia swung her arm so violently that tea splashed on her spotless white bathrobe. "I liked spending time with Tommi. I have no idea why he suddenly started hanging on me so much last spring though. After Christmas at our choir retreat, he always wanted to dance with me and he claimed he was sick of entertaining the new children in the choir. All spring he acted like he was infatuated with me. Whenever we went to a bar after rehearsals, he came and sat next to me. He walked me to the bus stop. Sometimes he even came home with me. And he asked me out to movies and concerts and dinner when Peter was away. You must know how miserable it is to always go out alone or just with other girls?"

Now it was Pia's turn to look at me with disingenuous intimacy in her eyes. The misery in question was foreign to me, because hardly a week went by when I wasn't sitting alone in the corner pub, and I preferred to go to the movies solo than with a companion who made loud comments at the wrong moment and endlessly rustled his popcorn. But what point was there in telling that to Pia?

"Peter can be a little bossy sometimes. He knows what he wants. And that's what I fell in love with. He's a man of the world. Tommi was...different. He let me decide what we did and where we went."

A new trait in Tommi, I noted. Until that moment, I had thought he was pretty bossy too.

"If Tommi hadn't turned all lovey-dovey, we could have had so much fun. Peter didn't have any problem with my going out with Tommi either. He meets beautiful girls on his trips. It comes with the territory. It's OK to be friends with men too." Pia sounded defensive.

"But Tommi wanted to be more than a friend?"

"He started to claim he was in love with me!" I noticed that when Pia became overwrought, a North Karelian twang slipped into the refined urban dialect she had cultivated. "At first I didn't believe him—everyone knows his reputation, after all—but little by little I started to think it was real. And of course he flattered me." Pia swung her glossy brown hair back with a smile. "There would have been other takers too. In any case, it's nice to know that men don't consider you completely dead erotically, even though you're married. And I thought it was only right that he was getting a taste of his own medicine for once." Pia smiled wickedly, and for a second I almost liked her. "But sometimes it was irritating."

"How so?"

"Well, it was like he couldn't believe I didn't want to cheat on Peter with him! He started pushing too hard. He even barged in here one night, supposedly because he felt so lonely. I didn't have the heart to turn him away because he looked so pathetic, but then he thought...but I didn't want to..." Pia blushed with a modesty that amused me.

"Did he threaten to tell Peter that you had slept with him?"

"Not really. But once when he was drunk, he asked, 'What would that *Marlboro* mannequin of yours say if he knew I had spent the night in his bed?' But *I* wasn't in the bed at the time. I was on the sofa in the guest room," Pia said quickly.

"Did Tommi want to break up your marriage? Do you think he might have fallen for you just because you didn't fall for him?"

"Probably. That was exactly the kind of guy he was—he wanted everything for himself, especially whatever was hardest to get. And sometimes I got the sense that he may have been jealous of Peter. I imagine Tommi would have liked to be as good a sailor as Peter and Henri, but even he couldn't be the best at everything. Maybe he wanted me because I was Peter's. But I'm not as stupid as Sirkku was. I never would have made myself dependent on Tommi."

"Did Tommi blackmail you?"

Could it be Wahlroos money that I had found in Tommi's account? But Pia's expression didn't even flicker. She poured me more tea and answered with a shake of her head.

"No. He threatened to occasionally. But I guess in the end he believed there wasn't anything Peter didn't already know. And he wouldn't have been able to break up our marriage. I love Peter. We want the same things out of life. I'm graduating this fall, and after that we want children. I don't have to work if I don't want to. And I don't want to go teach Swedish in some elementary school. Peter wants just the kind of wife that I am. I wouldn't have wrecked my life for Tommi."

My first impression of Pia had been that she was a fragile and coquettish sort of girl, a porcelain doll. It was clear that I had missed the mark. She was offering me exactly the information she wanted to, and she didn't see any reason to hide that money was everything to her. She might even be willing to kill someone to preserve her standard of living—but had Tommi ever threatened that?

"There were all sorts of rumors going around in the choir, and Sirkku was far and away the most enthusiastic gossip. You were at rehearsal on Monday. I'm not a particularly amazing singer, but Tommi made me believe I could do something beautiful, if I just didn't get flustered. He said I had a pretty voice..." For a moment, the corners of Pia's mouth trembled, and she looked like she was choking back tears.

"You just said you weren't as stupid as your sister. I've heard several different versions of her stupidity. She told me herself that they had a passing fling on a trip, but someone else claimed that Sirkku was really serious about Tommi. What do you think?"

Pia rotated the rings on her fingers again. There was no
doubt that the small, glittering stones embedded in them were
diamonds. For all I knew, those rings could have paid off all my
student debt.

"Sirkku was pretty immature back then. She'd been dating
this guy Jari since high school, but that had begun to wear thin.
Jari still lived in Joensuu, which is where we're from, and I guess
he wasn't sophisticated enough for Sirkku anymore. I remember when we were in Germany in the restroom of this one bar,
Sirkku and I were doing our makeup side by side and someone
said that we looked exactly alike. Sirkku looked at me a little
spitefully and said 'Pia has always been the family beauty.' Then
she went on to tell me that if her romance with Tommi lasted,
I could stop tooting my own horn about my fancy boyfriend.
Poor Sirkku didn't realize that Tommi just wanted to show Jaana
that he didn't give a damn about her romance with Franz.

"When we came back to Finland, Sirkku broke it off with
Jari. Our parents were terribly disappointed—they had considered Jari a potential son-in-law. He was an electrical engineer
in the same construction company where our father is a carpen-
ter. Our mother is a nurse's assistant. To them, an engineer is
practically royalty. We're the first to go to college in our whole
extended family."

"So Tommi really humiliated Sirkku? It sounds like she may
have had reason to be angry at him."

"Well, I don't know. I think the infatuation passed pretty
quickly. And what reason would Sirkku have for being bitter
anymore? Things are going well for her. She's dating Timo now,
and before him there was another guy she knew from college."

The wind was whipping drops of rain against the large picture window. Despite the length of the day at this time in the

summer, it was almost dark outside, and the combination of the boats banging against the dock and the gloom made it look like autumn. The world Pia was describing made me feel cold inside.

"How did Sirkku and Timo's romance begin, then?"

"It began at that same choir retreat when Tommi started to hover around me. I think Timo had been interested in Sirkku for a long time. Sometimes I get the sense that he worships her. And Sirkku encourages him."

"What does Sirkku see in Timo?"

"Maybe Muuriala Manor."

"Muuri...What?"

"Muuriala Manor. You've seen Muuriala herbs and lettuces in the grocery store, haven't you? Despite his common last name, Timo is a future Lord of the Manor. He isn't swimming in money yet because his father is of the opinion that a young man should earn his own way. That's why he's selling tractors these days, though there would be plenty of work for him at Muuriala too."

That explained a lot, including Timo's posh digs. He might be as stiff as a hay pole, but if he was plated in gold, he might be husband material. I had met Peter once too. I could have gobbled him up even without the gold coating, though he was a bit self-important for my tastes.

"If Timo worships Sirkku, he must have been jealous of Tommi?"

"Yeah, his face turned red whenever he saw one of the Germany pictures where Tommi and Sirkku had their arms around each other. He didn't care for Tommi much otherwise either. But if you're implying that he might have killed Tommi because of that, I don't believe it."

I didn't either. But Timo could easily have had other motives.

"I called the boat today, by the way...The *Marlboro of Finland* that is. The Peltonens called Henri in the morning and told him about Tommi. Hopefully it won't ruin their race. They're still in the lead in their class."

I sensed that Pia didn't want to let me leave. I had stopped asking questions, but she went on chattering about this and that. Maybe it was gloomy being in that big house all alone. I wondered whether she and Mira had any friends outside the choir.

It was already ten o'clock by the time I made it home. I had stopped at McDonald's on the way, and devouring the greasy grub on an empty stomach sapped the life out of me. I passed out on my bed in the middle of a mystery show and dreamed restless dreams.

11

But in dreams how dear it is to say

My fantasy of a leisurely Sunday morning spent slowly drinking my coffee as I lounged with the newspaper was just that—a fantasy. The phone rang before six, and I was soon off to interrogate a rapist and interview his victim. I guzzled my coffee on the run, crammed down half a yogurt and an orange, and then smeared waterproof mascara on my nose in the rush, which I then had to spend an eternity scrubbing off. I wished I had an understanding wife who could be waiting with a pressed shirt and sack lunch for me. As it was, I had to settle once again for the tight blouse with the precarious button, which now boasted sweat stains in the armpits, and hope that I would be able to sneak in a damp vending machine sandwich or a slice of cold delivery pizza at some point later in the day.

Koivu, who had been awake for the better part of twenty-four hours by then, gave me the basic rundown of the rape. He had been at the Kaivohuone Club until four. "I came straight from there to the station because I got some information I wanted to jot down right then—which I'll get to in a minute—and then I got roped into this rape investigation."

Koivu no longer looked especially young or fresh after being up all night, but he was clearly pleased with himself. Despite my morning wooziness, I was curious. Koivu said he had already typed up the report and left it on my desk. The rape victim had just come from the doctor and was waiting for me in the hallway, so I sent Koivu home to get some sleep. He promised to call me that afternoon.

The girl, Marianna, was young, barely eighteen.

"Can't I go home yet?" she asked, on the verge of tears. Her shiny black stockings were torn, her miniskirt was smeared with mud, and her face still bore the remnants of her makeup, though she had clearly tried to wash it off. There was a bruise on her cheek and another had formed at the corner of her eye. She looked cold, and I realized that she too had been awake all night. I started the dictation recorder, since there was no one to take notes. Someone could transcribe it later.

"Hi, I'm Detective Maria Kallio. We'll try to get through this quickly so you can get home to sleep. I have your initial statement here. We also have the results of your examination. Would you like some coffee and a sandwich?"

"Do you have any tea?" the girl asked barely audibly. I wondered whether the police examiner had the sense to give her any sedatives.

I asked the duty officer to bring tea and sandwiches. In the meantime, I asked the girl a series of routine questions about her life in an effort to get her to trust me. Marianna was from Kouvola. She was about to enter her last year of high school and was working at the Hietaniemi cemetery this summer. She had been out partying the night before and returned to her summer apartment in Vallila on the last bus. She bought a hamburger from the hot dog stand next to the bus stop.

"This guy was in line ahead of me...Maybe he was on the same bus with me. I don't remember. So he was standing there waiting for his hot dog, trying to talk to me, but I was tired and I wanted to get to bed...Then he grabbed my ass and said something about my cute miniskirt. I told him to get his hands off me, and he left. After getting my burger, I headed through the park and forgot all about him. Suddenly he jumped out of the bushes and asked if he could walk me home. I told him to get lost, but he just started walking along beside me and began calling me all kinds of names...I was a whore because I was wearing a miniskirt and earrings, that sort of thing. Then he grabbed me and threatened to kill me if I didn't let him...you know." The girl swallowed her tears and glanced fearfully at the bearlike duty officer who plunked a cup of tea—spilling some—and a wilted bologna sandwich down in front of her.

"Put a lot of sugar in your tea," I suggested as I took a sip of my own. The girl obediently dropped four lumps of sugar into her cup and took a sip. She frowned and then continued.

"So he pushed me against a tree and started pulling my skirt up and undoing his pants. That was when I finally realized what was happening, and I started to scream. I remembered there had been people at the hot dog stand. He tried to strangle me and poke...like, you know, himself...inside me and tried to hold me in place, and I think I bit his chin. But no one came. So he finished doing his thing, even though I was shouting and fighting the whole time, but then we heard the sirens...I guess the guy at the hot dog stand called the police. And then they got him. He climbed a tree, but one of his shoes fell off—" The girl suddenly started to laugh hysterically. She was shaking with cold, and I gave her my jacket.

"Yeah, it looks like we've got him in a holding cell." Mixed in with the other preliminary investigation papers that had appeared on my desk was the rapist's rap sheet. He'd already been convicted twice for the same crime, and had gotten off first with a fine and then with a suspended sentence. "This is a simple case. You don't even need to identify him. The doctor's statement will come in due course. Rape is a complainant offense, so you have to decide whether you want to press charges or not. You don't have to decide now," I explained in answer to the girl's frightened eyes. "I imagine you probably want to put the whole thing behind you as quickly as possible, but I recommend that you go ahead and press charges once you have the energy to think about it. You aren't this man's first victim. Maybe he'll go to prison this time."

"Would I have to go to court? Would I have to pay for a lawyer?"

I explained the trial process to her, though I didn't know how much of what I said got through to her in her current state. She looked frightened, tired, and very young. I thought of myself at eighteen. Would I have made it through a rape without going off the deep end?

"I…I don't want my parents to know about this…'cause they would just yell at me about my going to bars and walking around in clothes like that…" The girl wiped a tear off her bruised cheek and then flinched at the pain.

"Listen, Marianna. In the last rape case I investigated, the victim was a sixty-year-old woman who was on her way home from a meeting at the Salem Pentecostal Temple in Hakaniemi. Idiots like this don't look at your clothes or anything else. Even if you were stumbling down the street dead drunk and naked as the day you were born, no one would have the right to rape you." I was clearly getting too worked up. "Do you have someone you could call to stay with you today? A friend maybe? I can take you home now if there's a car available."

"Well, there's my oldest sister...She probably won't get all preachy."

I let Marianna use my phone, and then took her home in the department's most beat-up Lada.

"You were very brave to scream and fight and then still have the energy to make it through the doctor's exam and these interviews," I said. I wanted to cheer her up, but she suddenly burst into hysterical sobbing.

"What if he has AIDS? Or what if I get pregnant? That doctor was so big and rough that I didn't dare ask him anything. He just gave me a pill and said it was emergency contraception and told me to take a couple more."

"They've done all those tests on you, and on the rapist. As soon as the results come in, I'll give you a call. Was the doctor rude to you?"

"His exam...hurt...And he asked me all kinds of things, like when I had last been...with a guy. And I have never been...He probably thought this was all my fault."

I knew the police physician, Pekka Nieminen, and I could imagine that a gynecological exam with him might almost feel like a second rape. While we had been investigating the previous sexual assault, the language Nieminen used had infuriated me. I tried to assure Marianna that what happened wasn't her fault, and I gave her the numbers for the Abuse Victims Alliance and the rape crisis group. When she looked uncertain, I also gave her my own phone number and told her to call any of the numbers on the list if she needed to talk to someone. I felt horrible about leaving her alone in her apartment—her roommate was away— but she said that her sister would be there soon.

"I just want to take a shower and go to bed," Marianna said listlessly. I hoped her older sister would be sensible. I was about to leave when the doorbell rang. I recognized the woman who entered before she even introduced herself. Sarianna Palola. Antti's ex-girlfriend. I had seen several pictures of her in Tommi's photo albums. She didn't seem to recognize me, however.

After Marianna went to shower, I briefly explained the situation to her. Sarianna was shocked and furious on her sister's behalf, but she seemed like a levelheaded person and I felt that Marianna would be safe with her.

When I got back to the station, I started interrogating Pasi Arhela, Marianna's rapist. Though he had practically been caught in the act, he tried to be cavalier and deny the whole thing. He was an engineer, just like Tommi, and tried his best to shield himself from my accusations. I could easily imagine how such a smooth operator had succeeded in walking away so easily after his prior convictions. All he needed were good lawyers. When I didn't accept his claim that Marianna had lured him from the hot dog stand, he started to lose his composure. It was his word against Marianna's. The hot dog stand operator might be able to convince the judge, and there was no way that Arhela would be able to deny the sperm and cell samples. It riled him that I wouldn't let him smoke in the interrogation room. He hadn't slept all night either, but I didn't feel the least bit sorry for him.

"All those fucking little whores ever do is beg for it," he finally snapped. "This one was walking around with her skirt above the water line and her face all painted like a working girl. They should put them all in a goddamn cage. Seeing a little piece like that would get anybody up, you know?" Arhela winked at Virrankoski, who had come in to act as recorder. Arhela had been directing most of his outburst to him in an "us boys" sort of spirit. Virrankoski did not conceal his smile, which irritated me.

"So you admit to raping her?" I asked, wanting to get rid of Arhela as quickly as possible.

"The hell I raped her. It was just a little quickie. She should be happy with what she got."

"You admit that you forced Marianna Palola to have sexual intercourse with you?"

"Yes, yes...Fuck, when was the last time you got some, baby? You wouldn't bitch so much if you got laid a little more often. Or are you some kind of fucking lesbian, since you have to do men's work and try to defend every little whore who sashays by?"

I haven't been forced to use violence often in my work. I've used my weapon only once; people who are being arrested are generally calmer around a woman. I've had to hit someone only a few times. But right now, I felt like beating Pasi Arhela's balls to a bloody pulp. If the other person in the room had been, say, Koivu instead of Virrankoski, I probably would have. I imagined what it would feel like to smash my fist into his face and hear the cartilage in his nose snap or to kick him in the testicles so that they swelled up like balloons. I realized I was shaking.

"Take him out for a smoke and then back to his cell," I said to Virrankoski, and then retreated to the ladies' room one floor up. I felt like vomiting. If it were up to me, Arhela would sit in that holding cell for every last second the law allowed.

Why did he upset me so much? I tried to pretend it was some noble impulse, that I was angry on behalf of Marianna and all of Arhela's other victims. But I was also angry on my own behalf. Did everyone have the right to come in and slander me just because I was a woman and a cop?

What if I became an attorney or legal aid counsel, as I had planned to do after graduating? What would I do if I had to defend guys like Pasi Arhela?

Virrankoski and Arhela were still in the corridor when I
returned to my office. I tried to keep my face neutral.

"This dude says he knows the Peltonen kid who was murdered last week. Aren't you on that case? He says he fixed him up
with women sometimes," Virrankoski explained.

"Arhela got women for Peltonen?" I said without looking at
the rapist.

"No, Peltonen did for me," Arhela said. "He was, like, an old
army buddy. We ran into each other around town every now and
then, and a couple of times he introduced me to some really nice
Estonian whores. They were good, but expensive."

There was nothing to be done but to ask Arhela back into
the interrogation room. Once inside, he immediately tried to
strike a deal with me: if he told me anything that helped with
my murder investigation, we wouldn't charge him with rape.
When I refused the exchange, he showered me with more abuse.
I forced myself to stay calm and was already starting to order him
back to his cell when he started to talk. He was clearly the type
who enjoyed feeling important.

According to Arhela, Tommi had been an intermediary for
the Estonian girls. Though he was not an actual pimp, he had
taken some commission from the girls and served as some sort of
go-between for these high-class private entrepreneurs.

"They weren't any thirty-mark train station whores either.
They were totally clean, healthy girls."

"There were several of them?"

"Well, I saw two, and I screwed one of them a couple of
times."

"Names?"

But Arhela said he couldn't remember because he'd been
so drunk at the time. He did, however, tell me that he'd found

Tommi with his girls at the Hesperia. I sent him back to his
holding cell to work on coming up with the names, though I
didn't actually believe I would get anything more out of him.
I could always send him to the Hesperia Club with Koivu and
Virrankoski to refresh his memory if necessary.

Koivu's report from the Kaivohuone Club confirmed the
prostitute angle. He had managed to talk to a couple of girls who
were obviously professionals, and they had recognized Tommi,
who had evidently hung around by the bar occasionally at the
end of the night. According to one of the women, Tommi had
definitely been a pimp and had tried to lure her into his racket
once too, but, as she explained to Koivu, she didn't give it up
for money. Which was, of course, exactly what she would say
to a cop. Not that there was necessarily anything reprehensible
about a woman who went out with a different companion every
night. So far, the independent girls were still doing fine in the
metro area, but the position of prostitutes could easily worsen
if the eastern mafia were to start tightening their grip on the
market. That would mean the end of occasional tricks for college students.

One acquaintance of mine, a bisexual guy, preferred to turn
the odd trick instead of getting a regular job. Evidently, both
aging men and women paid well. Maybe it would be worth asking Janne if he had known Tommi, though he might be less
forthcoming now that he knew I was a cop again.

Alcohol and Estonian prostitutes. Tommi had been quite an
enterprising young man. What would we discover next? The
prostitution business opened up a whole new angle on the murder. Could his death have been the work of the Russian mafia?
That idea wasn't all that farfetched, given that crime in the city
had grown much more international in scope in recent years.

And Tommi had been working on that joint Finnish–Estonian project…Could it be that the murderer wasn't someone from the choir after all?

At the end of his message, Koivu had scrawled by hand, "They knew Martti Mäki. He meets a 'pretty' boy they call Tomppa pretty regularly. No sign of them this time though."

I immediately dialed the Mäkis' number, but no one answered. Tomppa, eh? This painted an even rosier picture of the Mäkis' marriage. Did Marja Mäki know anything about her husband's sexual proclivities?

Hunger was starting to gnaw at my stomach and the lack of coffee made my temples ache. I ran down the stairs to the café because I could get better coffee there than from the vending machine. The menu looked appalling—liver casserole or vegetable soup in milk broth—so I settled for a soggy Karelian pie, rice filling baked in a rye crust.

After paying the clerk, I found my old police academy classmate Tapsa Helminen sitting at the window table. He had applied to work Narcotics as soon as he could. He teased me relentlessly early on, but he'd stopped when I nearly broke his elbow during self-defense practice. I did it intentionally, though now I was embarrassed to think about it. To be fair, I had teased him right back—he had a fairly sizable nose, and I told him more than once that they wouldn't need dogs in Narcotics anymore once they had him to do the sniffing. He was an OK guy but a little overzealous—he didn't see a difference between a joint and a hundred grams of meth.

"I hear you've got a real mess over in Drugs," I said, sitting down at his table. "They asked us for help, but we can't spare anybody."

"Yeah, well." Helminen sighed. The shadows beneath his eyes told me he had slept as little as I had the past few nights.

"It's a real shame. These new rings keep cropping up, and all we got was one dealer and a couple of street runners, but that was it. Some of the stuff has been coming in over the eastern border, or I guess I should say the southern border, since Estonia is independent now. We jumped the gun on some arrests—if we had just waited a bit longer, we could have netted a couple of the bigger fish. The street sellers claim they don't know where it was from, and the dealer doesn't dare open his mouth. It feels like there's a pretty big organization behind all this though."

"Sounds like the big leagues."

"Yeah, this racket seems to be getting more serious all the time. It isn't college kids sneaking weed home on InterRail anymore—this is something completely different. We definitely need more men, I mean…uh…officers in our division, but there doesn't seem to be the money for them. How's the VCU?"

"Same thing. Overtime budget always in the red. By the way, do you know anything about Russian girl-runners?"

"Well, of course they're more Vice's area of expertise, but I guess some of them are on the drug side too. You can never touch them. They even talk about each other in code names. X and M and shit like that."

Something clicked in my head.

"M? In what context?"

"He was some guy who was calling his dealer's answering machine and asking where they could meet to make a swap. Why?"

"There's this murder I'm working on. Somebody named M also made an appearance on my victim's answering machine. Any chance we could compare tapes?"

"Mine is in the lab. Should be back tomorrow. I'll let you know when I get it. You have any leads about your M's identity?"

Then it clicked.

"Wait, what did you say? Em! Of course. Not Emma, just M. Sorry, Tapsa, but I've got to go. I may have just figured something out."

Although I couldn't get in touch with Anu from the choir right away, the coffee and the new information from Tapsa made the day more bearable. It seemed that the line from that rock song was complete now: "Money, liquor, women, and drugs..." Maybe it was time to focus on that last subject.

Riku wasn't home, so I called his work, and they gave me his car phone number.

"Maria Kallio here. Drop by Pasila once you've finished your deliveries. Yes, your boss knows. And you'd better come if you don't want me to arrest you."

Riku arrived at my office a little over half an hour later. People must order anchovy and *mettwurst* pizzas to raise their spirits on Sunday mornings, because those were the smells that wafted in with him. Or maybe he had just raised my own spirits with them. I was hungry again.

"You don't happen to have any extra pizza in your car, do you?" I asked hopefully. Riku shook his head. He looked hungover and nervous.

"Did the rest of the funeral last long?" I asked.

I indicated that he should sit across from me, so that he couldn't fail to notice the EFSAS account ledgers spread out on my desk. Luckily, I had the sense to bring them in to work with me despite all the commotion that morning.

"Me and Tuulia were at the Roba until at least two last night," Riku explained feebly. Was he even fit to drive? Would it be irresponsible of me not to breathalyze him? I picked up the ledger and explained why I'd brought him in.

"I've been reading through these accounts pretty carefully and comparing receipts and bank statements. You didn't tell me the whole truth about your debts to Tommi. I could charge you with embezzlement and fraud. Tommi discovered the scam when he was checking the books, but promised to loan you the money to cover it up and hide it from Antti, the other auditor. Why would he do something like that?"

Riku's pale face had turned blotchy.

"He was my friend. He knew I would put the money back eventually. But then the annual meeting was coming up, and we had to get the accounts cleaned up, and I didn't have any money...So he promised to loan me what I needed."

"And made himself an accomplice by writing up a falsified audit report? Why on earth would he do that? And why did he start demanding his money back?"

"It sounded like he was leaving for somewhere," Riku said, clearly pained. "What I told you about that Thursday was mostly true. But he also threatened to tell the cops I'd been siphoning off choir money. He said you could get probation for that; he knew a guy who had for less."

"When were you supposed to give him the money?"

"He gave me till Monday."

"How were you going to get the money together?"

"I was supposed to pawn everything I could. My stereo, my TV, even my leather jacket..." Riku explained, sounding depressed.

"But Tommi died on Saturday, and so you were in the clear. If you whacked him because you were drunk and angry, then you'd better confess right now! You'll get off easier if you confess voluntarily."

Riku buried his head in his hands. I almost felt sorry for him. Murderer or no, I should probably hand over the cooked books

to the White-collar Division to deal with. Maybe the shame
would teach Riku a thing or two. A few grand was small potatoes compared to everything you heard was happening in bank-
ing circles all the time. But that was how it was: you could lose
billions, and even get caught, and at most you'd lose your job but
still get full retirement. Nicking a few thousand, however, could
land you on probation. And poor Antti had also unsuspectingly
put his name on the audit report that Tommi had manipulated,
thus unwittingly participating in the fraud. Did I really have to
sic the prosecutors on Riku? Did I have a right not to?

"I didn't kill Tommi," Riku said, his voice teary. "I was
just so damn disappointed when he started being so difficult all
of a sudden. But I would have gone and pawned all my stuff on
Monday. I would have gotten the money from somewhere...
And Tuulia promised to loan me some."

"Did Tuulia know about this?"

"I just told her that Tommi wanted his money back."

"Listen, Riku. The duty officer has an Breathalyzer. Let's go
have you blow in it, and if it registers anything, you call work
and tell them you can't come back in today. Then you get in
touch with Antti and work out this mess. He already knows all
about it. You and EFSAS can decide how you want to handle
it. But one more time: if you killed Tommi, admit it right now.
You might still get off with manslaughter. We're going to find
out sooner or later. Fraud and murder are a nasty combination."

I knew how hollow my own words sounded.

The duty officer's Breathalyzer registered zero, so Riku
went back to work.

I decided to try reaching the Mäki family again. Martti
Mäki was home this time. I told him what we had found out,
and he didn't even bother trying to deny it.

"We spent that night at the Vaakuna Hotel. I imagine you can find our names in the hotel register."

"It would be best for you to give me this Tomppa's full name and address so we can check your alibi."

"Oh hell…Is that really necessary? Tomppa isn't going to get in any trouble over this, is he? He's such a nice boy."

"I don't suppose he's done anything criminal," I said dryly. I didn't want to start snooping into whether Mäki had paid Tomppa. Mäki gave me Tomppa's contact information.

"Um…you don't have to tell my wife about this, do you?" Mäki asked me as I was about to hang up.

"You can work out your relationship problems on your own," I said, more angrily than was strictly necessary, and hung up the phone. The Mäkis must have a ball together.

I tried to reach Sirkku and Timo, to no avail, then switched over to finishing up the rapist's statement and worked on some other paperwork. Actually I was free to do as I pleased—I was only on call—but since I had time to spare I figured I might as well catch up on a few things. My next commitment wasn't until that evening.

I left work just after three and walked through Central Park in the fog, around Töölö Bay, and then made my way home from there. In the interim, I had had to go look at a middle-aged woman who had hanged herself from the carpet beating rack on her balcony, after which I needed some fresh air. Along the way, I bought a large ice-cream cone from a kiosk.

At home I changed my clothes and then ran over to the women-only gym where I had a membership. Wrestling with weights usually energized me, and my muscles had had time to recover from the other day. The run had been a good warm-up, so I just stretched my arms for a few minutes before getting down to business. It was arms and back day because I'd already tortured my legs and abs the previous Friday. As always on Sunday afternoons, the gym was almost empty.

As I did my lat pull-downs, I thought about Tommi: charming, talented, and generous, but also selfish, power hungry, and narcissistic. Criminal? Bootlegger? Pimp? Drug dealer? Had he suggested that Riku turn a couple of tricks with some aging gay men to pay his debts, and made Riku so angry that he killed him? Or had Pia done it out of fear of unpleasant revelations? And which of Tommi's businesses had Tuulia gotten mixed up in? Certainly something. It was hard for me to imagine her being taken advantage of in any way or selling her beautiful body. There was no way she would have agreed to become a prostitute. What about Sirkku? And could Antti have gotten so angry over being taken advantage of that he struck Tommi in a blind rage? Yes. Even though he looked like the stereotypical pacifist: he'd skipped the military for civilian service, had a ponytail and everything. Could Antti have connections to the drug trade? And I couldn't rule Mira out either.

I moved on to the arm curl bench. Hitting Tommi had obviously required some strength. That seemed to rule out Pia and Sirkku, and possibly Riku too. I could definitely have taken Riku in a fight, since he weighed considerably less than I did. Timo had the requisite strength, but could he have snuck out of his room without Sirkku's knowledge?

My biceps were burning, so I shifted to the bench press. "Who wants to live forever," asked Freddie Mercury's ghost from the speakers in the ceiling. Tommi hadn't been given a chance to choose. "And we can love forever." Had Tuulia been in love with Tommi? Didn't she trust me enough to have told me if that were the case? That thought made me feel lousy. The bar I was lifting was heavy—I had put on ten pounds too much. I did this frequently—overestimating my own strength.

I jogged back home, showered, and started to clean my apartment. The workday was behind me, and I was done with my weight training, but the hardest part of my day still lay ahead. I was supposed to go to the train station to meet my parents and then put them up for a night at my place before they left for their annual two-week summer vacation in the Greek Islands. They almost never visited me otherwise. Though they had both studied in Helsinki years before, the city felt big and frightening to them these days, and they didn't know how to make their way from the station to my place without help.

"I like having a police escort," Dad said with a grin as we climbed onto the tram.

"Have you been able to study at all?" Mom asked, clearly concerned. I had bluffed them into approving of my temporary gig at the VCU by claiming that I would be able to take some of my exams on the side.

"I've been getting ready for one of my tests."

That wasn't actually a lie. I had picked up the books for my criminal justice final from the library, and my parents believed what they wanted to hear. Uncle Pena wasn't an alcoholic—he just drank too much sometimes. The students weren't intentionally mean—they just had hard home lives. I would go back to law school, get a good job, and find a nice husband. My parents weren't actually interested in me so much as in the façade of my life.

My freshly cleaned apartment felt hot, cramped, and dusty. I had made ham and onion quiche and salad for dinner, and now I steeped some tea. The last time I had seen my parents was at Christmas, which I had dutifully spent at their house. Over the last six months, several more wrinkles had appeared on my mother's forehead, and my father's shoulders had slumped significantly. Fall semester was becoming more unpleasant for them each time it came around, but they still had a couple of years to go before they could retire.

My parents gave me an update on everything that was happening back home, none of which I particularly cared to know. Ten years had already passed since I left home, and I didn't even run into people I knew from there anymore. Then they asked politely about my work, and I replied just as politely—and vaguely—appealing to professional discretion. They told me about their plans for Greece and showed me a picture of their hotel from a travel office brochure. Then we watched the news and sports report on TV. We drank the rest of the kiwi liqueur, but even that didn't do anything to relax the tension in the air. We were all relieved when Dad observed after the ten o'clock news that it was probably time to head to bed. Their flight was at seven the next morning, so we would have to be up before five.

Though I hadn't gotten much rest the night before, I couldn't sleep. As I lay there listening to Mom's snuffling and Dad's occasional snoring from my creaking sofa bed, I realized how strange it felt to be sleeping in the same room with someone. It made me sad. On every form I filled out, I put my mother's name as my next of kin, but were we really anything more than strangers to each other anymore? What did I know about my parents, and what did they know about me? If I died suddenly, as Tommi had, would they recognize the person whose things they would have to sort through?

It was my fault. I visited only a couple of times a year, and while I was there, I always adopted a distant, self-assured stance. We hadn't revealed any of our thoughts or feelings to one another for years, and I only ever heard about their reactions to the twists and turns in my life from my sisters.

I had never really forgiven them for not wanting me. They wanted a boy and had even picked out a name for him. Mom had been sure that the person in her womb was a Markku, since he kicked so enthusiastically. I had tried to be their boy because all I had were little sisters, and had even gone so far as to choose every little boy's dream job.

It was only a couple of years ago that I started to grasp that my parents weren't responsible for the messes in my life. I had even made a few attempts at drawing closer to them, but it was too late. The polite status quo between us was unlikely to change. Occasionally, when I listened to my mother and little sisters gossiping gaily together, I felt like a child who had been shut out of a fun game for no reason.

12

That spring will come again and a new dawn yet will break

I put my parents on a bus to the airport at five fifteen and then returned home and crawled back into bed to sleep for a couple more hours. In my restless dreams, I saw myself with a fishing pole, reeling in a body that had been beaten beyond recognition out of the sea. It was my mother. But when I finally got her out of the water, my mother had turned into Tuulia, whom I tried hopelessly to revive by kissing her.

I rode my bicycle up to Pasila. The fog had started to lift, and the Ferris wheel came slowly into view as I pedaled past Linnanmäki Amusement Park. I hoped there would be something symbolic about this dawn. I braked at a stoplight just as my chain derailed. As I fiddled with it, I managed to get grease on my best jeans. The chain fell off once more after that, so I didn't make it to the station until ten after eight. As I passed by Kinnunen's office, I glanced inside, but it was empty. Was he still out on drinking leave? A message from Heikki Peltonen and an order to see the captain had already appeared on my desk.

I called Peltonen first, who was looking for Tommi's car keys and thought we still had the spares.

"I've never seen any except the one set—the ones that were in the ignition. We didn't find any others, at the villa or in Tommi's apartment."

"Strange. I'm quite certain that there are at least two other sets of keys somewhere. We'd been meaning to sell the car as soon as the estate inventory was complete, but now we'll have to have the locks changed."

I remembered the phone message from this M person asking to borrow the car. Did M have the missing keys? What had M done with the car? Transported drugs? Why would he have used Tommi's car? I tried to assure Peltonen that the investigation was progressing, but avoided telling him how unpleasant the truth about his son's life was turning out to be.

Tapsa still hadn't received his tapes back, so I grudgingly went to see the captain to report on my current cases. He blew cigar smoke in my eyes and listened to me theorize about Tommi's involvement in various trafficking businesses with an incredulous expression on his face.

"Aha. How much of this information do you have actual evidence for and how much is made up—or should I be calling it women's intuition?"

I told him about Koivu's outings, about the rapist, and about the bottles of moonshine, which we would be getting analysis on that afternoon.

"So it's possible that the murderer was someone from the outside, then?"

"Not necessarily. I think some of my current suspects were at least mixed up in the bootlegging."

"Theories are all well and good, but we need results!" Another cloud of smoke wafted into my eyes. "You have until

Friday. Make an arrest by then. I've had my hands full keeping
the tabloids quiet about this case."

"So am I still the lead? What about Sergeant Kinnunen?"

The captain got an uneasy look.

"Well, Kalevi…" he started to mumble but then rallied. "Yes,
well. All the work that happens in your section is Kinnunen's
responsibility, of course. However, we spoke this morning about
trying to delegate more authority to junior officers. Of course
you should also be reporting to Kinnunen, but you've already
gotten pretty far with this case, so go ahead and wrap it up on
your own."

So Kinnunen was back from sick leave, but it seemed that
the situation was tense. I decided it might be best for me to talk
to him myself.

We spoke briefly about the other cases I was working on.
When I asked the captain for permission to use Koivu as my
main assistant, he agreed.

Then, seemingly in passing, he said, "The end of September
isn't that far off anymore. Saarinen called last week to say that
his back is so bad that his sick leave might turn into permanent
disability retirement. At the very least, he'll be out until the end
of the year. Have you thought about staying on?"

"No, I haven't had time," I said evasively.

"It would be good for the unit to have at least one woman
on staff, even if it's just for our image. And you seem to be able
to keep up with the boys," the captain said, oblivious to the fact
that he had just said precisely the wrong thing. Fortunately, his
secretary put an urgent call through from some higher-up right
then, and I was able to slip out.

In the meantime, a round package from the lab had appeared
on my desk.

Before I even had a chance to open it, my phone rang. It was Anu, the second soprano from the choir, returning my call.

I got straight to the point. "You told me that when you overheard Tommi on the phone, he said something to the effect of, 'Listen, Emma, I can't talk now.' Could it have just been, 'Listen, M' instead of "Listen, Emma?"

Anu thought for a moment.

"Yeah, I think you might be right."

"Good. And this M wanted more of something than Tommi had?"

"That was the impression I got."

I told Anu I might need an official statement from her later. She sounded relieved that was all.

Then I turned my attention to the package from the lab. It contained one of the bottles of moonshine from Tommi's apartment, along with another bottle, the lab results, and some photographs. I looked at them and whistled. This was starting to get interesting. I stuck the moonshine in my desk drawer so that it wouldn't create any temptation for the boys in the department, especially Kinnunen. Now I had the office bottle I had been wanting.

I reserved a department car for myself and Koivu, who was refreshed and in good spirits. I praised his accomplishments from Saturday night, and he laughed with satisfaction.

"Yeah, that place was full of fresh meat for sale. Girls or boys if you had the money," Koivu said. "Do you remember that Estonian woman who got arrested for robbing a client? It was a couple of days before Peltonen's murder. She might know something."

"Good boy, Koivu! Will you find out if she's still in custody and get permission to talk to her? But before that let's tackle these other interviews," I said as Koivu started monkeying with the car phone to get the scoop on the Estonian. It turned out she was still remanded in Pasila.

First we made our way to Koskela to look up Tomi Rissanen—otherwise known as "Tomppa." A beautiful boy with hair like an angel opened the door after several rings of the bell. He was rubbing his eyes as though he had just woken up. He wore only a skimpy white G-string, which emphasized the tan of his muscular body.

"Koivu and Kallio, Helsinki PD," I said and showed Tomppa my badge. "We have some questions about one of your...friends."

Tomppa looked more confused than afraid. Had Mäki warned him? On closer inspection, he looked more like a school-boy. I wasn't the least bit surprised that he found takers, but this kid didn't have any business hanging around the Kaivohuone Club. I could see that a face like that would be lovely to look at and touch though. The Mäkis, both Tommi's boss and her husband, seemed to have the same taste in men, since Tomppa looked like he could have been Tommi's little brother.

Tomppa confirmed that he had spent the whole night with Mäki at the Vaakuna Hotel. Since the guest register at the hotel had also confirmed this, it looked like Mäki could be crossed off the list of suspects.

"You were nice to that kid," Koivu said with a grin as we walked back to the car.

"How could I be hard on a cutie-pie like that?" I snorted. "But seriously, I saw enough of those guys in Vice. They never believe your friendly advice or threats until it's too late."

We drove north to Ring 3, making our way to the farm equipment store where Timo worked, which I found without Koivu's help. Tractors and threshers stood gleaming on the lot, bringing back distant memories of piling hay with my Uncle Pena when I was a child. I had bragged that I was able to lift a bigger pile of hay on my pitchfork than my cousin, who was a couple of years older than I was and a boy. While my little sisters had been content to help our mother work in the kitchen, I had ridden the horse and driven the tractor. Mother had never enjoyed our summers in the country because she was always shut up in the kitchen. Since Uncle Pena wasn't married, she had been responsible for preparing all the meals for everyone working on the harvest. No doubt she would have preferred to lie on the grass reading Agatha Christie all day. At the time, I thought she had chosen her place in the kitchen; in those days, I still believed that adults did only what they wanted.

When we pulled up, Timo was moving a load of fertilizer sacks into the sales yard with a tractor. He was clearly confused when I ordered him to come with us. I explained to Timo's boss that I urgently needed Timo's help with an investigation. I didn't want to needlessly sully his reputation, but at the same time I wondered why I was bothering to be so nice.

"I would have interviewed you and Sirkku last night, but you weren't in town," I said to Timo in the backseat. "Didn't we talk about you informing me if you went anywhere?"

"We were just in Muuriala, at my parents' house, I mean..." Timo explained, bewildered. "We didn't think you would need us over the weekend anyway."

We drove downtown. I parked the car illegally on a sidewalk and left Koivu with Timo while I headed in to the cosmetics counter of the large department store where Sirkku worked. Her makeup was showy, as I would have expected given her place of work, but it was not especially flattering. She wore too much of it, for one thing, and I didn't think pink lipstick suited her. The artificial lighting of the store made her look like an overgrown doll. Then I saw myself in a magnifying mirror and quickly averted my eyes.

"Hi, Sirkku. It looks like I need you to come up to Pasila for another interview. Who is your boss? I'll tell her."

Sirkku braced herself against the sales counter in such a way that a perfume bottle display that was set up on it collapsed to the floor with a clatter. She glanced around with such a frightened look that the department manager, who looked like she should be on a soap opera, came to ask what was the matter.

"I need a little help from Ms. Halonen on an investigation. I'll bring her back within the hour."

Sirkku went to hang up her work coat and punch her time card. I wondered whether they would dock her pay for the time she was gone, then realized it was stupid to think about something that petty. I escorted Sirkku to the car. When she saw Timo, she turned so pale she looked ill. I ordered Koivu into the backseat with Timo and made Sirkku sit next to me. Her pink nails were trembling at the tips of her fingers. Actually, I didn't even need to ask my questions anymore. Sirkku had already confessed everything through her demeanor.

She calmed down a bit when we got into my office and she could hold Timo's hand. Koivu brought them coffee, and a cup of tea for me. He sipped a Coke. I pulled the bottle of moonshine out of my desk cabinet, and Koivu made a hopeful gesture. I gave him a grin that indicated he should behave himself, though the thought of fortified tea sounded pretty good to me too all of a sudden.

"Is this bottle familiar to you two? Or do you need to sample the contents first?"

Timo and Sirkku glanced at each other. Finally Timo said weakly, "Yes, I recognize it." Now Timo's face was surprisingly pale too.

"Well, why do you recognize it? I imagine you know what's in it."

"Moonshine," Timo said, forcing the words out.

"And might I ask who made it? We found this bottle and dozens more like it in Tommi's apartment, but we didn't find a still there or in the villa in Vuosaari. If I need to, I can get a warrant for both of your apartments."

"But it isn't..." Sirkku began quickly, then squeaked when Timo squeezed her hand.

"But what isn't what? The still isn't put together anymore? We found both your fingerprints on the bottle samples," I lied. I figured we would probably find Sirkku's fingerprints on the ones in Tommi's attic storage locker. But my simple ruse worked on Sirkku in her frightened state.

"They can't have my fingerprints on them! Timo's the one who bottled it!"

"Idiot," Timo sighed, shaking his hand free of Sirkku. I bit my lip to keep from laughing. Sirkku's loud makeup looked grotesque in the light of day, and Timo's expression was defeated.

"Where did you make it, then?" I directed my words at Sirkku, but Timo had clearly decided he should take over from here. He spoke slowly and deliberately, as though carefully weighing each and every word.

"We've been cooking our own moonshine out at Muuriala for decades. My granddad's dad probably started making it during Prohibition, and then we just kept up the tradition. Every once in a while, I brought in bottles for choir or student association parties. Then last summer, Tommi asked if I could get him a little more if he paid me. I asked my father about it, since he's the one I've been making it with the last few years, but he was totally against it. We've never sold liquor at Muuriala; we just made it for our own use. I was annoyed of course, because Tommi thought that we could make upward of two hundred percent profit, since the grain was basically free from Muuriala. He said he wanted to sell it to friends at work.

"I considered building my own still in the city, but it seemed too complicated. Then, after I started dating Sirkku, Tommi brought it up again at a party one night."

"Tommi was always luring people into all sorts of things," Sirkku said angrily. Timo took her hand again.

"Yeah, Tommi was always propositioning Sirkku too. In any case, Sirkku promised to help me put the materials together—Sirkku is a chemist after all—and we made our first fifty liters of moonshine. We gave half of it to Tommi and kept half for ourselves. It's actually amazing mixed with Coke," Timo said to Koivu. I detected a note of professional pride in his voice.

"And then?" I asked, angry that I was being shut out of "men's business" once again.

"Then we made another batch for the choir's spring party, and we just finished the third a couple of weeks ago. That last batch was twice as big because we had a new pot."

"Where did you get the bottles? It looked like they were all the same."

"Some of them are old Muuriala bottles, and Tommi got the rest somewhere else."

"Who came up with the idea of using fennel to flavor it?"

"Tommi. I told him once that one of the things we grow at Muuriala is fennel, and Tommi said it would give the liquor a more refreshing flavor...like anise."

"And you sold some of the moonshine to Tommi?"

"Yeah, even though..." Timo looked bewildered. "It was a bit strange because he kept demanding that we make more all the time. I didn't want to spread it around too much. I don't think it's a crime if you just make liquor for yourself. Everybody does it where we're from," Timo said defensively. "Tommi just wanted so much of it. And he wouldn't tell me where he was selling it."

"Did he pay you up front?"

"Yeah. Except this last time..." Timo suddenly clammed up, and Sirkku stared at him, looking frightened.

"Go on," I said, trying to inject my voice with authority. I was surprised that Timo was from Eastern Finland because his slow, clumsy manner of speaking more closely resembled the stereotype of someone from Central Häme.

"Tommi called Thursday night," Sirkku said, suddenly annoyed. "He said he needed all the liquor we had in storage right away. He didn't have the money to pay just yet, but he promised to pay us on Saturday in Vuosaari once he'd sold it. He came by that night to pick up the bottles and told us that he was heading out to sell them right then."

"But the liquor was still at his house after Tommi died, and he didn't pay you on Saturday," I said. "Did you have a fight about the money?" Timo and Sirkku looked at each other, as though they couldn't decide who should answer. Timo began.

"Well, yeah. We thought about what to do that night when we were in the sauna. We didn't have any way to get the money out of him, but it would have been a loss of a couple of grand, which isn't small change for us. Tommi was acting strange all evening, and it was obvious he was avoiding us."

"And when we tried to go in his room to talk to him after the others had gone to bed, the door was locked!" Sirkku interjected indignantly.

"We decided to try again the next day," Timo continued. "But then Sirkku woke up in the night and went to the bathroom and...It's best that you tell what happened next yourself," Timo said to Sirkku, who was looking frightened again.

"Yes...well, I went to use the upstairs bathroom, and it smelled just awful. Riku had probably just been in there puking. When I went to open the window, I saw that Tommi was out on the dock. I decided not to wake up Timo but just to run down to the water and demand the money right then." Sirkku paused to catch her breath and downed the rest of her coffee, which had already grown cold and tasted horrible, judging from the look on her face. Or maybe Sirkku was grimacing at her own memories.

"But Tommi didn't have your money," I said, egging her on. "And he didn't even tell you that he hadn't sold the liquor yet."

"No. He just laughed and said we shouldn't be so gullible. Then I lost my temper and hit him."

"Hit him?" I asked, dumbfounded. "With what?"

"My hand. Or my fist. I don't remember. In the face. Tommi swore at me, and I ran away. I didn't stick around to see if I'd hurt him or not. But then in the morning...He couldn't have died from my hitting him, could he?" Sirkku asked frantically.

"Don't worry. He was hit on the head with an ax before he died," I said to console her.

"But Sirkku and I thought that maybe Tommi somehow fell on the ax and hit his head and then fell in the water," Timo said, miserable.

I thought about the reports from the lab and the pathologist. Was it possible? I didn't really believe that Sirkku could hit anyone hard enough to make him fall over. But what did I know? I was a lot stronger than I looked. It would explain the lack of fingerprints of course. Salo had said that one of the facial bruises had obviously been inflicted prior to death. That supported the theory that Sirkku's blow didn't knock Tommi down. But it was also true that he had been drunk. So was it that simple? Sirkku had killed him by accident? Should I arrest her now? I felt downright sorry for the poor girl.

"Come here," I said, standing up. Sirkku obeyed submissively. I raised my hand like I was taking an oath, tensed my arm muscles, and said, "Hit that. Hit my hand the same way you hit Tommi, as hard as you possibly can."

Sirkku punched my hand. The force of the blow was nonexistent. My arm didn't even budge. Sirkku could simply be faking it though.

"Sit down. I don't really believe you could have hit Tommi hard enough to lay him out. We'll still have to check whether it was even possible for him to have died that way. You saw the ax on the dock?"

"Yeah...It was there, with the blade sunk into one of the posts."

Of course it was possible that Sirkku was still lying, that she had used the ax and then still had the presence of mind to hide the weapon and wipe her fingerprints off it. But why wouldn't that have wiped the other prints off too? No, Tommi's killer had been wearing gloves.

"Did Tommi say what he was doing outside?"

"He didn't have time because I started ripping him a new one right off."

I dug the rest of the contents out of the packet from the lab and laid them all out on my desk.

"Are you sure that you've told me absolutely everything you know about the bootlegging? Tommi told you he was selling it to his friends?"

They nodded.

"When our lab tested your moonshine, the chemists discovered that exactly the same stuff, flavored with fennel, has been showing up on the street."

I picked up the other bottle from the package. The bottle itself was exactly like the one from Tommi's apartment, but it had a different cork and a Russian label, which claimed it was Siberian anise vodka, 94 proof.

"Do you have any idea where these labels are from?"

Both of them looked flabbergasted. Timo recovered first and asked, surprisingly quickly, "Someone's been selling this on the street? Who?"

"An Estonian dealer. He swore up and down that he'd brought it in from Russia. He had several bottles of it."

"What price was he asking?"

"Seventy per half."

"What the hell! Tommi was paying us twenty for half a liter. So he was skimming. He told us there was so much Russian vodka around that it had driven the price down."

"That's true." I was starting to believe that Timo and Sirkku hadn't known anything about where their product was ending up. After asking them a few more follow-up questions, I asked Koivu to take them back to work. Then I ordered them forcefully not to leave the city without telling me.

"Are we going to get charged with anything?" Timo asked nervously on their way out. "I just mean…I wouldn't want my dad and Muuriala to get mixed up in this."

I considered the fate of the still. If Sirkku and Timo had the least bit of sense, they destroyed it as soon as they heard about Tommi's death. We would have to interrogate the dealer again to see whether there was any possible connection to Tommi. Then it would be time to decide what charges to press.

"Oh, you'll probably just get off with a fine," I said encouragingly. We might even be able to overlook the whole thing, but I couldn't promise them that.

My phone rang just as Koivu was stepping out with the lovebirds. I thought it would be Tapsa about the tapes, but it turned out to be Tuulia.

"Listen, Maria, you have Jaana's address, right? I was just thinking I'd go visit her since I'm going to be bumming around Europe on the train later this fall."

"Yeah, wait a sec while I look it up." I dug my address book out from under the stacks of paper cresting on my desk. I was sure there was something I wanted to ask Tuulia, but I couldn't remember what it was. I gave her Jaana's address in Germany.

"So how's it going? I gather the memorial service was pretty awful," I said sympathetically.

"Luckily that's over now. It hadn't sunk in that Tommi was really dead until the funeral." Tuulia swallowed. "Anything new in the investigation?"

"I think we're getting there. It's slow going though." Though I wanted to reassure Tuulia, I didn't dare say any more than that.

"Let's go out for beers again sometime, OK?" Tuulia said with a hopeful note in her voice and then hung up before I had a chance to agree. Sometime. Sometime when the case was solved. Sometime when the suspects have permission to start living normal lives again.

Tapsa didn't answer my call. I listened to Tommi's answering machine tape one more time. "It's Tiina. The plans are ruined now. You're a cheap man. I can't trust you. Come to my place on Sunday." "M here. Sunday night. I'm taking off tomorrow. Call me now."

Finally it dawned on me that the word I had been interpreting as "cheap" translated as "bad" in Estonian. Well, well, the mysterious Tiina might just be one of Tommi's Estonian girls.

The members of that drug ring and the Estonian prostitute had been arrested only a couple of days before Tommi's death. How much did these three events have in common? Sirkku had been awake in the early morning, so she would surely have heard if someone had come ashore on a boat or driven up in a car. And we hadn't yet found any sign of someone having been on the dock who wasn't supposed to be there—a waste of expensive fiber analysis. But we had to put the possibility of an outside murderer back on the table.

Or maybe...I had already discovered plenty of surprising things about my suspects lurking just beneath the surface. If Tommi was mixed up in the drug trade and pimping, then why couldn't one of his other friends have been too?

Tapsa Helminen knocked on my door while I was still lost in thought. In his hand was an envelope containing an answering machine tape fresh from the lab.

We listened to the messages in succession, starting with the one for Tommi: "M here. Sunday night. I'm taking off tomorrow. Call me now." The voice on Tapsa's tape was clearly the same: "M here. I'll have another car full of merchandise on Thursday. Name the place." Though the phone and the recording altered the voice somewhat, the intonation at the beginning of the message was exactly the same.

"You think maybe it's M for Murderer?" Tapsa asked excitedly.

"Not really, but this has to tell us something. At the very least I want Tommi's car inspected again; they only checked it superficially before. I want a full workup this time around." I told Tapsa that Koivu had gone to interview the Estonian prostitute and that Tommi might be a link between the two worlds.

"You try to squeeze your drug dealers about how Tommi was involved in all this. Here's his picture. And I want to know who M is. Give them the third degree if you have to. Knowing that is going to help us both out."

I realized I was giving orders to Tapsa, though I didn't have any authority to do so. He seemed a bit confused for a moment too. I had met Tapsa's wife once and doubted she ordered her husband to do anything more than to occasionally run down to the laundry room to get the clothes out of the dryer. But Tapsa had known me a long time, and he had the good sense not to turn this into a turf war.

We arranged to meet later that night. I made the necessary calls to get Tommi's car back in for a more thorough inspection—Tommi's father was less than pleased—and then continued to catch up on the previous day's paperwork. The weekend had been surprisingly quiet, just a couple of routine assaults in addition to the rape and suicide. The phone rang while I was still mired in paperwork. My esteemed immediate superior, Kalevi Kinnunen, from two doors down was requesting an audience. Oh joy.

Kinnunen had clearly been sober for at least a day. There was still an obvious tremor in his hands though, and his eyes resembled half-ripe strawberries. Beet-red blood vessels crisscrossed his puffy face. The stench of his Boss aftershave barely masked the underlying reek of a body poisoned by years of boozing.

I reported on my activities of the previous week. Kinnunen wasn't any more interested in the Peltonen case than in any of the others—i.e., not at all—and he perked up only when I mentioned the word liquor. I wondered what it would feel like to realize that your subordinates got along better without you.

I went to the corner store to buy some rye bread and coleslaw, and munched on them while basking in the sunshine on a bench alongside the path leading to Central Park. Then I stopped at an ice-cream stand to buy a double fudge chocolate cone and was just savoring my first licks when I ran into Mira. We greeted each other awkwardly. Mira was never going to forgive me for knowing things about her life that she herself wanted to forget. Seeing her made me remember what I was supposed to have asked Tuulia.

"Listen, I'm glad I ran into you," I said with feigned good grace. "Do you remember whether Tommi got any calls out at the villa? Or did Tommi call anyone from there?"

Maybe the mysterious drug dealer had arranged a meeting. That might explain why Tommi had been so tense that night, sensing what was going to happen.

"Calls?" Mira's eyebrows went up. "All I remember is Tommi's parents calling when we were in the sauna. Tommi heard the phone they have installed outside and went up to the house to answer it."

"Who else was with you in the sauna? Was anyone up at the house who could have heard what Tommi said?" I was a little surprised about the coed sauna, though a mixed sauna packed with people was an extremely chaste place. I thought naked men mostly just looked stupid with their flaccid Johnsons flapping around like inedible mushrooms pushing through moss. A mixed sauna had never inspired in me the least temptation to sin. Two people alone in the sauna was a different matter.

"Antti was with Tommi when he came back to the sauna. Timo and Sirkku didn't show up until everyone else had left."

"So Timo, Sirkku, or Antti could have heard Tommi's call?" The ice cream was dripping onto the front of my blouse, and I hurriedly licked the edge of the cone.

"I wouldn't be so sure about Timo and Sirkku. They went out in the rowboat at some point. I think Antti was the only one in the house at that point."

I made a mental note to myself to call Antti and said goodbye to Mira. My ice cream had begun to melt more rapidly and was dripping everywhere, so I shoved the remaining half of the cone into my mouth all at once. I was quite a sight with my pants covered in bicycle grease and my ice cream–stained shirt. Back in my office, I was just dialing Antti's number and debating whether to dig my uniform skirt out of the cabinet when Koivu came bouncing in like an eager blond dog. His expression told me that he had made another breakthrough. I hung up the phone again. Antti could wait.

"Well?"

"Yes," Koivu said with a grin. "The Estonian chick knew Peltonen. Her name is Tiiu Välbe—no relation to Jelena. The cross-country skier," Koivu explained when he saw the confusion on my face. "In fact, sometimes she worked for him, for Peltonen I mean. One night at the Kaivohuone Club, he roped her into a romp with some of his French guests, and after that he had Välbe work in his company's sauna a couple of times, helping with the...uh...bathing. Peltonen fixed her up with odd tricks from time to time, apparently for company guests again, but she didn't really know."

"When did this happen?"

"It started sometime last summer. The last gig was in May."

"But Tommi wasn't her actual pimp?"

"No...More like a middleman. He wasn't so much taking her money as lining her up with good jobs."

"Strange form of charity," I said. It didn't really fit with my picture of Tommi's character. But on the other hand, I was beginning to discern a pattern. At first, he had just been helping Riku out as a friend, and he helped Sirkku and Timo turn a profit bootlegging. And Tommi had paid for Mira's abortion without complaint. Was Tommi really more or less a "good guy"?

"This Tiiu thought that one of her colleagues, name of Tiina, was also one of Tommi's regular girls. Didn't a Tiina leave a message on his answering machine? Tiiu claimed that Tiina also had some connection to the drug trade."

"So where do we find Tiina? Do you have an address?"

"No, but apparently on Monday nights in the summer she works the Little Parliament. I got a description."

"Can you handle another long day? Try to find this Tiina."

"Is she the murderer, then?"

"I doubt it. But she might hold the key to this case. Call me at home right away if you find her, and arrest her if you have to. I'll come down to the station to talk to her. Call me either way when the bar closes. I think we can go ahead and use the overtime the boss has been promising on this case."

After Koivu left I tried to reach Antti at the university again, but all I got was the department answering machine. I called Antti's direct line—no answer—and the library number, where a guy who was half asleep told me he didn't think Antti had been in the building all day. Though my reason for calling wasn't terribly important, I was still annoyed. Maybe university researchers got to go to the beach on beautiful days like this. Or perhaps

Antti had gone to visit his parents and Einstein at their cabin—
without notifying me.

Tapsa came back to the station sooner than I expected, his
long nose all aflutter with excitement. "I just issued an arrest
warrant for a Mauri Mattinen, also known as M in certain circles. He hasn't been home for a while, and he's on vacation from
work."

"So you found out who he is? What was his name? Mattinen!
Hell, yeah! The same name shows up on Tommi's consulting
bills for work. Does he have a record?" I was already dialing as
I spoke.

"Mattinen, Mauri. Born 1949. One six-month stretch for
possession of marijuana."

I called the lab and asked them to look specifically for
Mattinen's fingerprints in Tommi's car.

Next I called Marja Mäki, who, after thinking for a moment,
told me that she thought Mattinen's company had been survey-
ing transportation subcontractors in Estonia.

"So my husband has been cleared of any suspicion?" Mäki
asked.

"Yes. His alibi has been confirmed by several different
people."

"So where was he?"

"He can tell you that himself," I replied, trying to bring the
conversation to a close, but Marja Mäki didn't give up that easily.

"He was with some boy, right?" Her voice swelled with
uncontrollable rage. "How old was he this time?" I was stunned.
Why did the Mäkis have to drag me into their business? Suddenly
I understood.

"You listen to me, Dr. Mäki! You never suspected your husband of killing Tommi Peltonen, did you? You just wanted to

use the police to trace where your husband had been. Next time hire a private detective!" I slammed the phone in her ear. Lovely. Maybe Marja had just used Tommi as a pawn to get back at her husband. I wouldn't have to watch *The Bold and the Beautiful* for a while now—real life was just as warped.

I gathered up my papers and headed over to Tapsa's office, where we started trying to line up what we knew. Another narcotics cop joined us, a man in his sixties named Makkonen—whose hastiness had been the cause of the premature arrests—and Koivu, who had just had time to go home and pull on his bar-trolling clothes. In his sky-blue shirt and white pants, he definitely looked like a man who could attract the attention of girls beyond the nice brunettes he was so sick of.

"Should we inform Kinnunen?" Makkonen asked scrupulously.

"He headed up to Haaga with Virrankoski a couple of hours ago," I said quickly. I couldn't deny that I was protective of my case. This was the first murder case I'd handled on my own, and I didn't want some alcoholic boss messing it up.

After several cups of coffee and half a box of smokes in the hallway for Makkonen, we had assembled all the facts we had up to this point. Tapsa had just received confirmation from the lab that they identified Mattinen's fingerprints on the driver's side door and around the trunk lock of Tommi's car. Koivu had just begun to read a summary of our conclusions when the phone rang.

"It's for you, Maria. Some Mrs. Sarkela."

"This is Marjatta Sarkela. How do you do?" asked a sophisticated-sounding, middle-aged woman with a hint of alarm in her voice. "You are the policewoman investigating Tommi Peltonen's murder, correct?"

"Yes. And you must be Antti Sarkela's mother."

"Yes. I don't know whether I'm overreacting, but it seems that my son has disappeared."

"He isn't at your place in Inkoo?"

"No...Did he say he was coming out here?" Antti's mother explained that they had picked up Einstein from Antti's apartment on Saturday night and then left for Inkoo. She tried to call Antti on Sunday to tell him that the cat had woken them up at six in the morning by dragging a mole into their bed. Antti's roommate told her that Antti had gone out somewhere Saturday night and hadn't come back. Now it was Monday, and no one had heard from him.

"I can't help but be concerned, given what happened to poor Tommi...And Antti and Tommi were such good friends. What if whoever killed Tommi has done something to Antti?"

I tried to calm Mrs. Sarkela down, though I was immediately concerned myself. I recalled Antti's words from Saturday: "If only I...if only I knew which things were significant and which weren't." And later: "Whoever killed Tommi might be unpredictable. You ought to be careful too." Had Antti been careless himself? Or was he on the run?

13

That from atop the fells, come winds of days soon to wake—

"What now?" Tapsa asked curiously when I hung up the phone.

"Oh hell. It looks like one of my prime suspects is missing." I remembered that Monday was the EFSAS *kyykkä* night at Kaisaniemi field. Antti might be there, or at least I might find someone who knew something about his whereabouts. I decided I needed to go pay them a visit.

The cars were all booked, so I jumped on my bike, fervently praying that it wouldn't start acting up again. I booked it all the way down the hill to Kaisaniemi in fifteen minutes. The evening was still warm, and I wished I was wearing shorts instead of greasy jeans. I realized that my neck was stiff, and my head was reeling from all the new information.

Tapsa's dealer had finally agreed to give up M's identity. Here's what I knew about the mysterious Mauri Mattinen: one conviction for marijuana possession and sale; fines for importing human growth hormones across the Russian border; currently the principal shareholder and CEO of Mattinen Consulting; and missing, just like Antti.

Mattinen had delivered the goods to the dealer, who always had to pay in cash. According to the dealer, Mattinen had had a relatively large batch of cocaine in his possession, which Mattinen had been selling slowly in order to keep the price high. Luckily there wasn't much cocaine available on our market. It had been top-notch stuff, evidently out of the Middle East, and had arrived in Finland "on a boat from Tallinn," according to the dealer.

After hearing that little tidbit, I put in a call to Heikki Peltonen—how many calls had I made today?—but no, Tommi hadn't stopped in Tallinn on the *Maisetta* this past sailing season. I had been disappointed when that nice little theory fell apart. But then Peltonen remembered that Tommi had been there earlier in the summer with Henri and Peter Wahlroos on a test run of the *Marlboro of Finland*. Henri and Peter were getting the feel for the new boat, as every member of a crew did before a big competition. Peltonen couldn't tell me who else had gone on that trip, but he guessed that at least Pia and Antti would have accompanied them.

The *Marlboro of Finland* would certainly have been an excellent hiding place for the cocaine. There had been such a fuss about the boat all spring that it was likely quite a familiar name even on the other side of the border. There was no way customs would have done anything more than a perfunctory inspection. Tommi and his possible accomplices had taken a pretty big risk, but the risk had paid off—for a while.

According to the dealer, Mattinen had brought him the cocaine in his car, the same Opel Vectra that showed up a couple of times in the pictures that Makkonen's team of investigators had taken before arresting the dealer and the street runners. The Department of Motor Vehicles hadn't been able to find the plates that appeared in the pictures, so they must have been fakes. And Tommi's car was exactly the same color, make, and model.

I wondered why Mattinen had specifically used Tommi's car. Maybe his own was too easy to recognize. At least that was

Makkonen's guess. In any case, we now had an APB out on
Mattinen, and Forensics was going over Tommi's car with a
fine-tooth comb. I was irritated at myself for having let the lab
just do a cursory search originally.

I found the choir on the grass next to the tennis courts.
There were about twenty of them present, including Hopponen
and all my suspects—all, that is, except Antti.

Kyykkä didn't appear to be a particularly fast-paced game, and
the players didn't look very sporty with their beer bottles in hand.
Kyykkä seemed to be some sort of Finnish version of lawn bowl-
ing with sticks. After watching for a while, I realized that one
team was trying to use one piece of wood to knock the other
team's pieces of wood out of the square. When it was Tuulia's turn
to throw, she took her position, her bobbed hair swinging, and
neatly sent three of her opponents' *kyykkäs* flying out of the square,
receiving enthusiastic cheers for her accomplishment. There was a
fascinating elegance to Tuulia's movements, which were simultaneously boyish and feminine. I turned my eyes away. As Riku was
cheering for Tuulia, he noticed me standing nearby.

"Hi, Maria," he said lamely. "Did you come to watch the
game?"

"Have you seen Antti?" I asked. Riku's expression turned
to alarm.

"Um, I've been trying to call him, but he hasn't been at
home or at work. I thought he would be here."

Riku seemed to think I was asking after Antti because of
his own mess. If he wasn't here, where the hell was he then? I
motioned to Pia, who had been glancing over curiously, and we
stepped away from the game.

"You were on the *Marlboro* in Tallinn this past spring, right?"

"Yeah, at the beginning of May. I think it was Mother's Day weekend. It was really cold. Why?"

"Who else went along?"

"Peter and I. Peter's dad. Henri and his girlfriend. Niklas Bergman, who's racing with them now. Sirkku wanted to come sailing too, and of course she brought Timo. And then Antti and Tuulia came along too."

"Ten people?"

"Yeah...We went to an Estonian Philharmonic Chamber Choir concert that night that Tommi was dying to hear."

"Do you remember what your customs inspection was like when you came back?"

"Customs inspection? There wasn't any. They don't usually check racing boats."

It looked like a drug run on the *Marlboro* was a distinct possibility. I asked the choir members to tell Antti to call me. None of them seemed the slightest bit disconcerted by his absence, and no one knew where he was. I noted that none of them looked nervous or acted guilty.

No one had heard anything from Antti since he left my place to go meet his parents on Saturday night. On Saturday night after the funeral, Mira and Pia had been home—I could attest to that myself—Sirkku and Timo had been on their way to Muuriala or were already there, and Riku and Tuulia had gone to a bar together. Had any of them also seen Antti that night?

I cycled back to the station. It was only a little before eight. Tapsa had left with Koivu for the Little Parliament. On my desk was a curt message: "We went to hunt down Tiina. Mattinen flew to London the Monday before last. Shit. Interpol on him. Koivu & Helminen."

Mattinen hadn't left the country until after Tommi's death. What if he was the murderer? If he'd already been in London for over a week, finding him would probably be impossible, even with Interpol's help. Annoying. Just minutes before, I had been so jazzed about discovering all these new connections, but now it looked like they weren't going to give me anything solid.

Antti's roommate answered when I called his apartment. He hadn't actually seen Antti Saturday night. He'd been asleep in his own room because he had a night shift coming up at the hospital. He vaguely remembered having heard Antti giving Einstein to his parents and then leaving some time later. And neither roommate had seen him since then.

"No one came to pick him up?"

The roommate wasn't sure of anything except that the doorbell hadn't rung.

"It usually wakes me up. Same with the phone. That didn't ring either," he explained.

"Did Antti call anyone?"

He couldn't say. Nothing was missing from Antti's belongings aside from his tennis shoes and a jacket, but the roommate said he wasn't all that familiar with Antti's belongings.

I called the Sarkelas' cabin. Antti's parents were very concerned at this point and wanted to put a missing persons report in the newspaper and on the radio. They appeared to believe that the same person who had killed Tommi had also attacked Antti.

"But Antti isn't dead," Marjatta Sarkela said at the end of the call. "Animals know things like that. Einstein isn't any kind of genius, but he would sense it if something had happened to Antti. As it is, he's acting completely normal, sitting here purring hopefully at my feet. In fact, it's his dinner time."

I hoped the cat was right, though that might mean that his owner was guilty of murder and was now on the run from the police. Poor Einstein. Neither option looked good for him.

It was just barely 9:00 p.m. The guys probably wouldn't be back from the Little Parliament Club until around midnight. We had arranged that they would give me a call once they were done for the evening, so I decided to head home and try to get some sleep before then.

I flew home on my bike, changed into my workout clothes, and went out for a run. As usual, I felt like molasses for the first few minutes, but then I started to get into my groove. The cool air flushed out my lungs, and my stiff shoulders relaxed. Sweat poured down my temples, and my steps felt lighter and lighter. I went all the way to where the bridge goes out to the Seurasaari Island Open-Air Museum—nearly two miles—before forcing myself to turn back. I had to get some sleep.

When I woke up, the sun was high in the sky. It was eight thirty in the morning, and I had slept almost ten hours. The guys hadn't called. What the hell happened?

Then I realized why my phone had stayed silent. I had disconnected the cord the previous morning, fearing that my mother would call at 6:00 a.m. just to tell me she had left her toothbrush on the edge of the sink. I cursed, set the coffee on to percolate, and called the station.

"No sign of Koivu or Helminen," the person at the main desk said coldly. The duty officer for my unit, however, had a message for me from Koivu: "We found Tiina and heard all sorts of charming stories. We had no reason to arrest her. Are you out hunting Sarkela? I'll be in at eight."

I gulped down my coffee and what little was left of the ham and onion quiche. My best jeans were still greasy, so I pulled on my other pair, which were faded and patched at the crotch. I didn't want to risk getting them dirty so I took the tram to work. Having overslept, I was now late, hungry, irritated—and curious.

When I arrived, Koivu was off with Kinnunen investigating some robbery, and Tapsa was busy executing yet another search warrant. I hoped it was for Mattinen's apartment. Then, just as I was getting settled in, I got a call ordering me over to the Cholera Basin at the harbor to have a look at a drowning victim. I didn't get back to Pasila until after noon. At that point, Koivu had come and gone, but I caught Tapsa and we arranged to meet for lunch in half an hour.

The lab worked fast. In addition to locating Mattinen's fingerprints, they had now found traces of cocaine in the first aid kit in the trunk. Apparently some small amounts of it had been stored recently between the packages of gauze. Most of the fingerprints were on the license plate, which, judging from the scrape marks on the paint, had been screwed on and off repeatedly.

I realized I was starting to feel ill from lack of food and all the tension. The taste of onion rose in my mouth as I jogged down the stairs to the cafe. There was no sign of Tapsa yet, so I forced myself to choke down some salad and roasted vegetables. Then Tapsa showed up in the food line, freshly shaved and wearing a pressed shirt. He set a tray full of food down in front of me: five potatoes with hamburger gravy, two glasses of milk, and three pieces of bread. Apparently, this was going to be a long meeting.

"I just came from Mattinen's apartment. Were you looking for these?" Tapsa took a small plastic baggie containing a set of keys out of his shirt pocket. I could see the familiar letters

through the plastic: Opel Vectra. I would have been willing to
bet quite a bit that those were the missing keys to Tommi's car.

"On the way to the lab, we found Mattinen's own car in the
parking lot. It's a beat-up VW that wouldn't have even fit the
new-size plates we found in the apartment, the same ones that
were in Makkonen's pictures."

"So Mattinen was using Peltonen's car to move his merchandise in order to throw us off his trail."

I had already told Tapsa my theory about the *Marlboro of
Finland* being used for smuggling, and he had thought it plausible. We had to work back and trace Mattinen's movements. He
might have been in Tallinn at the same time as the *Marlboro* and
delivered the cocaine to Tommi on the boat.

"What about last night? I gather you didn't make any arrests."

"We got what we needed without having to arrest anyone. I
went over with your boy Koivu, since my old school buddy is a
bouncer at the Little Parliament, and I thought he might recognize Tiina. I haven't spent a whole lot of time hanging around
bars lately."

Tapsa had a wife and two small children, one of whom was
only about six months old, if I remembered correctly. There
were probably days when Tapsa left before they woke up and
came home after they went to bed and he didn't get to see his
kids at all. I had occasionally wondered what it would be like to
be a cop's wife, and figured it must practically be like being a
single mother.

"At around ten, Masa, the bouncer, came to say that Tiina
had arrived. She was clearly looking for company."

"How did you know that?" I asked, simply curious. Next
time I was in a bar I would know to behave exactly the opposite.

"Well, she was alone, dressed to the nines, glancing around, smiling. You know. Koivu strolled over to chat her up. After only a few minutes, they had arranged to go to a hotel, but Koivu said he needed a little pick-me-up first. He's a good boy," Tapsa said with all the eminence afforded him by a difference in age of barely ten years.

"And Tiina knew where to get some?"

"Tiina said the market was in kind of bad shape right now. All she had on her was a little weed. At that point Koivu brought her over to our table. She was somewhat surprised to find that there were two men now. I showed her Mattinen's picture and asked whether we could get something a little harder from him. At that point she guessed who we were. We agreed we wouldn't haul her in for possession if she gave us what we needed."

I admired the ease with which Tapsa had gotten used to cutting deals. In Narcotics, investigations were all about making trades with the smaller crooks to nab the bigger fish. Maybe I had been wrong about him; he didn't get worked up over a few grams of weed anymore.

"After cursing out Koivu for a few minutes, she turned coop-erative. Koivu is a pretty boy—maybe he would have been a nice customer." Tapsa's face suddenly turned neutral again. Maybe he still remembered that treatment I had given his elbow so long ago at the academy. I had never been on the same easy terms with Tapsa as with Koivu when it came to joking around, and he probably thought of me as some sort of scary feminist battle-ax.

"In any case, she recognized Mattinen and Peltonen. She was even the one who introduced them. Apparently, last fall, Mattinen had been looking for someone to bring cocaine in from Estonia to Finland, and Peltonen had agreed to do it. Over the winter, Peltonen brought in small amounts through customs while he was on business trips. It would be interesting to know how he pulled that off," Tapsa said darkly.

"As Tiina understood it, Mattinen had sold some, and Tommi got the rest. Tiina suspected that Tommi cheated Mattinen sometimes, because he once had some junk for sale that Mattinen didn't know anything about. In May, Tommi brought a larger batch over. Mattinen had been in Tallinn at the same time, so he probably arranged the deal."

Tapsa thought they had probably stored the stuff in Tommi's apartment.

"We should take the dogs over there. You'd probably also be interested to know that Peltonen brought some goods over to Tiina's place in his car once. Tiina threw the key out the window to him so he could let himself in and saw that there was someone else in the car with him. She was upset with Peltonen for being so careless, but Peltonen just said that whoever it was knew all about it. They had been along on the Tallinn gig too."

"Did Tiina say what this person looked like? Male or female?"

"Tall and thin. A man, a friend."

"Some women can pass for men, at least from a distance. Did she see a hair color?"

"No. Another thing that may interest you is that Peltonen had promised Tiina a gig for Friday night. The client came, and Tiina did the job, but she never got her money from Peltonen."

"Was that why she called Tommi?"

"Evidently. Maybe she got so ticked off she went out to Vuossari and put an ax in Peltonen's head?"

"I doubt it. I'm still sure the killer came from the house. It isn't Tiina or Mattinen. No, it's definitely one of the choir members. And one of my suspects is missing now. Our perp is either him or one of his friends." I sighed, worn out. Though it was frustrating that Mattinen had gotten away, I had still hoped he was Tommi's murderer.

I carried a big cup of coffee up to my office and started to sift through all the documents and notes I had amassed over the course of the investigation.

Tommi had been selling alcohol, drugs, and women. He had sold Finnish moonshine as Russian vodka, swindling both his customers and Sirkku and Timo. Maybe he had gotten the labels on some trip to Russia. You could buy anything there these days. Tommi probably found them at some stall in an outdoor market, remembered the Muuriala moonshine, and easily combined them in his mind. He sold the bootlegging idea to Timo and Sirkku as an innocent little side business, even though it had been something else entirely.

Tommi had also been pimping women. Maybe not actually pimping, but he had been skimming money for himself. Regardless, it certainly hadn't been a charity operation. Tiina had probably needed money for drugs, and the other girls had almost certainly required cash for other things. Tommi's own sexual and emotional life had always been confused. He had wanted to own his women. Pia had presented a challenge to Tommi because she was married. If Pia had agreed to a relationship with him, he would almost certainly have lost interest in her. Had the same thing happened to Tuulia? Had they just been "friends with benefits" at first and then she fell in love with him and became a drag?

Finally, Tommi had been running drugs. Those pirate games they'd played when they were kids had turned strangely real. The ME hadn't found any traces of hard drugs in Tommi's own system, so he'd probably just smoked the odd joint now and then. It was unlikely Tommi had been playing honestly with his business partners in this matter either. He had probably been skimming, or even outright cheating Mattinen.

On his last day alive, Tommi had needed money badly. He had been afraid. The news about the drug ring getting nailed and the arrest of the Estonian prostitute had spooked him. He had obviously been planning to flee the country. He couldn't have been in a total panic yet because he didn't just make a run for it. No, he had stayed on and tried to scrape together as much money as he could before he left.

Maybe I would never know all of Tommi's dealings. Or understand why he had done what he did. What did he want to accomplish with all of this? Was he looking for adventure, or power? From all appearances, he was the epitome of a successful, handsome, and wealthy young man. Tommi had an advanced degree and an interesting job, and he had found "good" hobbies in music and sailing. None of that had been enough for him though, and in the process of going after what he wanted, he had pulled someone else down with him into his twisted world.

Riku and Mira hadn't been along on the Tallinn trip, so I could count Mira out of the drug running. Riku could have been the friend in Tommi's car though. He wasn't tall, but who could accurately judge the height of a person who was seated?

Timo and Sirkku had been on the trip. But you couldn't call Timo thin, and there was no way anyone would mistake Sirkku for a man, even in the dark. How much weight could I give Tiina's testimony, given that we could haul her in for solicitation the second we didn't like what she was telling us? Tommi's companion could also have been Peter Wahlroos, in which case Pia would have had an obvious motive for killing Tommi—he could have been blackmailing them over the drugs. Or Tuulia, who could pass for a man in the dark, or Antti, the tallest and thinnest of them all.

I read through all of the papers several times, and gradually the pieces started to fall into place. However, I didn't like the picture that was coming into focus. I had seriously misjudged one of my suspects.

14

Or have they lied?

By four o'clock that afternoon, I was sure. I made a few calls and checked my papers one last time to verify my facts. At six o'clock, I went into motion. I still hadn't heard from Antti, and the thought of what might have happened to him was weighing on me. If Antti was dead, it would be my fault. I hadn't figured out the truth soon enough.

I parked my car a couple of buildings down from my target's home. I hadn't called to see if she was home, but I was ready to wait all night if I had to. I climbed the stairs to the second floor of the old wooden building and rang the doorbell. The steps that came to the door were not the least bit hesitant. If the woman who answered was surprised to see me, she didn't show it.

"Hi, Maria! I hoped you'd return the visit. I just put some tea on. The water's probably already boiling. Do you want some? Come in, come in." There may have been a bit too much bustling energy in her voice.

"Thanks. I'd love some." I walked into the kitchen, which had a round red dining table that made it feel cramped. The aqua blue of the drapes matched the chairs and the tablecloth, and the indigo-colored tea setting was a handsome contrast. I sat down at the table and put my shoulder bag on the windowsill.

"Have you heard anything from Antti?" Tuulia asked as she set some thin slices of cake on the table.

"I could ask you the same thing. Tell me right now if you know where he is. It will save us all a lot of time and effort."

"I don't have the foggiest idea. Do you think he's the murderer?"

"No. I think he knows who is though."

Tuulia poured my tea. Her hands didn't shake, and not a single drop of the jasmine-scented liquid splashed on the saucer. There we sat with our teacups between us like two old ladies having a social visit. Outside, the evening sun was shining, and I could hear the eager shouts of children in the distance.

"I came to get Tommi's car keys. Would you give them to me?" Tuulia didn't protest—she just disappeared for a moment into the other room and then returned with the familiar Vectra keys.

"Do the Peltonens intend to sell the car? I guess they need all the keys for that."

"I don't know if the car will make it to the lot now. The insurance may or may not pay for the damage to the interior now that we've turned the whole car inside out. Why did you have the keys?"

"I have copies of all of Tommi's keys. He was afraid of losing his own and thought it would be good for one of his friends to have spares."

"Your fingerprints were all over that car. I guess you drove it a lot?"

"Now and then, when I needed it."

"Was Mauri Mattinen one of Tommi's trusted friends too, since he had the third set of keys?"

I noticed how the hand holding Tuulia's teacup shook as she said quickly, "Mauri who?"

I looked at Tuulia's hands. She had on a long-sleeved T-shirt, whose sleeves had stretched some. Evidently she was in the habit of pulling them down to cover her hands when they were cold. On her right fourth finger was a ring that would have eaten at least a month's worth of wages as a cop. I had thought it was high-quality kitsch, but apparently it was real.

"Don't you know Mattinen? You must have met him on Mother's Day in Tallinn when he turned over that shipment of cocaine to you and Tommi. And I imagine you took Tommi's car to the door of Mattinen's garage a few times when Tommi couldn't take it himself. That must have been what the 'No Tuulia Monday' on Tommi's notepad meant. You couldn't take the car to Mattinen because he was afraid he was being watched."

"Who told you that? Was it M, I mean Mattinen?" Tuulia noticed her slip too late.

"That's for me to know. Though you had a good cover, quite a lot of people knew about different parts of this mess. Tommi just had to get his hands into everything. I don't know where he first met Mattinen—maybe in some nightclub where Tommi was running girls. Mattinen had good contacts with the drug runners in Estonia and distribution channels ready here in Finland, but he needed someone clean to bring the merchandise through customs. I imagine Tommi brought a few deliveries of marijuana through over the winter. He was probably surprised by how easy it all was and started to think he could handle some bigger jobs. Around the same time, Mattinen learned there was a big load of coke available. Henri and Peter were planning their test run on the *Marlboro*, and it was easy for Tommi to talk them into going to Tallinn under the cover of listening to that choir concert. Everything went just as you had planned. You and Tommi probably just disappeared into the city together for a few

minutes, during which time you met Mattinen and took possession of the goods."

Tuulia smiled at me the way one smiles at a small child who
says they've seen monsters in the forest.

"Maybe Tommi was mixed up in all that. All I knew was
that he sold a bit of black market vodka and arranged escorts for
people now and then. Even if he did bring drugs home on the
Marlboro, why would he have dragged me into that?"

"You were Tommi's trusted sidekick. I'm guessing it probably all started a couple of years ago with Tommi's prostitution
business. You had a chronic shortage of cash, and you agreed
when Tommi suggested going to bed for money. Not all of his
women were from across the border—he also had normal Finnish
student girls. Like you. But you had had enough pretty quickly.
You know better than I do what it's like. It's not the most enrich-
ing way to make a living. But you still needed money. You told
me yourself when we were together at the Elite what kind of
life you want to live. Wild, free, not getting stuck in the usual
ruts. And I envied you then. So when you told Tommi about
your money problems, he offered you a different kind of work.
You carried marijuana to Mattinen, and it looks like you sold it
yourself a few times too. Then Tommi needed an assistant on
the boat job since it isn't safe to walk around alone at night in
Tallinn anymore. The two of you probably also had some sort
of plan for how to make it through if customs got too interested
in you. Then I imagine that Tommi must have gotten greedy.
Mattinen was taking too much frosting off the cake, so Tommi
wouldn't give him everything he had brought all at once, and
instead parceled out small amounts at significant commissions.
He wouldn't even meet with Mattinen, so he made you drive his

car to and from Mattinen's place. Mattinen agreed because he didn't have any alternative."

"And so Mattinen killed Tommi because he got so greedy?"

"No, Mattinen didn't kill Tommi. Mattinen called Tommi's answering machine on Sunday night. He was skipping the country. You killed Tommi. And for nothing. Mattinen didn't get caught. No one could have burned you or Tommi."

Tuulia suddenly looked tired. I wondered how long she was going to have the energy to resist. All I had against her was circumstantial evidence. If I wanted to charge her with Tommi's murder, I would have to get her to confess. Did I want Tuulia to confess? I had to keep pushing myself, my own feelings, aside the entire time. I was a police officer investigating a murder. Nothing else mattered now. I took a swig of tea and continued my monologue, which seemed to glance off her without any effect. Tuulia was smiling sort of crookedly, as if she were watching a boring TV show and waiting for whatever idiotic thing the pathetic comedians were going to say next.

"Tommi had gotten wind of the arrests on Thursday, presumably from Mattinen, who figured it out when his dealer didn't show up," I continued. "He got worried and started arranging his affairs in order to leave the country. The news on Saturday exaggerated somewhat about a drug ring being rounded up, and Tommi probably panicked. He wasn't a very good loser. You arranged to meet him that night. You had to talk. You knew that if Mattinen had been arrested, you were both in deep shit. While you were talking, you got into some sort of argument, and you hit Tommi with the ax. Maybe you thought Mattinen didn't know your name. So with Tommi dead, there would be no one left to expose you."

"I slept through the whole night. Everyone can tell you that. Remember how they all said I was snoring so loudly? I always do that when I'm a little drunk. And why didn't the famous ax have my fingerprints on it if I used it to hit Tommi?"

"It was your snoring that did you in actually. According to Riku, you were sleeping comfortably on your back snoring. But Mira said she tried to turn you off your stomach to stop you snoring. Don't people usually only snore in one position? Your act wasn't quite flawless. And the fingerprints—your hands were cold while you were standing out there on the dock so early in the morning. You simply grabbed the ax with the sleeves of your shirt, which you'd already stretched out over them, and you carried it up to the sauna the same way. You showed me that last week too. But of course, you thought I wouldn't catch on." I couldn't hide the indignation in my voice. "When we went to the Elite, you just wanted to find out what I knew. All your fun stories and everything you said about friendship and how alike we were—it was all just a game. And to think I took you seriously!"

"It wasn't a game," Tuulia said, looking out the window. "I really thought you understood me."

"Did you think I would approve of you supporting yourself by dealing cocaine?"

"I didn't know it was cocaine!" Her violet teacup clinked angrily against the saucer. Tuulia stood up to pour herself more tea and then slowly, weighing every word carefully, said, "I guess that's it, then. It's probably best that I tell you the whole story. Then at least you'll be able to understand it a little better. Do you want more tea, by the way?" I nodded, and she poured some in my cup, then set the pot back on the counter and sat back down at the table. Her movements were heavy, like those of a wounded animal, and her voice was quieter than usual. Tuulia stared out into the yard. A white wagtail landed on the windowsill, looking hopefully through the window for breadcrumbs, and then flew away. Tuulia finally began to tell her story.

"You were mostly right. It all started by accident," Tuulia said, snorting at her own memories. "A couple of summers ago I was with Tommi at the Kaivohuone Club listening to a rock band. I was more dressed up than usual—a lot of makeup, my hair up, high heels, a miniskirt. Toward the end of the evening, this lost-looking middle-aged hick came up to me and asked me how much I cost. At first I didn't get what he meant. Then I said—just joking, of course—that I was one grand, and that he had to pay up front. He practically started waving the money right under my nose. I barely had time to say 'ciao' to Tommi before we were in a cab to the guy's room at the Meri Hotel.

"Of course I told Tommi about it, and a couple of weeks later, one of his work friends needed some company. Tommi set me up with him, for money again. We tried to make a business of it, just kind of playing around for a while. It was fun. Back then the market for girls wasn't what it is now, and guys would pay anything. Tommi lured a few other girls in, because he'd started to develop a reputation in business circles as someone who could get you a good, clean one-night escort."

"I did all that for a little over six months, but then I started to get sick of it. It wasn't as easy as it looked; in fact, it was actually pretty damn hard, and how I felt about my own body had started to get weird. So I told Tommi I was quitting. He didn't argue, because he had enough girls at that point even without me.

"For about a year, things went just fine, but then I ran out of money again, completely this time. I borrowed money from Tommi for a while, and then he told me that he now had all

sorts of different businesses going and that he was making even
more than before. He'd met this guy Mattinen through a girl
named Tiina, and they were smuggling weed into the country. I
went and sold it in the clubs a few times, but it was a pretty risky
business.

"Right after May Day, Tommi called to say he had a big
load coming in over the Baltic. So we came up with the idea
of that trip on the *Marlboro*. The only mistake we made was
claiming that the reason we were going was to see the Estonian
Philharmonic Chamber Choir concert, which made Antti and
Timo and Sirkku want to come along. We had a hard time shaking them, especially Antti.

"Though I was really nervous, our plan went off without a
hitch. The others thought I was seasick, but I was really throwing up out of fear. Tommi was pretty nervous too. Once we
got the stuff into the country, Tommi decided not give it all to
Mattinen at once. He gave it to him in small batches, including
his car in the deal, for a much higher price than they'd originally
agreed. That scared me a little—I knew that Mattinen had all
kinds of connections—but Tommi just laughed and said he was
a whole lot smarter than Mattinen. I asked Tommi whether I
could trust him since I could see that he was always cheating
everyone else at everything. He pulled me close and said I was
his best friend; I was a special case. He would never lie to me.

"I only knew what Tommi told me. And I really did think
it was just marijuana! Then he called me Thursday night and
said that I should be careful because one of his regular dealers
had been nabbed. We all knew the name of the game: you cops
are always ready to make a deal with the little guys to catch
the bigger ones. And everybody always just tries to save their
own skin. So now Tommi was trying to unload all the stuff on

Mattinen at a discount just to get rid of it. He was totally panick-
ing on Thursday. By Friday he'd calmed down a bit. Mattinen
had bought the stuff from him, so he had his money and things
were good.

"Then on Saturday when we were on our way out to the
villa, we heard on the news that several more members of the
cocaine ring had been arrested. I just laughed, thinking that
didn't have anything to do with us. I mean, *we* hadn't been selling cocaine. I didn't get to exchange more than a few words with
Tommi that afternoon, but I could see that he had tensed up and
was avoiding me. I eventually managed to ask him if that news
story was about the people we knew, and he admitted it. He told
me that if Mattinen had been caught by the cops, we were up
shit creek too."

Tuulia poured the rest of her tea down her throat. Rage and
anguish burned in her eyes, and I found myself wondering once
again what her true feelings had been for Tommi.

"I finally got him to promise me that we would talk later
that night when everyone else had gone to bed. I lay awake until
four thinking about how Tommi had betrayed me. You don't
get it, I'm sure; to you weed and coke are probably both the
same. But everybody's smoked a few joints at Roskilde or in
Amsterdam. Personally, I prefer a good binge. Cocaine is a different matter entirely though. I never wanted to get mixed up in
anything like that. And I had trusted Tommi. I had known him
my whole life, and he had never betrayed me before.

"I waited and waited. People were wandering all around the
house. When Tommi went out to the dock, I started to get up, but
then I heard Sirkku going out to talk to him. At first I thought
Tommi had arranged that just to avoid me, and by the time Sirkku
came back inside, I was beyond furious. I could barely keep from

screaming when I saw Tommi sitting there on the dock, dangling his feet in the water and admiring the sunrise, looking as though he didn't have a care in the world. When I asked him why he hadn't told me the truth, he just laughed at me. He said, 'Did you really think we could get that kind of money from weed?' How was I supposed to know? What did I know about the drug market! He had been bullshitting me too, just like he did everyone else, always. It turns out I wasn't any kind of *special case* in his life after all. I tried to kick him, but then he caught me by the foot and tried to drag me down into the water. So I grabbed the ax and hit him on the head. I wasn't thinking at all. I heard sort of a crunch, and then he fell in. I only saw a little blood coming out of his head."

Tuulia was staring far beyond the landscape visible through the window, and I knew that she was seeing it all again, had seen it many times already, and would see it forever.

"And then?"

Tuulia woke up as if from a daze.

"I rinsed off the ax because it had gotten blood on it. Tommi was lying facedown in the water. I said to him, 'Stop playing around.' He moved a little—though it might just have been the waves rocking him—and I took off running. I guess I threw the ax behind the sauna as I went. I don't remember. I felt nauseated. I went to the outhouse behind the sauna and threw up. Then I washed my face in the sauna and noticed the ax. I kicked it under the sauna with the tip of my sneakers and went back to bed. I was sure that Tommi was just playing around. In the morning, I waited for him to come down the stairs grinning. I even went and knocked on his door. I was sure he was sleeping in there and that it had all just been a bad dream. But then Riku came up from the water and I saw right away from his expression that Tommi hadn't been playing after all."

"You should have confessed right then. You would have gotten off with manslaughter."

"You wouldn't have believed me. You don't believe me now either."

"Does it matter what I believe anymore? This whole time you've been feeding me different things. You knew how to manipulate me, and I let you. I guess my parents raised me to be just like them because I really did see you as the Tuulia I wanted to see. When you came to me to find out how much I knew, I really thought you wanted to be my friend. I haven't had that much fun in ages."

I felt tears welling up in my throat, but I couldn't give in to those feelings until this job was done. It was easy for me to believe Tuulia's story. I felt the same way now as she had felt then: I had been betrayed too; I had been used too.

"I didn't mean to manipulate you," Tuulia said meekly, fingering her cup. "I like you, and I know you like me." Tuulia looked at me, all but pleading. "You came to arrest me, but why did you come alone? Maybe deep down you hoped I would get away. Give me one day. I'll do exactly what Tommi planned to do. I'll leave the country. I have all his money. I managed to grab it along with his address book from his room while we were waiting for the police. Give me a chance." There was fear and pleading in Tuulia's eyes. I averted my gaze; I didn't dare look at her. The plan she was proposing was an option. After all, did I really want to send her to jail?

"What did you do to Antti?"

"Antti? I haven't done anything to Antti. I have no idea where he is. You don't really think I would have done something to Antti, do you?" Hysteria was creeping into Tuulia's voice. "You aren't going to let me go."

"No, I'm afraid not. You're under arrest. Collect your things. We'll go down to Pasila so you can make an official statement." I stood up from the table. There was no point in prolonging the agony.

Tuulia was faster than I was though. She grabbed a bread knife from the counter, the same one she had just used to slice up the cake. She wrapped her arms around me so the knife was now poised to slice my throat. I felt the iron grip of Tuulia's cold hands, the coolness of the steel against my carotid artery, and the rapid beating of both of our hearts. Time stopped. Tuulia smelled of lemon.

"You came alone, without a weapon. If you don't let me go willingly, then I'll have to force you to let me go. Walk slowly over there to the bedroom," she said, forcing me down the entry hall.

"Don't be stupid," I said. "You don't have a chance. Do you really think we don't have guards at the airports and the harbors?"

"Be quiet! You can always get out of this country. I'm going to tie you up, and then you're going to get just a little bonk on the head—don't worry, it'll be much smaller than Tommi's. When you wake up, I'll be long gone."

I tried to slow my breathing in order to calm down. I wasn't going to get out of this by rushing. Tuulia slowly slid the knife from my neck down between my shoulder blades.

"Open the cabinet in front of you. Good. On the bottom shelf are a couple of jump ropes. Bend your knees slowly to reach them...Yes, like that. Hand them to me. Thank you. Now walk over there to the bed and lie down on your stomach. This knife is going to be resting between your shoulder blades the whole time. If you try anything, you die. I read somewhere that the second one is a lot easier." Now Tuulia's voice really was hysterical. I knew that sound; it was the desperate growling of an animal driven into a trap. She was capable of anything.

I bent over onto the bed. Out of the corner of my eye I saw that the hand holding the knife was shaking uncontrollably. Instead of lying down, I gave Tuulia a swift kick in the thigh.

Then several things happened at once. The knife arced away and landed on the floor, as Tuulia collapsed against the half-open window. Then Koivu and Kinnunen rushed into the room.

Of course I hadn't gone off to arrest a murderer all by myself— I had double backup. And of course Kinnunen had wanted to take part in the collaring. Koivu had been waiting in the stairwell the whole time, and Kinnunen had retrieved the spare key from the building super to open the door while Tuulia and I were talking. I had wanted to start by talking to Tuulia alone because I was sure she would speak to me more openly without other officers present. Convincing Kinnunen that this was a sensible plan had been a bit of a chore though.

Kinnunen aimed his gun at Tuulia's shins. I didn't know he'd even brought one with him. It looked as though Tuulia hadn't seen his weapon because she lunged for the knife. I saw Kinnunen pull the trigger, and time slowed as I watched the bullet hit Tuulia in the shoulder instead of the leg and throw her through the open window straight down into the yard. Since the window was only one floor up, she should have made it through the fall without further injury, but she landed on the hood of the car of a neighbor who was just pulling out and slid from there under the tires.

Someone screamed. I charged down the stairs. Tuulia was lying in a strange position, and blood was leaking from her mouth. Someone was still screaming and tears were dripping down onto Tuulia's body. I didn't realize they were my tears until Koivu shook me.

"Maria! There's no point in trying CPR on her. The ambulance is on its way." Koivu gently wiped the blood from the side of my mouth, while Kinnunen tried to calm the driver. Curious neighbors were streaming toward us, and I heard the ambulance siren in the distance. Everything was still happening in slow motion, and the film kept going dark and then light again. As Kinnunen approached me, I smelled the stench of gunpowder and drunken sweat on him. An uncontrollable rage exploded inside me.

"Why the hell did you shoot, you fucking drunk? Nothing was going to happen! She couldn't even reach the knife!" I punched Kinnunen right in the jaw. Taken by surprise, he collapsed, landing partly on top of Tuulia. Koivu rushed between us and slapped me in the face like I was some kind of hysterical woman in the movies. The pain helped me forget everything else for a moment.

I gradually pulled myself together. The ambulance arrived, and the paramedics loaded Tuulia into it. We promised to follow them to the hospital once we'd calmed the neighbors down. I went upstairs to get my bag. Inside it was the recorder that contained Tuulia's confession. Koivu had heard all of it, and Kinnunen a good part of it. The case was solved.

I was moving as though in a dream. We dropped Kinnunen off at the station to report to the captain and left the tape for transcription. None of us was especially talkative. The responsibility for the miscalculation was mine, of course. I hadn't imagined that Tuulia would turn violent. I knew that Kinnunen had been aiming at her legs, that he had been trying to help me.

Women can't get along on their own, you know. I knew he would tell the captain something like that.

By the time we arrived at the hospital, Tuulia was already in the ICU. She had a concussion and a spinal fracture. They didn't know yet whether she would pull through. We promised the nurses that we would notify Tuulia's parents of the incident.

"Are you OK now?" Koivu asked, clearly concerned, as we drove across Kuusisaari Island toward North Tapiola, where Tuulia's parents lived.

"I'll be fine. I keep asking 'what if.' What if I had just let her tie me up? You two would have caught her anyway. What if I had just waited? What if Kinnunen hadn't started waving his gun around? Why can't they just find a desk for that idiot to sit at! He can push paper even when he's hungover."

"It was hard for us to tell just from your voices how serious the situation was in there," Koivu said defensively. "Is this where I should turn?"

"Yeah. Third house on the right," I said, looking at a map. "I can do the talking."

Explaining what had happened to Tuulia's parents was just as appalling as I had imagined it would be. I also had to explain why I had been arresting Tuulia, and they just couldn't believe it. I watched the life drain out of their faces as they sat on the handsome leather couch in their sweet little row house. There was nothing comforting to say. I gave Tuulia's parents the number for the intensive care unit and then left as quickly as I could. I didn't start to cry until Koivu was turning off of Kalevantie onto Ring I.

"Am I taking you home?" Koivu asked. I was glad he didn't start fussing over me.

"No thanks. I need to make a report, talk to the captain, and probably call Peltonen's dad." I wiped my cheeks on a hamburger stand paper napkin that I had found in the glove box. It still smelled a little like mustard. "Do you still have work to do?"

Koivu snorted. "I need to help you write your report."

"How about three pints minimum to finish off the workday? Solved cases deserve a little celebration. Or have you spent too much time loitering around bars lately?"

We cobbled together what would pass for our report. I took it to the captain, who seemed satisfied that the case had been solved, even if the end result was an embarrassment for the police. He glossed over Kinnunen's actions by observing that "these things happen," and I didn't have the energy to argue. Then I called Heikki Peltonen, who didn't want to believe what I was telling him at first either. He shouted that I was just shoveling shit at him, and only calmed down once I repeated five times in succession the list of evidence pointing to Tommi's dealings. Peltonen's ire raised my own adrenaline level, and I grew even more irate when the next call was from a tabloid reporter. I had just promised Peltonen that I would keep a low profile with the media, but the driver of the car that Tuulia fell on had clearly wanted to get some publicity and called the reporter. I could already imagine the headline: POLICE NEGLIGENCE KILLS SUSPECT. I answered the reporter's questions curtly. Talking all evening had made my mouth feel like sandpaper.

By nine thirty, Koivu and I were seated at the Old Cellar restaurant. Koivu ordered a pint, and I asked for a Jack Daniel's. I downed the first one without even tasting it, and then ordered another. The aging waiter didn't even raise an eyebrow. He had seen thousands of liters of whiskey flow down his clients' throats, and I was hardly the thirstiest one he'd ever seen.

A warm feeling coursed down my throat to my stomach, then rose mysteriously back up to my head. Koivu sipped from his mug, complaining about how hungry he was. We ordered greasy steaks and more beer. Koivu commented on the success of the Finnish athletes in the recent Olympics. I made some disparaging remarks about our country's male competitors, to which he responded by criticizing the women's legs. I couldn't see anything wrong with them—just so long as they beat the Swedes, I couldn't care less how they looked—so we argued about that for a while. We went on chatting desperately about all kinds of trivial things. Koivu must have sensed the distress behind my apparent joviality, but he didn't have any desire to start that conversation.

After the two pints I drank with my meal, and a third whisky, I thought Koivu was starting to look even more adorable than usual.

The thought of falling asleep in those kind arms, gazing at that flaxen hair and those blue eyes was tempting. However, I knew that it would be a bad idea in the long run. I would need a good partner for at least another couple of months, and it would be pointless to ruin such a good team for one drunken roll in the hay. I gave Koivu a tired smile and said I was going to crawl home to bed. Koivu convinced me to order one last drink. We spent the rest of the time debating several future Olympic athletes' chances. We shared a taxi home. Koivu tried to invite himself into my place, but I packed him off home, pulling rank and then assuring him he would be happier in the morning if he followed orders.

Despite my drunken state, I couldn't go to bed until I called the hospital. They had operated on Tuulia's back, and she would probably live. The liquor and greasy food churned in my stomach. I took two ibuprofen and knew that tomorrow would feel even worse.

FINALE

Drifting on the tide

The city was preparing for a dreary fall Friday night. It was cold, foggy, and rainy, precisely the kind of weather that most people hated. However, I didn't mind it and decided to take a stroll on the shores of the Baltic Sea. I wanted some time to think. I had just finished the paperwork for the Tommi Peltonen murder, and court proceedings would begin the following week.

The trouble was that the accused would not be appearing in court. Tuulia had survived, but she would not be able to travel to any courtroom anytime soon. Fractures in her spine had paralyzed her lower limbs. The doctors still thought she might recover, but only after several operations.

I didn't know whether Tuulia would ever recover psychologically. She had systematically refused to speak ever since the incident. Doctors hadn't found anything physically wrong with her vocal chords, and she behaved completely normally otherwise: she ate and slept, read the books she was given, and even did some writing from time to time. But she wouldn't talk.

I tried to visit her. They had allowed me into her room. She had signed the confession Koivu had brought her, a transcript of the tape I made during my visit to her apartment. However, I still had a few questions, and Narcotics and Vice were also interested in what Tuulia had to say. I didn't know at that point that Tuulia wasn't speaking to anyone, and I imagined that she would have the easiest time talking to me.

Of course I wanted to see her. Her face had been tormenting me: the expression on it before she fell out the window, her laughter over beers at Elite, her cold hands slapping against my own...I had thought and thought about what I actually felt for Tuulia, and I was still uncertain about it now.

I had walked down to the end of the hall, where Tuulia was locked in a private room. Legally speaking, Tuulia was incarcerated. I asked the nurse to let me go in alone. The room was small and spare. A pale red potted rose was blooming on the windowsill, and a copy of the collected poems of Edith Södergran lay on the nightstand next to a candle. In the corner across from the bed was a television. The room looked like a cell. Tuulia lay on the narrow iron bed looking small and insubstantial despite her height. When I stepped through the door, she did not even turn her eyes toward me; she just continued to stare at her hands resting on the blanket. I wondered ironically whether her hands were cold. I wanted to take hold of them, to warm them, but I didn't dare.

I spoke to her, trying to get her to look at me.

"Tuulia. It's Maria. I have some things I want to ask you."

Tuulia's gaze remained fixed on the blanket. I tried for five minutes, maintaining my role as a police officer, though I would have much preferred to just be myself, Maria. After five minutes, the head nurse knocked on the door and I let her in.

"She isn't likely to talk to you," the nurse observed, thinking that I was just any cop. She didn't know Tuulia and I had almost become friends.

The next day I called the psychiatrist who was treating Tuulia. He rattled off a list of terms and explained that Tuulia would return to normal only if she herself wanted to. Between the lines he was saying she didn't. Why would she want to get better if she was only going to spend years in prison?

The Narcotics Unit had been making some important arrests lately. They had discovered that the rumors of the eastern mafia's tightening grip were only partially true—most of those involved were still Finnish. In the end, Tommi had been a minor player and Tuulia merely a pawn. Mattinen's trail had gone cold in London. He had presumably acquired a false passport and disappeared without a trace. It was possible that Tommi could have done the same, and Tuulia probably never would have been caught if Tommi had successfully fled the country. Maybe she and I would have met in some bar and would be walking in the fog together right now.

I had run into Mira when I was leaving work a couple of weeks earlier. We had been walking to the same tram stop, and chatted stiffly all the way to the stop, despite the fact that the conversation was clearly unpleasant for both of us.

Mira told me that the choir had decided not to formally accuse Riku of anything. Recovering the money was the priority. Mira herself had decided to leave for London after Christmas to study and finish her thesis. Sirkku and Timo had become engaged in September, and Pia had traveled to San Francisco to meet up with Peter. Life continued on as it had before. The only one Mira didn't mention was Antti, and I didn't ask.

Although I had seriously screwed up with Tuulia's arrest, the captain asked me to continue on as Saarinen's replacement. I said thanks, but no thanks, and I now had only two weeks of work left. An uncommonly brazen and violent taxi robber had been keeping me and the whole unit busy lately. At least one rape a week had been coming in as well, and somehow they usually ended up on my desk, even when I wasn't on duty. In my free time, I had been working out and hitting the books for my criminal justice exam. My intent was to graduate by the end of the year and start my court practicum the following fall. I didn't dare think any further ahead than that.

Pasi Arhela's trial had taken place the week before. As a habitual offender, he received three years in prison. Marianna had been brilliant on the stand. I almost cried with pride listening to her. She had been attending a therapy group for rape victims, and I met up with her a few times before she returned to Kouvola for her last year of school. Although the incident had hit her hard, Marianna was clearly on the road to recovery. Luckily there hadn't been any pregnancy or disease transmission to worry about. Marianna said that she already felt comfortable walking outside at night again.

The rain drew me along the southern shoreline. Now and then I passed people running to escape the downpour, some laughing under shared umbrellas. But most were bad-tempered, as if they considered the rain a personal affront from nature. I had no need to run away from the rain, because my oversized bicycling poncho and Wellingtons were keeping me warm and dry, but also cut me off from my surroundings.

On the shore by Kaivopuisto Park, the fog was so thick that even the closest islands just off shore were invisible. The sea was an enormous gray mass that sighed strangely. The fog transformed the sounds, making them unfamiliar. I was walking in a strange country whose language I did not know. From a distance, I heard a rattling and creaking that made me think of a baby stroller, but a stroller couldn't possibly sound like that. But fifty yards farther on, that was precisely what emerged from the mist. Perhaps the odd rustling coming from the shore was the sound of the waves on the sand, or perhaps it was something else. Maybe I didn't need to know.

I had solved a crime. I knew who did it, and I knew her motive. I also knew a great deal about many other people's lives. But I still felt I didn't know anything. I would just have to learn to tolerate not knowing what certain things meant, and that I might never know. I had made a few decisions about my life, but those were hardly final. I knew that in a few years I might want to change course again.

I walked toward the pier, and then continued out onto it. The shoreline quickly disappeared, and suddenly there was no reality beyond the pier and the fog, my rubber boots glistening with moisture and the wet curls on my forehead. It felt strangely calming. I felt both lonely and whole.

I heard a new sound, once again distorted by the fog. A moment later, the sound took shape and became steps. Large rubber boots appeared, and a tall, thin figure loomed above them. An aquiline nose was visible beneath the hood—Antti.

I hadn't seen him since the day of Tommi's funeral. A couple of days after Tuulia's arrest, a phone message had appeared on my desk during my lunch break. "I was camping. Sorry for the hassle. Antti." I hadn't had any reason to contact him since then.

When I went to return Tommi's effects to the Peltonens, I kept Antti's letter. It was still in my desk drawer, and I didn't know what to do with it. It might be best to destroy it and forget that I had ever read it.

"Oh hi, Maria," Antti said formally once he recognized me under my poncho. "I've been meaning to call you."

"Did you have some business to discuss?" I asked, more coldly that I meant to. I was still annoyed with him for the confusion caused by his disappearance.

"I guess I owe you an explanation," he said slowly. "Should we walk so that we don't get cold?"

We walked along side by side for some time, not saying a word. The silence felt calming, and Antti broke it only once we turned away from the shore toward the city.

"I was pretty messed up after Tommi's funeral. I didn't know what I was supposed to do. I just wanted to get away for a while, to have time to think without any disruptions. So I grabbed my camping gear and jumped on the bus and went out to the forest in Nuuksio to think things over."

"You knew the whole time?" It was a statement more than a question. Antti looked uncomfortable.

"I knew in a way. More than I realized, I guess. I've known Tommi and Tuulia almost my entire life. I could see that weekend that something was wrong between them. I had had some idea about Tommi's drug dealing, but I had no idea he was in as deep as his dad says he was. Silly." Antti shrugged under his raincoat, and drops fell onto his shoes.

"My first reaction was to feel hurt. I was hurt because he hadn't told me what kind of life he was living."

We walked through Tehtaanpuisto Park to the end of Albertinkatu. The fog wasn't as thick in the city, and I could see a long way down the street. It was starting to get dark, and cozy lights were burning in the windows of the apartments above the shops. A window opened somewhere, and music flooded out. Mick Jagger inviting us to spend the night with him.

"I guessed it was Tuulia, but I wasn't sure why she had done it. I couldn't tell you my suspicions, though I suppose I should have. And I didn't dare talk to Tuulia. I wasn't afraid for myself, but I was afraid she might do something to herself. And in the end she did."

"Have you been to see her?"

"I tried. The nurse went in to ask her whether she wanted to see me. She still isn't talking, so she just shook her head. Do you know what kind of sentence she'll get?"

"It depends on a lot of things. If she goes on being like she is now, they'll probably commit her to the psych hospital out in Sipoo."

We had come to the corner of Iso Roobertinkatu. Tommi's former apartment was a block away.

"I just moved into Tommi's old place," Antti said as if in answer to my thoughts. "The Peltonens sold it to me dirt cheap. They just wanted to get rid of it. I've been pretty sick of living with roommates in little student apartments for a while now; I'm getting too old for that. And Einstein will like being able to go and wander around in Koff Park." Antti looked at me thoughtfully and then said, "My shoes are soaked through; I'd better head inside. If you don't have anything else to do, why don't you come with me?"

The door said Sarkela now, instead of Peltonen. The apartment itself looked different as well, mainly because it was full of stacks of books.

"I'm still working on building more bookshelves. Do your best to squeeze through." Antti dove through the piles of books to his bedroom in search of dry socks.

The biggest cat I had ever seen lazed on a blue armchair. It was clearly the cat's favorite spot, as it was covered in hair. The cat's underlying color was white, but it had a pattern of dark brown hair on its back and head. The tail went from gray stripes to midnight black at the tip. The creature jumped from the chair and sidled over to rub itself, purring, against my legs. It took only a moment for its nuzzling to leave trails of white hair on my black pants. I bent down to pet it, and the volume of the purring increased.

"He treats anyone who comes in as a potential source of food," explained Antti, who was now wearing oversized gray woolen socks. "I'll make us something hot."

The cat scuttled into the kitchen after Antti. I inspected the stacks of books. Antti had a Henry Parland that I hadn't been able to find in any of the secondhand shops.

"Could I borrow this?" I asked when he came out of the kitchen carrying two steaming mugs.

"Sure. There's a little alcohol in this; I hope that isn't a problem." I took a sip and recognized the strong anise flavor of Muuriala moonshine mixed in with the tea.

"Hard tea costs twelve-fifty, fourteen, fifteen—depending on the place," I said, quoting Parland.

"We're in the lowest price range here," Antti said, laughing, clearly recognizing the reference. I shifted a couple of piles of books off the corner of the sofa to the floor and sat down. Antti collapsed into the armchair, and a moment later Einstein, looking injured at the theft of his chair, jumped up next to me. He deftly found a comfortable hollow for himself among the remaining stacks of books.

"Could you tell me what really happened in Tuulia's apartment?" Antti asked seriously. I took a hefty swig of the burning tea and began to talk. I had spent dozens of nights going over and over it in my head, but I still couldn't talk about it without getting emotional. My voice started to tremble, and then the tears followed. By the time I reached the end, we were both crying.

"I feel like somehow I'm to blame," Antti said. "If I had just told you in time…"

"I've tried to tell myself over and over that there isn't any point in what-ifs, but I realize that's easy to say to someone else. Do you have any more of this fennel liquor?"

"Oh, you recognized it. Yeah, I still have half a bottle. Probably the last of the batch. Timo was complaining about how much of it went down the drain at the police station." Antti retrieved the bottle from the kitchen, along with a roll of paper towels, which we used to dry our eyes. I felt like touching him, and for once, I did exactly what I wanted. We hugged long and hard.

Then we continued drinking moonshine and petting the cat. We talked until late, about Tuulia, about Tommi, about sorrow, about cats, about everything under the sun. Finally the bottle was empty, and I stayed and fell asleep between Antti and Einstein.

CAST OF CHARACTERS

THE COPS

Maria Kallio...Helsinki VCU detective
Rane..VCU detective, Maria's old partner
Pekka Koivu...............................VCU officer, Maria's new partner
Kalevi Kinnunen..VCU sergeant
The Lieutenant...............................Head of Helsinki PD VCU
Tapani "Tapsa" Helminen.................Narcotics detective, Maria's
academy classmate
Makkonen...Narcotics detective
Salo...Medical examiner
Savukoski..VCU sergeant
Virrankoski and Miettinen...................................Other VCU cops

THE CHOIR

Tommi Peltonen..Bass
Riku Lasinen...First tenor
Antti Sarkela..............................Bass, Tommi's childhood friend
Sirkku Halonen..............................Alto, Timo's girlfriend
Timo Huttunen....................................Tenor, Sirkku's boyfriend
Pia Wahlroos...Second soprano
Mira Rasinkangas..First alto
Tuulia Rajala................First soprano, Tommi's childhood friend

Anu..Second soprano
"Hopeless" Hopponen...Choir director

SUPPORTING CAST

Jaana....................Former choir member, Maria's ex-roommate
Heikki and Maisa Peltonen.......................................Villa owners
Henri Peltonen.............................Sailboat racer, Tommi's brother
Peter Wahlroos...............................Sailboat racer, Pia's husband
Dr. Marja Mäk...Tommi's boss
Martti Mäk...Dr. Marja Mäki's husband
Mrs. Laakkonen..Tommi's secretary
Jantunen...Tommi's coworker
Tomi "Tomppa" Rissanen...................................Male prostitute
Tiina...Estonian prostitute
Mauri Mattinen..Drug dealer
Marianna Palola...Rape victim
Pasi Arhela...Rapist
Toivo Kuula...Finnish composer
Marjatta Sarkela..Antti's mother
Einstein..Antti's cat

ACKNOWLEDGMENTS

The translation in Chapter 9 of "Song of My Heart" by Jean Sibelius, which takes its text from the novel *Seven Brothers* by Aleksis Kivi, borrows from previous translations of the novel by Alex Matson (1929) and Richard Impola (2008).

ABOUT THE AUTHOR

Leena Lehtolainen was born in Vesanto, Finland, to parents who taught language and literature. A keen reader, she made up stories in her head before she could even write. At the age of ten, she began her first book, a young adult novel, which was published two years later. Besides writing, Leena is fond of classical singing, her beloved cats, and—her greatest passion—figure skating. She attends many competitions as a skating journalist and writes for the Finnish figure skating magazine *Taitoluistelu*. *My First Murder*, now translated into English, is the first installment in her best-selling Maria Kallio series, which has already been successfully adapted for Finnish television. Leena currently lives in Finland with her husband and two sons.

ABOUT THE TRANSLATOR

Owen F. Witesman is a professional literary translator with a master's in Finnish and Estonian area studies from Indiana University. He has translated over thirty Finnish books into English, including novels, children's books, poetry, plays, graphic novels, and nonfiction. His recent translations include the satire *The Human Part* by Kari Hotakainen (MacLehose Press), the thriller *Wolves and Angels* by Seppo Jokinen (Ice Cold Crime), the 1884 classic *The Railroad* by Juhani Aho (Norvik Press), and the children's book *This is Helsinki* by Aino Havukainen and Sami Toivonen (Otava). He currently resides in Springville, Utah, with his wife and three daughters, a dog, a cat, and twenty-nine fruit trees.